MURDER
AT
CHATEAU SUR MER

Books by Alyssa Maxwell

Gilded Newport Mysteries

MURDER AT THE BREAKERS
MURDER AT MARBLE HOUSE
MURDER AT BEECHWOOD
MURDER AT ROUGH POINT
MURDER AT CHATEAU SUR MER

Lady and Lady's Maid Mysteries

MURDER MOST MALICIOUS
A PINCH OF POISON
A DEVIOUS DEATH

Published by Kensington Publishing Corporation

MURDER
AT
CHATEAU SUR MER

ALYSSA MAXWELL

KENSINGTON BOOKS
www.kensingtonbooks.com

KENSINGTON BOOKS are published by

Kensington Publishing Corp.
119 West 40th Street
New York, NY 10018

All Kensington titles, imprints, and distributed lines are available at special quantity discounts for bulk purchases for sales promotion, premiums, fund-raising, educational, or institutional use. Special book excerpts or customized printings can also be created to fit specific needs. For details, write or phone the office of the Kensington Special Sales Manager: Attn. Special Sales Department. Kensington Publishing Corp., 119 West 40th Street, New York, NY 10018. Phone: 1-800-221-2647.

Library of Congress Card Catalogue Number: 2017940679

Kensington and the K logo Reg. U.S. Pat. & TM Off.

ISBN-13: 978-1-4967-0332-3
ISBN-10: 1-4967-0332-4
First Kensington Hardcover Edition: August 2017

eISBN-13: 978-1-4967-0333-0
eISBN-10: 1-4967-0333-2
First Kensington Electronic Edition: August 2017

10 9 8 7 6 5 4 3 2 1

Printed in the United States of America

To the wonderful people at the Preservation Society of Newport County, for their tireless and invaluable work in preserving the city's heritage and sharing their knowledge and expertise with countless visitors each year, myself included. Thank you for your generosity in twice now allowing me the honor of signing my books at the Mansions Gift Shops. It's been a thrill, and your support of this series means the world to me.

Acknowledgments

My continued gratitude goes to everyone at Kensington who has believed in this series. Many thanks to John Scognamiglio, Morgan Elwell, Susie Russenberger, Darla Freeman, and so many others!

I'd also like to thank Larry James Bettencourt for his help in locating some invaluable source material on Newport's history, including information on Lower Thames Street and the wharves.

Chapter 1

Bits of grass and earth pelted the air as a thunderous pounding rolled down the polo field. Long-handled mallets swung after a ball no larger than a man's open palm. *Crack!* Each time a mallet connected with the ball, ponies and riders raced in a fresh, ground-shaking burst of speed.

With my pencil and tablet in my hands, I stood just beyond the sidelines, out of danger of being hit with the ball, yet with a view worthy of the highest-paying spectators. As the action sped from one end of the field to the other, about a dozen other reporters and I hurried to follow, back and forth, attempting to discern every pertinent detail of the match and keep an accurate record. The wind and my own momentum plucked at my wide, leg-o'-mutton sleeves and rippled my summer-weight skirts. My hat, at least, I needn't worry about, for at home Nanny had pinned it to my coif and securely tied the ribbons beneath my chin. Her last words to me were, "Try to bring it home intact please, Emma."

The skies over Aquidneck Island had finally wrung out their clouds and cleared to a vibrant, porcelain blue. Bracing ocean breezes counteracted a warm sun, making this a day for sportsmen and spectators alike to rejoice. An exuberant crowd of local Newporters blanketed Morton Hill in a teeming medley of hats and parasols, while closer to the sidelines, the wealthy cottagers from Bellevue Avenue occupied seats in the covered grandstand or lounged on lawn furniture beneath shady pavilions. From wicker hampers drifted the savory aromas of roasted meats and baked delicacies, while copious quantities of champagne for the elders and lemonade for the young people flowed from crystal pitchers.

Most of those present cheered each time the mallet of a Westchester player connected with the ball. The Westchester Polo Club had officially made Newport their home a decade ago, and familiar names occupied the team list. Today they played the Meadowview Polo Club of Long Island, not only the season's favorite, but also last year's champions.

Grumbling had heralded the opening of the game, a controversy stemming from the belief many held that one of the Meadowview players should have been upgraded in his skill rating. Had the Polo Association officials done so, the Meadowview team would have been assigned a two-goal handicap, thus putting the two teams on a competitive par. Had clandestine funds changed hands among the Polo Association's Competition and National Handicap Committees, resulting in Meadowview's rating remaining the same? Such a transgression could be difficult to prove.

I didn't know who had been the most disgruntled when the usual handicaps were announced, the Westchester players, the wealthy gentlemen who were known to place hefty wagers, or the working men watching from Morton Hill, who risked a day's pay or more in hopes of doubling or tripling their money.

Another thwack sent the eight riders, four in red shirts, four in blue and white stripes, about-facing and hurtling down the field yet again. I admit I cringed often, so certain was I that men and beasts couldn't possibly avoid pulverizing one another. Perhaps it was because, as a reporter covering the event for the Newport *Observer*, I daren't look away but must carefully view every swing and every advance across the field. The sure-footed ponies—horses, really, most being a mix of Thoroughbred and quarter horse and standing between fourteen and fifteen hands—never collided, and somehow those mallets never sent anything but the ball and grass flying.

Still, it was to my relief that a bell rang out, indicating the present seven-minute period, called a *chukker*, was nearly at its end. It was enough time for James Bennett of the Westchester team to recover the ball from Meadowview and send it, with the help of his teammate Oliver Belmont, across the field and through the Meadowview goal. The halftime horn sounded amid uproarious cheers from the grandstand and the hill beyond. Ladies clapped while gentlemen rushed to one another shouting new odds for the eventual outcome of the match.

The horses were walked off the field into a fenced pavilion where they would be unsaddled, watered, and rubbed down. Another set of eight would replace them for the next chukker following the break. In the meantime, gentlemen in morning coats and top hats escorted ladies in colorful day dresses and wide, beribboned bonnets onto the field. A six-piece band struck up a lively tune. The stomping of the divots began, accompanied by a good deal of laughter and lighthearted shrieks.

Replacing dislodged bits of earth to the field hardly interested me, and I had already recorded the most notable of fashions sported by today's gathering of the Four Hundred— that magical number of guests who could fit inside Mrs.

Astor's ballroom and thus claim their place in illustrious society. The latest designs of the likes of Worth, Redfern, Rouff, and Doucer were well represented. I therefore moved off the sidelines toward the surrounding pools of shade cast by sweeping beech, elm, and ash trees, where other spectators went to stretch their legs. Perhaps, if I paid careful attention, I might discern the seeds of a real news story.

"Emma! Emma, do come and join us!"

The hail came from a stunning young woman dressed in pale green silk that set off the brilliance of her auburn hair. She wore the latest from Worth, of course. She always did. I changed course to greet her beside a bright blue pavilion sporting golden tassels that flashed in the sun.

"Grace, how lovely to see you." I tucked my pad and pencil into my purse. "When did you and Neily arrive in Newport?"

"Emma, don't be so formal." Grace Wilson Vanderbilt, my cousin's wife of one year, drew me into an embrace and kissed my cheeks in the European manner. "We came in only yesterday and are staying with my parents. We knew we'd find you here reporting on the match." She drew back to hold me at arm's length. "Do you never tire of it? Reporting, I mean?"

Before I could answer, my cousin Cornelius Vanderbilt III excused himself to the others beneath the pavilion. I recognized Grace's brother, Orme Wilson, and his wife, the former Carrie Astor, and Carrie's brother, John, and his wife, Ava. They glanced over at me, each raising a hand in casual salute.

Neily paused to pour a glass of lemonade from a frosty-looking pitcher, then ducked beneath the flapping canopy as he stepped out to join Grace and me. As he handed me the glass, the cool condensation against my palm made me realize how thirsty I'd become, scampering along the sidelines. Thank goodness for the recent rains that prevented the billows of dust often raised during a polo match. Holding the glass, I returned his quick embrace with one arm. "How are you, Neily?"

However much I tried, I couldn't keep the concern from my voice. Though my cousin stood as tall and slender as always and was still a couple of weeks shy of his twenty-fourth birthday, he appeared older than his years, world-weary. The bright sun brought particular attention to the fatigue dragging at his features. I would have thought the opposite, that, having achieved his heart's desire in marrying Grace, he would have flourished this past year of their marriage. Yet he looked to me nearly as he had in those days before his wedding last summer, when difficult choices had thrust their weight onto his shoulders and forever changed his life.

"I'm well, Emmaline," he said with neither enthusiasm nor dispiritedness, nor, I noted, a direct look into my eyes.

"Have you seen—"

He shook his head before I could finish asking. "I haven't seen my parents. They know I'm back but they've made it clear I'm not welcome at The Breakers, nor in New York, for that matter."

"I'm so sorry, Neily." His parents had objected vehemently to his marriage to Grace. They considered her family beneath them, and Grace herself to be a gold digger. Ridiculous, for the Wilsons were as wealthy as any members of the Four Hundred. Neily and his father had nearly come to blows over the matter, and would have, except that before Neily's eyes—and my own—his father had collapsed from a stroke from which he still hadn't recovered.

"It's all right," he assured me quietly. "We're staying with the Wilsons."

Grace slipped her hand into the crook of Neily's arm. "Mother and Father are thrilled to have us. And you must join us for dinner soon—quite soon. I'll send an invitation." Her eyes twinkled. "You may bring the delectable Mr. Andrews, if you like."

Neily blanched at his wife's forwardness, but I laughed it off. "I'll come alone, if you wouldn't mind, Grace."

"Oh?" She leaned in closer, our hat brims nearly touching and enclosing us in secrecy. "I had so hoped you and he might . . . you know."

"I haven't seen him in a year," I told her. "His planned return from Italy last spring was postponed. I have not had word from him in several weeks."

Grace looked thoroughly dissatisfied, as if the day suddenly threatened rain. I said the first thing that sprang to mind in an effort to cheer her.

"There is someone else I could bring, if I may. Jesse Whyte." My friendship with Jesse, a longtime family friend, had blossomed through the winter and spring, and he now occupied an important place in my life.

Grace made a slight clucking noise in her throat. "Are you speaking of that local policeman?"

"Detective," I clarified.

Her pretty lips turned downward. "It's nothing serious, I hope." She didn't wait for my reply but continued on. "You could do so much better. Neily, surely you agree. Tell her." Neily quirked his eyebrows and shuffled his feet. With a slight shake of her head, Grace turned back to me. "There is no lack of eligible young men in our acquaintance, Emma, and if—"

"Thank you, Grace, but no. Leastwise, not at present." Goodness, didn't I have enough to do, warding off the matchmaking efforts of my two Vanderbilt aunts, Alice and Alva?

I certainly didn't need Grace adding to the fray. "I must be moving on now. The match will be resuming in a few minutes and I'll want a good position beside the field."

"Yes, all right. I'll call on you soon, Emma." Grace embraced me again, but I felt a hesitancy that hadn't been there when she'd first greeted me. I had clearly disappointed her and no doubt left her wondering what was to be done with a stubborn, misguided young woman such as myself. Though Grace and I had grown close last summer, I sometimes expected too much of her. As the daughter of one of America's great banking families, she had never known privation, and had rarely been told *no*. Though kindhearted and generous to a fault, as she had proved countless times, she had nonetheless grown up in circumstances vastly different from my own, and therein lay a gap between us that could never fully be breached.

I squeezed Neily's hand, imparting my loving acknowledgment that all was not well with him, and my willingness, no, eagerness, to lend a sympathetic ear if he should desire one. Of all my Vanderbilt cousins, I felt closest to him. We didn't need words to make our sentiments clear. He smiled bravely back at me and nodded.

Before I moved away, he said, as if suddenly remembering, "Brady is here with us. He and Miss Hanson went for a walk."

I turned back to him, beaming with pleasure. "Brady is here with Hannah?"

Neily responded to my rhetorical question with a genuine smile. He didn't know Hannah Hanson well, but he obviously approved of my half brother's interest in her. When we were children, I'd often brought her with me when invited to visit at The Breakers. Another lifelong friend of ours from the Point neighborhood where Brady and I grew up, Hannah had only just returned to Newport the previous summer after several years away. I scanned the colorful crowd, craning my neck to see around the pavilions.

Brady and Hannah. What a lovely thought. And a surprising one, though perhaps it shouldn't have been. Brady's position at my uncle Cornelius's New York Central Railroad brought him in contact with some of the highest levels of society but, like me, Brady was a Newporter born and raised. And like me, monetary considerations played very little role in his affections.

I didn't spot them presently, but I would make a point of finding them later, during the next intermission. For now, with only a few minutes left to roam the grounds before the next chukker, I tipped my hat a bit lower over my brow. I had worn a day dress given to me by my cousin Gertrude Vanderbilt Whitney, Neily's sister. Though of simple design and a year out of date, the garment nonetheless boasted the quality needed to fit in with this summer's creations of Worth or Paquin—or well enough. Typically, female society reporters clad themselves in modest attire as a way of acknowledging the superiority of those about whom they reported, but today I wished to blend in with the crowd. If I had learned nothing else in the past several years as a reporter, it was how to render myself invisible.

As I strolled, I assumed a leisurely pace as if I hadn't a specific destination in mind. In this way, I moved from group to group without drawing attention to myself—and without prompting sudden breaks in conversations. For it was often such conversations that most interested me at any social gathering, whether it be Mrs. Astor's season-opening ball or a tournament at the Newport Golf Club or one of Newport's many yacht races. During the earlier intermissions I had gleaned hints of several illicit affairs, learned of a dispute concerning James Bennett's desire to expand the Newport Casino, and witnessed the desperate pleas of a compulsive gambler for a loan—a request his elder brother curtly denied him.

I hadn't long to wait for another interesting snippet. I passed a group of men handing round a silver flask. They attempted to be discreet, but I caught the flash of sunlight on the metal surface. The word *burglary* drifted to my ears. I tilted my head to hide my face beneath my hat brim and pretended to be searching for an item in my drawstring bag.

"There's been quite a rash, and one wonders when these scum will decide shops aren't lucrative enough and come after bigger game. We'll be lucky not to be murdered in our beds." The man who spoke sported a mustache that wandered across his cheeks to meet the bushy profusion of his sideburns.

The thin fellow next to him slapped his shoulder. "Come now, Warner. You think these brigands would have the unmitigated gall to intrude on Bellevue Avenue? They're cowards, preying on the weak."

"Five break-ins in as many days, all along Lower Thames Street," another of the group said. "With accompanying vandalism. That points to thugs with plenty of gall." He shook his head while accepting the flask from the older man on his right, who had his own opinion to share.

"Seems we might be dealing with a single criminal, and these burglaries are not random but in fact part of a pattern."

The others harrumphed noncommittally, but I tended to agree with that last assessment. The robberies they spoke of had occurred at a milliner shop, a purveyor of leather tack, a general mercantile, a bakery, and an apothecary—the one I sometimes stopped in at to purchase Nanny's headache powders. In each case, there had been acts of vandalism that had nothing to do with the actual theft, such as the gouging of countertops and the breaking of glass cases kept empty at night.

I hadn't covered these break-ins for the Newport *Observer*. Mr. Millford, the paper's owner and editor-in-chief, had judged the incidents too distressing for a woman's delicate sensibilities, and had sent my co-reporter and nemesis, Ed Billings, instead. Not that I hadn't covered similar stories in recent years. I most certainly had. But I knew his decision had little to do with my sensibilities and everything to do with the letters he had received in the past year chastising him for allowing a woman—me—to expose herself to life's more disagreeable occurrences.

Disagreeable, indeed. My nape bristled ever so slightly, as it had when I read each account of these break-ins in the *Observer*'s morning editions. Now, as then, I couldn't shake the sensation that both Ed and the police were missing some vital clue that connected these crimes and pointed to a single individual.

I reminded myself that these were not my stories to cover. I had my assignment—today's match—though if I happened to stumble upon a more interesting news item, could I be blamed?

I moved on. Gathered beneath the overhanging branches of a giant weeping beech, three men speaking in rumbling tones drew my interest. The foliage that draped like a lacy tent between us partially obscured me from their view, and they from mine. Nonetheless, bright red hair and a mustache of equally fiery color identified one of these men as Stanford Whittaker, an architect who designed many of Newport's opulent cottages, as well as the Newport Casino. The other two, Robert Clarkson and Harry Lehr, were well known to me as well; all three were members of the Four Hundred. I stopped a few yards away, turned my back to them, and pretended to be enjoying the view of Morton Hill, the colorful pavilions, and the stomping of the divots.

"I tell you frankly, gentlemen, the Dingley Tariff will be the death of fair competition in this country and will result in the stagnation of international trade." The speaker was Robert Clarkson, a man several years my senior who, in the last election, had won a seat in the Rhode Island State Senate. He was one of the youngest men currently serving as senator, yet Mr. Clarkson's receding hairline and somber manners belied his age.

"You're not telling us anything we don't already know. But the question is what are we to do about it?"

With my back to them I couldn't see the speaker of this last comment, but I knew the voice to be Harry Lehr's. At twenty-eight, Mr. Lehr was a man of youthful good looks, vigorous energy, and a clever tongue—with very little else to recommend him. My Vanderbilt relatives considered him a fortune hunter and had taken pains to veer their daughters well clear of his path.

I'd heard of this tariff they spoke of, for lately it had been an ongoing item in the newspapers, and the U.S. Senate was set to vote on it next month. Passions ran high both in favor and against, leading to accusations on both sides and threats of an impending end to free American enterprise as we knew it. Obviously, these men were against the proposal that all imported goods should be taxed higher than the current rate.

"The devil take George Wetmore and his cronies. They're drunk on power, is what they are. They need to get off their high horses and listen to reason." Again, I didn't need to turn around to recognize the voice of Stanford Whittaker. My mouth turned down in distaste. He made men like Harry Lehr seem downright respectable. His antics were legendary.

Older than Mr. Lehr and Mr. Clarkson by some twenty years, Whittaker had publicly humiliated his wife, Bessie, with his lewd behavior more times than I could count. And then, of course, he carried on quite openly with that teenage chorus girl in New York. Rumor had it he maintained an apartment in the city where he often brought the young beauties he seduced. I shuddered to think of it.

Now he dared speak crudely of George Peabody Wetmore, a respected U.S. senator *and* one of Newport's most generous and esteemed residents. Even if this Dingley Tariff deserved Whittaker's and the others' disdain, out of a sense of indignation I found myself hoping the opposition won out in the matter. Intrigued, I turned my head slightly to block out the distracting sights and sounds of the polo grounds.

"I suppose Wetmore and the Republicans believe they're protecting American interests," Robert Clarkson murmured.

"What they're doing," Harry Lehr countered, "is creating American monopolies that will allow a very few select men to dictate supply and price."

"That is precisely what sticks in my craw. Wetmore's father made his fortune in the China trade, an international endeavor if ever there was one." Whittaker spewed an oath I would be ashamed to repeat. "Now he wants to prevent the rest of us from doing the same. It's insufferable." Whittaker's voice became a low growl. I strained to make out his words. "He can't be allowed to get away with it."

A chill swept my arms. Exactly what did he mean by that?

"Wetmore's not alone in his protectionist thinking." Harry Lehr gave a mirthless chuckle. "What do you plan to do, Whittaker, take them *all* down?"

A long pause ensued, and then Whittaker spoke again. "No. Not all."

Lehr laughed again. "Don't be ridiculous. Look, the bill might not pass, and all our grumbling will be for nothing."

"*I'm* being ridiculous?" Whittaker shot back. "Lehr, the only reason you won't actively take up the fight is because you're hoping Wetmore will let you marry his daughter."

My eyes widened. Harry Lehr and one of the Wetmore sisters? This was news. I could hardly fathom such a match, nor did I believe for one minute George Wetmore would consider it. The Misses Wetmore had been carefully educated and groomed to be respectable ladies. Great ladies, like my cousin Consuelo, who was now a duchess. Harry Lehr, on the other hand, was hardly known for his gentlemanly virtues or financial prospects. However charming he might be when he wished, rumors abounded concerning his many ribald antics and reckless business schemes.

What could he be thinking?

As if to answer my question, Robert Clarkson sniggered. "You'd sell us all out for Miss Maude's dowry, eh, Lehr?"

"And quite a dowry it'll be, my good man," Lehr said with a snide laugh. "You've seen how she dresses. Her sister, too. Neither one of them goes in much for French frippery, which means that much more to line my pockets."

While the others snickered, a sour taste filled my mouth. Yes, despite the Wetmores' wealth, it was true the sisters were governed by good old-fashioned, New England thriftiness. How dare any man seek to take advantage of their good sense?

So it was the younger sister, twenty-four-year-old Maude, he was after. Did he think he had a better chance of winning her than her older sister, Edith? Or did he consider Miss Edith too long on the shelf? Either way, more fool he. A man like George Wetmore wouldn't allow Harry Lehr within a hundred yards of either of his daughters. And in my opinion, both ladies were too sensible to suffer his attentions for long. Both had been courted in the past, but thus far neither had found a man enough to her liking to prompt her to spend the rest of her life with him. Unlike most ladies of the Four Hundred, the Wetmore sisters refused to marry merely for appearance's sake.

I could not blame them. After all, I lived according to the same principle.

From the field, the warning bell for the next chukker sounded. The spectators ceased stomping earth back into place and dispersed to their pavilions and seats in the grandstand, or climbed back up to their blanketed perches on Morton Hill. The eight players rode onto the field on fresh horses. Behind them came the two mounted referees. A stocky man in dark trousers, checkered cutaway, and a rather flat-crowned derby walked out onto the field. If nothing else, his hat identified him, for it had become his trademark, much to the chagrin of his more fashionable peers in the nation's capital. Where other senators sported top hats on their way into Congress, George Wetmore insisted on wearing his derby. They called it disrespectful, but that didn't deter Mr. Wetmore. He raised his arm and tossed out the ball, beginning the chukker and setting the riders in motion.

Time for me to return to my official business of reporting on the match for the *Observer*, where I ran my weekly Fancies and Fashions page during the Summer Season. Never mind that I had rather learn what the bitter triumvirate beneath the weeping beech was planning in response to the proposed import tariff. Mr. Millford expected an article detailing the match and today's fashion highlights on his desk first thing in the morning.

In no particular hurry, I moved away from the tree and strolled toward the field. A moment later the branches of the beech swished behind me as they were swept aside, and all three men strode in single file by me. Each tipped his hat in passing, and I received a clipped "good morning" from Henry Lehr.

As the others kept on, Harry Lehr suddenly stopped, pivoted, and pinned his gaze on me. He waited until only a few yards separated us. I stopped short at his abrupt step toward me.

"Miss Cross." He swept his top hat off his head and tipped me a bow—a mocking one. "Always on the lookout for a story, aren't you?"

A quirk of his eyebrow suggested that his question wasn't a rhetorical one. "I'm covering the match of course, Mr. Lehr."

"Are you, indeed? Then perhaps you should stay away from the trees, Miss Cross. The match is that way, on the field." He pointed with an outstretched arm.

"I'm on my way back now." I tried to keep my voice light, unconcerned.

He moved another step closer. "Listening in on other people's private conversations isn't very ladylike. I'd advise against it, if you don't want others to think ill of you. And you'd do best to keep whatever you think you heard to yourself."

"I assure you I was not—"

He didn't linger to hear the rest of my lie, but strode past me, shoving his top hat back over his straight, dark hair. I drew a rather shaky breath. Here I thought I'd been discreet, but I had underestimated Harry Lehr's powers of observation. Now that I considered it, it only made sense that a man like Lehr, a gentleman with little inheritance who had learned to live off the largesse of high society, would be keenly attuned to his surroundings at all times. He wouldn't want to miss an opportunity. Nor would he want me to give the Wetmores advance warning of his designs on their younger daughter.

I dismissed the incident when sharp voices resonated from a few yards beyond the foot of Morton Hill, both male and female and none too friendly. I raised my face to see from beneath my hat brim.

Two policemen blocked a woman's path as she seemed to be attempting to make her way toward the grandstand, which was reserved for the wealthy cottagers. Obviously, she could not have paid the costly admission fee, or the police would not have stopped her. I couldn't make out her identity, but even from a distance and in the glaring sun, I saw that she wore a tasteful day dress and matching Eton jacket of rose silk with plum trim. I made my way closer, slowly, pretending to scan the spectators in a general way. It was then I spotted the inconsistencies in the role the woman attempted to play: the slightly ragged quality of the ostrich feather in her hat, a complete lack of jewelry, a drawstring bag that tried but didn't quite match her ensemble. The closer I went, the more I realized the trim on her outfit had been added by a less-than-nimble seamstress, for the velvet embellishment rippled where it should have lain perfectly flat. What had appeared elegant from a distance revealed itself on closer inspection as shabby, almost garish, in ways no society lady would ever countenance.

My reporter's instincts came alert. As I looked on, she attempted to push past the two policemen. I moved closer, within hearing distance.

"You don't understand. I must speak with Mrs. Wetmore."

I halted. Had I heard her correctly?

One of the officers caught her elbow and spun her around. "I don't think so."

She tugged free and attempted another dodge past her pursuers. "If you'd allow me to see her for one minute, I'll say my piece and be on my way."

"Of course you will. Now, let's be a good girl and come along." The same policeman reached for her again.

I heard a breathless murmur behind me. "Lilah."

I peered over my shoulder. Harry Lehr, Robert Clarkson,

and Stanford Whittaker had circled back around and now stood not far behind me, watching the policemen's attempts to remove the trespasser. Which one of them had spoken? I could not have said, for the voice had been too low to identify.

I stole another glance behind me. A third policeman had apparently hurried to the grandstand and alerted George Wetmore, for with a deep frown the senator came striding across the lawn, the officer trailing him. I recognized the moment his gaze lit on the intruder, for he came to an abrupt halt and surveyed the scene with a baffled expression. Obviously he, too, wondered what a woman from among the spectators on Morton Hill could want with his wife. The woman with the ragged ostrich feather caught his gaze, but rather than call out to him, she looked quickly away and took a step back as if searching for an escape.

George Wetmore continued toward her. Did he know this woman who demanded to speak with his wife, and who seemed to be known by other men in his social circle? A possibility sprang to mind, one that left me gaping—that she was, perhaps, George Wetmore's mistress. It seemed impossible, based on all I knew about him. Upstanding, charitable, hardworking, and, as a former Rhode Island governor and present U.S. senator, dedicated to public service.

At the thudding of footsteps behind me, I turned to see Harry Lehr, Robert Clarkson, and Stanford Whittaker walking at a brisk pace back to the grandstand. Again I wondered which one had spoken the name *Lilah*. But perhaps all three of them knew her. Where would three well-bred gentlemen have occasion to meet a woman of such modest means?

As if she had heard the intruder calling to her, which of course she could not have from that distance, Mrs. Wetmore made her way through the crush and came in our direction.

Had she noticed her husband's departure from the match? Perhaps, for now she slowly followed in his wake, holding her skirts above the tips of the grass. Concern grew on her middle-aged but still attractive features.

Quickly I raised my own skirts and made my way to her. I'm not exactly certain why I felt it my duty to shield this society matron from potential unpleasantness. Perhaps the contemptuous conversation I'd overheard beneath the beech tree had raised a protective instinct or two. Hastily I closed the distance between Mrs. Wetmore and myself.

"Ma'am, there appears to be a trespasser making a bit of a scene, but it seems under control."

Mrs. Wetmore stopped beside me but her gaze remained on her husband. Her own frown deepened. The altercation continued, but the policemen were succeeding in bustling the woman away. George Wetmore lingered, watching. At the same time, a man in work clothes and a wide straw hat came down from the hill and trotted to catch up with the woman and the policemen who were ushering her away. He fell into step beside them and tipped his head to hers, obviously speaking. I tried to make out his identity but they were too far from me now, and his hat cast a shadow over his face. But the woman's pleading had stopped, and she allowed the policemen to escort her off the grounds without further ado.

"What on earth is going on, and why is my husband involved?" Mrs. Wetmore started forward.

"Ma'am, please, I don't think you should." I again scanned Morton Hill. Were there other reporters watching from among the common folk? These matches were typically attended by journalists from Tiverton, New Bedford, even Providence and New York. Not all of them were willing to practice discretion, as I did when circumstances warranted. Again, I half questioned my motives in trying to protect Mrs. Wetmore.

Most of the Four Hundred were quite capable of taking care of themselves. But the Wetmores were different. Perhaps because they were lifelong Newport residents rather than summer transplants, I couldn't help feeling a kind of kinship toward them—however removed.

George Wetmore, apparently satisfied that he had seen the last of that woman for the time being, turned about, saw his wife, and rushed over to us. When he reached us he caught his wife's hand and drew her several steps away from me. "My dear, it's nothing. An unfortunate miscreant wanting a handout, I'm quite sure."

"How do you know?" Mrs. Wetmore spoke in a calm, genteel tone. "Did she speak to you?"

"Indeed not. If she wishes something from us, there are proper channels she may follow. We do enough to succor the poor without their having to seek us out at sporting events. And I refuse to reward bad behavior."

"Will she be arrested?" Mrs. Wetmore appeared saddened by the prospect.

Her husband shook his head. "She's been warned not to attempt such a stunt again. If she is so bold as to seek us out a second time, then yes, she'll find herself behind bars."

"Us, George? You mean she came here specifically to appeal to you and me?"

"Uh, er, yes, she did. But never mind. Come, dearest, let us return to our pavilion before our friends begin to wonder what's happened to us." He spared me a glance. "Ah, Miss Cross is it? I hope I can depend on you not to—"

I held up a hand in a gesture of reassurance. "There is nothing here to report, sir, other than the match. As you said, an unfortunate woman decided upon an ill-advised undertaking."

Nodding, Mr. Wetmore offered his wife the crook of his arm and drew her toward the field. "But George," she said as he ushered her away, "why us? There are so many others here to whom she might have stretched out her hand."

"She must have heard what a tender heart you have, my dear."

I wondered about that. Mrs. Wetmore *was* known in Newport and throughout the state for her philanthropic efforts. She even supported St. Nicholas Orphanage in Providence, as did I. But she was not known as a woman who simply doled out money to all who asked. She expected something in return for her generosity, namely, that the recipients of her benevolence use the opportunity to better their circumstances. It was a philosophy to which I myself subscribed. It wasn't enough to simply feed someone, although at first basic sustenance might mean the difference between life and death. But after that, a person must learn to feed themselves if they are to achieve any dignity and fulfillment in this world.

I yearned to follow the trespasser and question her. She might have scoffed at me, but more often than not I have found troubled individuals willing to speak of their adversity. A way to lift part of the weight from their shoulders, at least temporarily, I supposed. But if Mrs. Wetmore was known for her philanthropy, I, too, was known in Newport for taking in young women in need of a haven. My home, Gull Manor, had become a stopover for any honest soul—or even not so honest—looking to escape regrettable circumstances and start afresh. The tradition had started with my great aunt Sadie, who had left Gull Manor to me in her will, and at the same time imparted to me the responsibility of helping my less fortunate sisters.

Sighing, I retrieved my pen and tablet from my purse. Yes, I took strays into my home, and with the help of my housekeeper, Nanny, I fed them, taught them skills such as reading, writing, mathematics, sewing, and cooking, and once they healed from whatever wounds had sent them to me, I gave them what cash I could spare and wished them Godspeed. I could do none of those things without an income of my own. My article for the Newport *Observer* beckoned.

Before I could take up position along the sidelines again, my half brother Brady stopped me. Having not seen him for several weeks, I tossed my arms around him. Like George Wetmore, he, too, had eschewed the traditional morning coat and top hat, and instead looked quite the sporting gentleman. A straw boater topped his sandy blond hair, and he wore tan linen slacks and a striped suit coat and waistcoat, perfectly tailored and crisply new. Working in Manhattan for my Vanderbilt relatives had given Brady new confidence to go along with his greater salary.

"What was that about?" he asked in an undertone. His eyes gleamed with interest. Leave it to my older brother to never miss a thing.

"I'm not quite sure." I told him the plain facts as I'd observed them, including Mr. Wetmore's claim that the woman had asked for money. She had made no such request in my hearing. And then I remembered the name I'd overheard. "Does the name Lilah mean anything to you?"

A slight flush bloomed on Brady's cheeks. "I, uh . . . Lilah, you say?"

I lowered my voice another notch. "Is she George Wetmore's mistress?"

"Good grief, no."

I leaned closer and peered up at him beneath the brim of his boater. "Don't toy with me, Brady. Who is she?"

"Well, Em, as you know, any number of women might be named Lilah. Just because I might happen to know one doesn't mean I know them all."

"Brady, please." Despite the polite word I used, I spoke through gritted teeth and with an implied threat he couldn't ignore. Brady might be several years my senior, but somewhere along the way I had taken up a parental role and helped keep my brother out of trouble more times than I cared to remember. That had changed the nature of our relationship forever and given me an upper hand I wasn't afraid to wield under the right circumstances.

His eyes narrowed. "How did *you* come by that name?"

Although I was growing annoyed enough to whack him with my notepad, I nevertheless replied, "I overheard it a few minutes ago. I don't believe the speaker meant to utter it. Rather, the shock of seeing the woman yanked it from him."

"Really. Who was this? Surely not Wetmore."

"No. I didn't see directly nor could I hear well enough to identify him, but either Stanford Whittaker, Robert Clarkson, or Harry Lehr."

"Humph. Doesn't surprise me one bit that it would be one of them." He glanced from side to side, and then over his shoulder to ensure no one would overhear him. With his hand cupping his mouth, he leaned close to my ear. "She works at the Blue Moon Tavern."

I gasped, but only slightly. In fact, it was more of an *I thought so* gasp than one of surprise, because if she wasn't someone's mistress, this explanation suited equally well. The Blue Moon held a notorious reputation in town, and the appellation of *tavern* was understood to be a polite euphemism for the truth. "Why on earth would she want to speak with Mrs. Wetmore?"

"*Mrs.* Wetmore?" Brady removed his boater and raked his fingers through his hair. "Good grief, Em, tell me they didn't speak to each other." Again he glanced behind him. He knew as well as I what kind of scandal would ensue should anyone learn a prostitute had asked for Mrs. Wetmore by name, as if they shared a prior acquaintance.

I shook my head. "No, I stopped Mrs. Wetmore from following her husband. I'm not even sure why I did it."

"I'll tell you why. You're too decent to let someone walk unknowingly into her own ruination. Not to mention her husband's."

"I think you're exaggerating the danger, Brady."

"Perhaps, but only a bit. You and I both know it."

"Well, disaster averted, I hope." A sharp thwack and cheering from the field reminded me of my obligations. Still, I lingered as I regarded my brother. "How was Uncle Cornelius when you last saw him?"

A shadow fell across his usually jovial face. He shook his head. "Not well, I'm afraid. Still bedridden, for the most part."

"And his speech?"

"Little improved. I believe his mind is as sharp as ever, Em, but it's as if he's trapped inside his own body."

"Oh, Brady, how dreadful. Cornelius Vanderbilt was the strongest man I've ever known, and to think of him as helpless and dependent . . ." A weight pressed against my breastbone. "I saw Neily a little while ago. Apparently they still blame him."

Brady set his boater back on his head. "Yes, I'm afraid so, at least where Alice and Gertrude are concerned. And the old man won't hear Neily's name mentioned. He makes that more than evident even without the power of speech. I might risk my employment by standing up for him, but Em, I can't just sit by and see Neily demonized for marrying a woman he cares so deeply about. Luckily, Alfred and even William see my side of it, even though outwardly they feel obligated to show Neily the cold shoulder."

By Alfred, Brady referred to Neily's younger brother, who had taken over for his father at the New York Central. William Vanderbilt was Cornelius's brother. I understood why they must appear to stand with the family in this matter—unless and until Cornelius and Alice relented—but I was glad for Neily's sake that he did have allies, even covert ones.

I returned to our earlier subject. "Tell me more about the Blue Moon."

"Good grief, Em, I'm not going to talk about that place with you."

"You may spare me the baser details, thank you. I merely want to know who is in charge should I need to speak with anyone."

"Absolutely not."

"It could be important if Mrs. Wetmore is harassed again. I'll . . . pass the information on to Jesse." I improvised that last assurance, knowing I'd gain more insight from Brady if he believed I'd let our mutual friend, Detective Jesse Whyte of the Newport Police Department, conduct any necessary interviews.

"Well . . . all right." Brady went on to convey the details I sought, and ended with a protestation that he had only come by the information through hearsay.

"Of course," I readily agreed. "How else? I'd better get back to work." I leaned in to kiss Brady on the cheek, then laughed as I remembered a happier detail. "Say hello to Hannah for me, if I don't see you again before the match ends. And come by the house for supper as soon as you're able—both of you. Nanny has been wanting to cook for you."

I awoke with a gasp, a ringing in my ears, and a warm weight pinning my legs to the bed. It took several moments before my sleep-befuddled mind identified both the ringing and weight, the former being the telephone in the alcove downstairs, and the latter my dog, who had crawled up from the foot of the bed to nudge me from sleep.

"*Woof.*"

Blinking in the darkness, I eased Patch, part spaniel and part mystery, off me and flipped back the covers. The telephone jangled relentlessly. I gazed at the gap I always left in the curtains to allow the dawn's first rays to awaken me, but no sun peeked in from the seaward horizon. What time could it be? Patch must have wondered too, for he tilted his head as he peered at me, his brown ear twitching forward while the white one simply hung.

All at once, the portent of a ringing telephone in the dead of night gripped me with its urgency. Frantically I swept my feet over the floor beside my bed, searching until I found my slippers. No good could come from the summons of a telephone at such an hour, and my mind turned over several possibilities with lightning speed. Brady was in trouble. Uncle Cornelius had passed away. Some accident had befallen Neily. Ill news from my parents. But no, that last, I reasoned, would come by telegram and not over the telephone lines, as Mother and Father had returned to Paris in the spring.

I grabbed the shawl I had tossed over a chair last night and threw my door wide. Patch leaped down from the bed and was beside me in an instant, his furry tail arced and waving. His nails clicked on the oaken treads as he preceded me down the stairs. Finally, my shawl half falling from my shoulders, I squeezed past him into the alcove beneath the stairs and snatched up the ear trumpet. "Yes? This is Emma Cross."

"Emma, it's Jesse. How soon can you be dressed and ready to accompany me?"

"Accompany you where?"

"Chateau sur Mer." It was all the explanation he offered. I

knew better than to press him when he spoke in that concise, authoritative manner.

"I can be ready as soon as you get here. Are you still in town?"

"No. I'm at Chateau sur Mer with the Wetmores. Don't worry, no one in the family has been harmed. I'll start out now."

He disconnected, and as I replaced the ear trumpet back onto its cradle, heavy thuds and creaking wood sounded from the staircase above my head.

"What was that?"

I left the alcove, nearly tripping over Patch in the process, and met Nanny at the bottom of the steps. She held her dressing gown closed over a faded nightgown, her hair in curling rags and covered by a kerchief. I had known Mary O'Neal all my life. She had been my nurse when I was a child, Brady's too, and when I left my parents' home in our harborside Point neighborhood to take up residence here at Gull Manor on Ocean Avenue, Nanny had come with me as my housekeeper. *Grandmother* seemed a more accurate term for the woman who had soothed me, scolded me when I needed it, taught me, encouraged me, and stayed steadily by me all these years. I kissed her cheek, velvety soft with age.

"It was Jesse," I replied, feeling a sudden chill and hugging my shawl about me. "Something has happened at Chateau sur Mer. He needs me there."

"You? Why?" She clucked. "Never mind. I've learned better than to ask. I'll put the kettle on to boil and heat up some johnnycakes."

"There may not be time. Jesse's on his way now."

"There's time. You go get dressed." She called to Patch. "Come on, boy. You'll be needing a trip outside and then some breakfast, too."

Some forty minutes later Jesse and I drove up the driveway of the Wetmore estate on Bellevue Avenue. A faint light shimmered on the horizon far out over the Atlantic. Standing beside another of those giant weeping beech trees whose branches undulated like seaweed on the tide, Chateau sur Mer possessed a solid dignity that spoke of tradition and distinction. If The Breakers and Marble House personified the extravagance and vanity of my Vanderbilt relatives, this Second Empire French chateau, built of granite blocks and sporting two towers and a steep mansard roof, just as surely exemplified the upright and dependable George Peabody Wetmore. Jesse had told me little in the carriage, except to confirm that the Wetmores were all still alive, and that an incident like those that had brought the two of us together last summer and autumn had once again occurred. I knew what that meant, and I shivered in the predawn chill.

Three other police wagons and an ambulance populated the lengthy circular driveway. Light spilled from every room on the ground floor, and a few of the second-story windows as well. Jesse maneuvered the carriage around to the side of the house, to the new entrance the Wetmores had built during their extensive renovations. We exited the carriage beneath a sheltering porte cochere.

Strained, bewildered voices reached my ears as soon as Jesse opened the front door. I needn't take many steps beyond the vestibule to discover why.

Two policemen crouched at the bottom of one side of the double staircase. Between the two flights rose a tree of life mural painted on the soffit where the staircases merged at the half landing and continued as one to the second floor. After the darkness of the ride over, I blinked in the sudden glare of gas lighting.

It took several moments for my eyes to adjust, and for the full impact of the sight before me to register. When it did, it struck with the force of a pony-driven polo mallet. I now saw what the officers crouched over. Brown hair, curled into spirals, tumbled across a white, lifeless face, and a plum and rose gown lay tangled around legs thrust at odd angles, as if by a fall. Yes, certainly the result of a fall. But it was the neck and the position of the head that drew a gasp of dismay from me, along with a name:

"Lilah."

Chapter 2

"You know her?" Only a hint of incredulity tinged Jesse's question, for he had grown accustomed to my activities in recent years and little I did could surprise him. "Is she someone you helped? Took in at Gull Manor?"

I shook my head, staring down at the lifeless face. One of the policemen brought a lantern closer. Her eyes were blue—the blue of shallow ocean waves in high summer. Except for where an odd streak of amber spilled across the iris of the left eye. I wondered, had people often commented on it? Was it something Lilah ignored, or did she peer into the mirror and wish the minor flaw gone? There was so much we didn't know about her, would never know.

"I never saw her before yesterday's polo match." I turned to gaze into Jesse's face—youthful despite his thirty-odd years, fair and freckled in keeping with his Scots Irish heritage—but I did so more to avoid looking any longer at the tragedy sprawled before me.

He laid a hand on my shoulder. "She's the one who attempted to push her way down to the privileged seating, isn't she?"

"Yes. She was insisting she needed to speak to . . ." I trailed off, staring through the wide doorway into Chateau sur Mer's Tapestry Hall. Voices continued to echo from a room somewhere across the way. I spoke lower. "She demanded to speak to Mrs. Wetmore, but the police officers hurried her away from the grounds and warned her not to come back." I exhaled, long and hard. "What happened here?"

"That's what I intend to find out. Come."

I hesitated, prompting Jesse to halt and turn back to me. Over the past two years my friendship with him had strengthened, but we had also formed a partnership wherein Jesse often consulted with me on difficult cases. I had more than proved my ability to string together clues and deduce theories, possibilities, even conclusions. But always in the past Jesse resisted seeking my insight until a mystery became particularly perplexing. He rarely sought me out at the onset of a case.

"Why am I here?" I asked.

"Because Mrs. Wetmore asked for you."

Without further ado he grasped my hand and led me through the Tapestry Hall, oddly named for it contained no such artwork. Three stories opened above us with rectangular galleries overlooking the hall, the underside of each repeating the tree of life motif begun on the staircase. High above my head, gas jets illuminated a stained glass ceiling as if lit by a sun that had yet to rise. A cold hearth gaped at us from within its carved mantel and decorative tiles. Gas chandeliers, reflected in numerous mirrors, brought out the shimmer of red silk wall coverings and heavily coffered wainscoting. Our footsteps seemed astonishingly loud on the herringbone parquet floor.

From here we passed into the library. Seated around a square table were Mr. and Mrs. Wetmore and their two adult daughters, Edith, named for their mother, and Maude. The dark woodwork continued here, now of burled walnut, with pilasters bisecting the walls every few feet. The overall effect was one of warmth, elegance, and stately endurance. George Wetmore was scowling at the policeman presently talking to him. The young officer and I were well acquainted, as we had grown up in the same neighborhood.

"At some point, sir," Officer Scotty Binsford said in a respectful tone, "we'll need to ask your sons whether they heard anything."

Mrs. Wetmore reached over and pressed her hand to her husband's wrist. "George, we mustn't involve Billy and Rogers. They're just children."

"We most certainly will not, my dear." Mr. Wetmore's expression had eased slightly at his wife's words. Now the full force of his scowl returned as he addressed Scotty. "It is bad enough, young man, that you insisted on questioning my daughters. They heard nothing, saw nothing, as they have told you more than once. We would greatly appreciate . . ."

Whatever he would have appreciated we were not to know, for as Jesse and I entered the room he fell silent. The four Wetmores turned haunted, stunned expressions up at us. Miss Maude, the younger sister, looked close to tears. The family resemblance between the three women was strong, though Edith, nearly thirty, favored her mother more closely, while Maude, at twenty-four, was fairer, her features more delicate.

Only the day before I had overheard Harry Lehr's intentions toward her. While certainly not homely, Miss Maude would not be considered a beauty, and Mr. Lehr's fondness for beautiful women was notorious. I vowed then and there to intervene should I spy the merest hint of Miss Maude falling prey to Harry Lehr's charms.

"I'll take over from here." Jesse gestured at the doorway,

and the uniformed officers took their cue to leave. "Close the door," he added quietly.

"Wait." George Wetmore stood. "Edie, Maude, go back to your rooms for now. Take the back stairs."

His wife winced at this reminder of the body lying at the foot of the main staircase. Maude started to rise, but her elder sister stayed her with a hand on her shoulder.

"Father, please. Maude and I aren't children. We're thoroughly capable of hearing what must be said."

"Girls." It was their mother who spoke. "Do as your father says. If you wish to be of use, then be on hand when your brothers awaken. They'll want to know why they aren't allowed downstairs." She turned a remarkably calm face in my direction. "We've posted a footman outside Rogers and Billy's room."

I merely nodded. The sisters paused another moment, silently conferring with a look that passed between them. Then both turned to scrutinize me, no doubt wondering about my presence there. Their chins jutted in nearly identical ways as they took my measure. Then, almost as one, they stood, leaned to kiss their mother on either cheek, spared a glance for their father, and swept by Jesse and me.

Their parents each released a breath of relief. Then Mrs. Wetmore stood and approached me. "Miss Cross, thank you for coming. Please, sit beside me."

Taking my hand, she led me to the chair Miss Maude had vacated, and then resumed her own seat. She continued to hold my hand even after I settled in next to her. I still couldn't fathom why she'd sent for me, nor could I ask in such deplorable circumstances. I trusted that the answer would unfold in the next few moments.

Apparently, George Wetmore felt equally puzzled by my presence. He glared at me from across the table and spoke quietly to his wife. "Why is she here, my dear? Don't you realize what this young woman *does* here in Newport?"

My pulse quickened. I didn't like being talked about as if I weren't in the room—or perhaps didn't warrant being spoken to directly. But then, not everyone in Newport treated me as my Vanderbilt relatives did. Though they acknowledged me as their poor relation, they nonetheless esteemed and respected me for the person I was. There were plenty of others among the Four Hundred who considered me of little account, who put up with my presence at their social gatherings because they enjoyed how I reported on the splendor of their homes and the lavishness of their wardrobes.

I had thought better of George Wetmore. I had believed that as a year-round resident of the city, except when his senatorial duties sent the family to Washington, he might hold his fellow Newporters in higher regard.

Mrs. Wetmore seemed to take issue with neither her husband's disapproval nor my status as a reporter. "I do, George, but that is not why I asked Miss Cross here. I will trust her to keep our confidence." She glanced at me. I nodded my pledge of discretion. But I was no less mystified than before.

A knock sounded and the door into the hall opened. A man with dark hair, silvered at the temples, took one stride over the threshold and stopped. He was dressed in formal black and wore white gloves. I noticed his shoes made no sound when he stepped in. The butler, I deduced, correctly. "Sir, the servants are all awake and accounted for." He spoke with a cultured English accent.

Mr. Wetmore, sitting with his back to the door, didn't bother turning. "Did you find everyone in their rooms?"

"Everyone, sir, except Lucy, who was already up and preparing for her day."

"I'll need to speak with this Lucy," Jesse said to Mr. Wetmore.

"Lucy's a good girl," the senator retorted. "She didn't do anything. Thank you, Callajheue, that will be all for now."

The butler bowed and retreated, closing the door behind him.

Jesse took a seat at the table. "Now then, sir, what can you tell me about the woman, Lilah Buford? She approached you at the match this afternoon?"

"Not exactly. She was attempting to make her way from the general seating on Morton Hill to the grandstand. The police stopped her, and one of them came to me and informed me of the matter."

"Did you see her face, sir, and if so, did you recognize her?"

"I did, and no, I'd never laid eyes on her before in my life," the senator stated as if sitting in a witness box.

Jesse's brows drew together. "Any idea, then, why she specifically asked for you by name?"

"She did not, Detective." Mrs. Wetmore's grip on my hand tightened. "She asked for me."

"Edith." Mr. Wetmore's voice hissed with warning.

She met his caution with a righteous lift of her eyebrows. "That is what you told me, George. We must tell the detective the truth."

"Had you ever seen her before, ma'am?" Jesse asked.

George Wetmore held out his hand to forestall his wife's answer. "Of course she hasn't. What can you possibly be thinking, asking my wife such a question? This woman broke into our home, undoubtedly to rob us and murder us in our beds, and . . . she fell from our staircase. Drunk, I suspect, as she must have been drunk earlier today at the match."

"She might have been inebriated tonight, sir," Jesse said evenly. "That's for the coroner to determine. But the officers who ejected her from the polo grounds reported no odor of alcohol hanging about Miss Buford. They made a point in their report to state she did not appear in any way incapacitated."

"Then how do you explain her behavior?" George Wetmore's voice rose to a near bellow.

"That's what we are going to find out." Jesse flipped open a notepad and set his pencil to the paper. "But as for murdering anyone in their beds, no weapon has been found on the body."

"Surely you haven't checked everywhere," Mr. Wetmore challenged. "It could be hidden . . . somewhere on her person." He darted a glance at his wife, whose face suffused with color at this indelicate reference to where on a woman's person a weapon might be hidden. "I'm sorry, my dear," he said sheepishly, and reached over to pat her hand.

Jesse repeated his question. "Now then, Mrs. Wetmore, had you ever set eyes on Lilah Buford before yesterday morning?"

"You don't have to answer that, my dear."

"No, George, it's perfectly all right. The answer is no, I have not. And I do not know what she could have wanted with me. Although, I am involved with numerous philanthropic projects here in the city. Perhaps she thought I might be persuaded to give her money for some cause or other."

Jesse's and my gazes met. While approaching a wealthy woman in a public place might seem more advisable than attempting to call on her in her home, where Lilah undoubtedly would be turned away, the prostitute's demeanor at the match had spoken of greater urgency than simply wanting a handout.

Jesse appeared to read my mind. "The servants will be questioned to make sure Miss Buford never attempted to visit you here."

"Preposterous." Mr. Wetmore scoffed. "If she had, don't you think I would have been informed?"

"Still and all, sir, it behooves the police to ask. Now then." Once more Jesse set his pencil to the page open before him. He had been jotting down his observations, which I knew from experience included more than simply the replies of those he questioned. He also recorded their expressions, hesitancies, gestures. "I wished to spare Mrs. Wetmore the more sordid details of this case, but since she insists on being present, I must now speak of Lilah Buford's activities in town." His own expression became apologetic.

The senator cleared his throat. "Must you?"

"George, let the detective speak."

George Wetmore appealed to his wife in what I expected was not the first, or even his second attempt to shield her from the unpleasantness. "My dear, wouldn't you rather leave this to the detective and me? Take Miss Cross into the Green Salon and ring for tea. I promise to apprise you of any revelations we might happen upon."

The truth suddenly dawned on me. Mrs. Wetmore didn't know how Lilah Buford made her way in the world. No one had told her. Nor, I assumed, did her daughters know. No wonder George Wetmore had wanted them away. No wonder he now gazed at his wife from beneath hooded lids, his complexion dark with foreboding.

She cast him a puzzled look in return, and said to Jesse, "Please go on, Detective, and don't feel you must spare me. I am not as delicate as all that."

Jesse drew in a breath and let it out audibly. "Mr. Wetmore, had you ever had occasion to call upon Miss Buford for the purpose of engaging her services?"

"No, I have not." At the same time he spoke, his wife said, "George, what does he mean by that?"

A growing dread forced my eyes closed. I longed to be home, eating Nanny's warm johnnycakes and drinking her strong tea, rather than in the middle of this domestic storm about to break over my head.

"George," Mrs. Wetmore repeated more forcefully, "what does the detective *mean*?"

Mr. Wetmore emitted a sound from his throat, part cough and part rumble, and poor Jesse darted glances back and forth between them, a corner of his lip caught between his teeth. It was I, finally, who explained.

"Mrs. Wetmore," I said, barely above a whisper, "Lilah Buford found it necessary to depend upon the patronage of gentlemen in order to make her way in the world."

"The patronage of . . ." Her hand flew to her lips and her eyes popped wide. "Oh! Good heavens, you mean . . . ?"

I nodded, and waited for the tempest. Yet, astonishingly, the storm did not break. Instead, I found myself anchored within the calm of the eye by Mrs. Wetmore's relentless grip on my hand. So tightly did she hold me that my eyes watered and the shelves of leather-bound volumes across the room wavered in my vision. She turned back to her husband.

"George, are you quite certain of your answer?" Her voice was flat, her expression blank, her eyes empty. She sat stoically straight in her chair, and once she had voiced her question she pinched her lips together.

"Edith . . . you must believe me. I've never set eyes on that woman before yesterday. Nor any woman of her ilk. I swear it on my life. On my love for you, my dear, and our children."

His wife didn't move a muscle, didn't bat an eye. Did she believe him? She had wrapped herself in dignity, and I guessed that from here on she would not reveal a hint of her thoughts—not if she entertained even the smallest doubt concerning her husband's integrity.

"Mr. Wetmore, where were you last night?"

The senator's attention snapped from his wife back to Jesse. "Here at home, Detective Whyte, where else?"

"All night?"

"Every moment once we arrived home from the polo grounds."

Jesse scribbled in his pad. "What time did you go to bed?"

"I believe it was ten thirty, perhaps a little after. I remember the long case clock chiming the half hour."

Jesse turned to Mrs. Wetmore. "Did you retire at the same time as your husband?"

She nodded, her lips tight. Much to my relief, her fingers eased slightly around my own.

"Did you both sleep through the night?" Jesse asked.

"Until a noise woke me." George Wetmore raised a hand to the bridge of his nose and pinched it. "I almost believed I'd dreamed it, but something didn't feel right. The *house* didn't feel right to me. I rose, put on my dressing gown, and came downstairs. That . . ." He broke off, swallowed, and shook his head several times in rapid motions. "That is when I saw her."

Jesse nodded coolly as he took notes. "And Mrs. Wetmore, when did you first realize something wasn't right?"

She breathed in sharply through her nose. For a moment I feared she would refuse to answer, but then she raised her eyebrows and said, "I awoke and discovered George's side of the bed empty." She blushed and lowered her gaze. Most wealthy couples maintained separate bedroom suites. I had no doubt the Wetmores each had their own bedroom, but perhaps had taken to sharing a room nonetheless. That alone spoke volumes about the nature of their marriage.

When she said no more Jesse prompted her. "You discovered your husband gone and then what?"

"Must you goad my wife, Detective?"

"I must get at the truth, sir. Ma'am?"

Mrs. Wetmore gazed over at me and I gave her a nod of encouragement.

She sighed. "Well, coming fully awake, I decided to go downstairs and find him. I thought we might sneak down to the kitchen and make tea or warm some milk. But when I turned at the half landing, there he was, kneeling at the bottom, leaning over that . . . that . . ."

"Don't, Edith." Mr. Wetmore scrubbed a hand across his face. "Please don't think of it. Don't think of *her*."

"We have no choice, George, do we? We must think about her, and how she entered our home and died."

There came a knock at the door, and it opened upon Scotty Binsford. "The coroner is here, sir." Jesse nodded his acknowledgment, and Scotty continued. "It looks as though she came in from the veranda and through the ballroom. One of the doors appears to have been jimmied open."

"Have you found where she likely gained entrance to the grounds?" Jesse asked him.

"Not yet. We're waiting for more light to search for footprints, but she could have entered anywhere along the perimeter. The walls aren't high enough to keep anyone out."

That was true. The stone walls surrounding Chateau sur Mer were far more ornamental than protective. While locked gates at the end of the main and service driveways would keep out vehicles, someone intent upon trespassing could simply climb over.

"Check the Moongate," I suggested.

"Why there?" Jesse's question didn't challenge my suggestion as irrelevant, but rather, sought the logic of it.

"She would not have been seen," I replied. It was true that Lilah could have scaled the low walls at any point along the perimeter. The Moongate, however, presented an inviting alternative. The circular, ornamental gate, flanked on either side by arcing stone steps that met at a seat at the top, was located on the south side of the property, on quiet Shepard Avenue, rather than on Bellevue where, even in the middle of the night, an intruder risked being seen by homebound partygoers. The gate itself was a rather flimsy affair of thin, waist-high iron dowels and a laughable lock. If Lilah Buford managed to pry open one of the ballroom doors, she certainly could have done likewise to the gate. "Also, since the Moongate is on the south side of the property, it's more in a direct line to the veranda."

Jesse smiled—just the barest curling at the corners of his lips intended for my eyes alone. He peered out the front-facing window. Gray light gathered over the lawn, revealing the mist-laden driveway and Bellevue Avenue beyond. "You should be able to see well enough now. Check for footprints. And check that veranda carefully." Before Scotty backed out of the room, Jesse vacated his seat and approached him. "See if you can discover whether Lilah entered the estate alone or not." Scotty nodded and left. Jesse addressed Mr. and Mrs. Wetmore. "I have to speak with the coroner. I suggest the two of you remain where you are until the—until Miss Buford has been removed."

Mr. Wetmore nodded, his face grim. Mrs. Wetmore shuddered. She had yet to release my hand and cringed when Jesse spoke my name.

"Emma, a moment, if you would."

Mrs. Wetmore's hand tightened around my own again. This only baffled me further. Although I had reported on family picnics, garden parties, and her daughter Maude's birthday ball, I had never had occasion to speak personally with Mrs. Wetmore or her husband. At each of the affairs that brought me to Chateau sur Mer, I had dealt with either the house-keeper or the butler. While I thoroughly understood why she had sent her two daughters upstairs, away from the un-pleasantness, I could think of no reason why *my* presence should bring her any measure of comfort.

She reluctantly released me and I followed Jesse into the Tapestry Hall. He closed the door behind us.

"What is your sense of the Wetmores' connection to Lilah Buford's death?"

I held out my hands. "I cannot say, other than that I don't believe either one of them is capable of murder. But as to what brought Lilah here . . ."

"Are you thinking blackmail?"

I compressed my lips and considered before replying. "In other circumstances, it would seem the most likely scenario. But what can a woman in Lilah Buford's position know about people like the Wetmores? They lead impeccable lives. I cannot think of a more upstanding and sensible family than the Wetmores."

"Everyone has secrets," he reminded me.

"Perhaps. Or perhaps Lilah only *thought* she knew some-thing about the Wetmores." I was thinking specifically of a false allegation made against my relative Frederick Van-derbilt last autumn, and the terrible price paid because of it.

Jesse bobbed his head at the memories we shared of that time. He smiled again, sadly, and raised a hand to graze my cheek with the backs of his knuckles. "But the fact remains, she entered Chateau sur Mer, and she died. Whatever her er-rand was, she either fell on her way up the stairs, or she was pushed."

"Are you sure the fall was the cause of death?"

Jesse shrugged. "It certainly appears so. We detected no

sign of blood, but the coroner will make the determination."

Scotty called to Jesse from inside the ballroom. "Sir, come look at this."

Jesse touched my elbow. "Why don't you go back in with the Wetmores."

"I will, *after* we see what your men found."

Jesse knew better than to argue. We walked through the French ballroom with its varying shades of gray, gilded moldings, and bright floral-upon-yellow silk furnishings. As soon as we stepped out onto the veranda, I saw what the policemen had discovered. A line of black scuff marks marred the flooring from the edge that bordered the lawn to the door that had been forced open.

"The Wetmores could not have caused these," I said immediately.

Jesse regarded me. "To be certain of that we'll need to know who walked here yesterday and what shoes they wore."

"Had any of the Wetmores caused these marks, a servant would have cleaned them before now. And surely no servant would be so reckless as to scuff his shoes on George Wetmore's veranda."

"What color boots is Lilah Buford wearing?" As Jesse asked the question, he flipped through his notepad. "Ah, black. Obviously, she left the marks." He gestured to Scotty and the other policeman. "Go and check the Moongate."

With the body removed, Jesse allowed the Wetmores to once again move freely about the house. Their young sons, Rogers and Billy, came down from their bedroom along with their sisters, and the family adjourned to the dining room for breakfast. Jesse and I spent the next hour in the butler's pantry, interviewing the servants one by one. That is,

Jesse interviewed them. I merely observed and shared my impressions with him afterward. Each denied any knowledge of Lilah Buford. I believed them. If Lilah's errand here had involved any of the servants, she would not have attempted to approach Mrs. Wetmore at the polo match. Women of Mrs. Wetmore's station never concerned themselves with the daily affairs or private lives of their servants. That was the housekeeper's or butler's job. Lilah Buford would have arrived at the servants' entrance and demanded to speak with one of them. For that matter, if her complaint had been with a servant, she would have found the service stairs last night rather than attempting to sneak up the main staircase. The scenario of Lilah breaking into Chateau sur Mer to confront a servant seemed unlikely.

We were finishing up in the butler's pantry when Scotty Binsford called Jesse's name. "The lock on the Moongate appears to have been smashed, sir. That's not all. There are carriage tracks on the side of the road beside the gate, and a good pile of manure."

Jesse and I exchanged startled glances. We had been assuming Lilah must have walked here from town. From Lower Thames Street the distance was just over a mile. This new information suggested Lilah had come by carriage.

Jesse voiced my thoughts. "Any clue as to where this carriage is now?"

"There's no sign of it, sir," Scotty said.

"Then Lilah couldn't have come alone," I said, "unless she neglected to set the brake and the horse wandered off."

Jesse leaned against one of the countertops. "Not very likely for a carriage horse to wander off unless something frightened it."

"It isn't," I agreed.

"We need to return to the station and review everything

we've learned here." Jesse pushed away from the counter and led the way out of the room. In the Tapestry Hall, Mrs. Wetmore beckoned from a doorway.

"I must speak with you."

Jesse nodded and changed course toward her. She shook her head. "No, not you, Detective. Miss Cross. I wish to speak with Miss Cross before she leaves."

Chapter 3

❧

Jesse agreed to wait for me outside. Questions sprang to my mind but I voiced none of them aloud. Soon enough, I would discover my reason for being here. Mrs. Wetmore scurried ahead of me through the doorway into another, smaller hall tiled in black-and-white marble, with the now familiar dark walnut woodwork. This marked, I knew, the original front entrance that had faced Bellevue Avenue before Richard Morris Hunt redesigned the house and added the north entrance and porte cochere. Several double-leaf doors opened onto adjoining rooms. She led me through one of them.

I found myself in a corner parlor decorated in the Louis Quinze style, with walls covered in a cool green damask. Several French doors looked out upon the veranda and the south and west lawns. The room held a distinctly feminine air, and given its proximity to the ballroom, I surmised it to be a ladies' salon. Mrs. Wetmore led me to a gilt-framed sofa near one of the French doors. We settled side by side.

"Miss Cross, I want you to know that I have the utmost faith in my husband."

Whatever I had expected her to say, it was not this. "I'm . . . glad for that," I stammered in reply.

"I can see that you do not understand."

An understatement. I waited.

Sighing, she shifted to peer out the doors behind us. When she regarded me again, a conspiratorial expression stole across her features. "I know all about you, Miss Cross. You must realize that your escapades are no secret, that you are whispered about in salons and service corridors alike."

Heat climbed my neck and into my cheeks. Had she brought me here to chastise me? "Mrs. Wetmore . . ."

"Your abilities are much admired—secretly of course, for none of us dares express an interest in activities of which our husbands would thoroughly disapprove."

"I see, ma'am." I'm sure she deduced by my frown that I didn't see at all.

"Miss Cross, I wish you to conduct your own investigation of what that woman wanted and why she . . . why we were greeted with such a sight at the bottom of our staircase this morning."

I took a moment to absorb what she was proposing. It certainly wouldn't be the first time I'd been called upon to delve into the heart of perplexing circumstances. My own aunt Alva Vanderbilt had had me conduct such an investigation two summers ago, because she couldn't risk the police, and more importantly her peers, learning details that would permanently erase her from the Social Register.

I studied the woman before me. Mrs. Wetmore would certainly be termed a handsome woman, with light brown hair, only slightly graying, pulled back in gentle waves to a simple coif. Were those waves natural, or the result of her lady's maid's efforts? If the latter, Mrs. Wetmore employed a woman of singular skill. My gaze lowered to a straight nose, bowed lips, and a soft yet determined chin, and then back up to the eyes. They were blue, clear and calm, almost serene, with a self-possession that spoke of an intelligent mind. She had wavered earlier in the library when she learned of Lilah's profession. At that moment her faith in her husband had slipped a fraction, but she had since regained full command of herself, apparently. I had no doubt of her resolve, or that she had given serious consideration to what she was asking me to do.

One question remained. "Ma'am, if you trust your husband, why would you wish anyone but the police to investigate the matter?"

She leaned closer to me, her forefinger pointing. "That is the crux of it precisely, Miss Cross. I trust my husband, but I do not fully trust the police." She shook her head when I opened my mouth to reply. "No, you must understand. It's not that I fear the police might implicate my husband in Miss Buford's death, or in her prior . . . activities. What I fear is that the police will rush through without proving or disproving a thing, simply to have done with the matter. My husband has many influential friends who will believe they are doing him and myself an enormous favor in tying the police's hands. That is the last thing I wish."

"Then what *do* you wish, ma'am?"

"I want every possible link between my husband and this woman scoured until no secret can possibly remain hiding. It isn't enough to say a deranged woman broke into our home to rob us and fell down the stairs to her death. We must discover exactly what she wanted and why she came here, so that my husband can be utterly and completely exonerated of any wrongdoing whatsoever. Only that will do. Anything less will hang over our heads the rest of our days. If the police are forced to sweep this matter under the rug, there will always be questions and insinuations. Suspicion will dog my family—my children—always. It will cause a permanent stain upon our legacy. And I cannot have that. I will not."

There, finally, was the reason I'd been summoned this

morning, why Mrs. Wetmore insisted I be present when Jesse questioned her and her husband, and why she sent her adult daughters from the room.

Her eyes widened with expectation. "Will you do it, Miss Cross?"

The answer wasn't nearly as simple as one might think, and certainly not as clear-cut as Mrs. Wetmore hoped, judging by her eager expression. Yes, I had investigated crimes before. I had worked with Jesse, and at times even against him, to dig at the truth. I had put myself in danger numerous times, sometimes knowingly, at other times quite unawares. But on each of those occasions, I'd had a personal stake in the matter. A relative, a friend, someone I cared deeply about. I understood Mrs. Wetmore's position, her fierce desire to protect her family. I sympathized. I believed that in her shoes I would be similarly determined.

I was not her, however, and the Wetmores were not my family. Perhaps that seems selfish of me, but at twenty-three, didn't I deserve to be the slightest bit selfish? Besides, I had a surrogate family to look after: Nanny; Brady; my maid-of-all-work, Katie; and my dear little dog, Patch. I also had a legacy to uphold. Upon inheriting my seaside home, Gull Manor, from my great aunt Sadie, I also assumed the responsibility she had taken upon herself. Aunt Sadie never married and had no children, but Gull Manor had always been open to young women in need. Former prostitutes, disgraced maids, victims of some abuse or another, even abandoned children had found shelter at Gull Manor under Aunt Sadie's care. When the house became mine, so did her vocation to aid the less fortunate.

I often asked myself, which other doors in this city were as open as Gull Manor's? Where else would society's castoffs be welcome? There lay my responsibility, my obligation, my sense of duty. Not here, at Chateau sur Mer, to a family I knew not at all beyond reputation and the occasional, impersonal encounter at social events.

"Miss Cross, will you do it? Please. I don't know where else to turn."

Ironic that my thoughts had drifted to all those others who truly had nowhere else to turn, whereas I felt quite certain Mrs. George Peabody Wetmore had a spare resource or two up her silk and lace sleeve.

Still, I owed her an answer, even if I had yet to make up my mind. "I believe the best course is to wait until the coroner makes his report, and Detective Whyte has had a chance to review all the facts." And to give me time to consider this unexpected and not-altogether welcome request, I added silently.

"But Miss Cross, don't you wish to discover the truth about poor Miss Buford? Whatever she might have done, or planned to do, does she not deserve to have her last moments in life understood by someone?"

Kind words, yet they made me bristle. I felt as if Mrs. Wetmore had looked directly into my mind and heart and glimpsed one of my foremost vulnerabilities. She said at the outset of our little chat that she knew all about me. Obviously, she hadn't merely referred to my investigative skills, but rather to my life at Gull Manor and those with whom I shared my home. I bit back a retort. I did not appreciate her using my own convictions against me.

And then I sighed. "You are correct, of course, Mrs. Wetmore. Lilah Buford does deserve the truth to be known, rather than being defined by uninformed speculation. Perhaps her reasons for being in this house were not nefarious, but explainable in some other way." I drew myself up. "Yes, she deserves the truth, in the same way we all deserve our lives to be understood once we are gone."

"Then you'll do it."

I held up a hand. "I didn't say that, ma'am. I maintain that we must wait to see what Detective Whyte and the coroner can deduce. After that . . . perhaps."

We left it at that. When I rejoined Jesse outside, I didn't tell him what Mrs. Wetmore and I discussed. For now, he seemed content not to pry. For that I was glad, although eventually he would wish to know what transpired behind the closed door of the ladies' parlor. I needed time to consider, to reach a decision. But as Jesse drove me home, a weight of obligation settled heavily on my shoulders. I found no relief throughout the remainder of the day.

Jesse came to see me at home late that afternoon. He arrived without notice, though his sudden appearance didn't take me aback. I'd expected to see him as soon as he'd learned anything important. I just hadn't expected it to be quite so soon.

The day had turned blustery, with high winds and deep banks of clouds hovering low over the tossing waves. The eaves of my shingle-style house creaked and a loose shutter banged annoyingly until my maid, the red-haired Katie Dylan, found a hammer and nails and went outside to silence the ruckus.

Jesse and I settled in the front parlor with a pot of Nanny's strong Irish tea. Jesse politely refused anything to eat. I could see by his bearing that he had grave news to deliver, though he took his time about it. That set me on edge, so much so I scalded my tongue rather than waiting for my tea to cool properly. Even Patch, curled at my feet, let out several low, plaintive wines, prompting me to gently nudge him with the toe of my house slipper.

"I spoke to the coroner," he said at length, as I had guessed he would. His eyes fell closed and then opened slowly, increasing the sense of apprehension that had been growing inside me since opening the door to him. "Lilah Buford's death has become a good deal more complicated."

I set my cup and saucer on the sofa table. He sat opposite me, and I raised my chin to meet his gaze. "Please don't keep me in suspense any longer."

"I'm sorry. But it's a difficult thing to speak of." He took a fortifying sip of tea, as if it possessed the bracing effects of brandy or whiskey. "Lilah Buford was with child."

The breath left me all at once. I had not expected *this*. Nearly a full minute passed before I found my voice. "How long?"

Jesse shrugged. "The coroner estimates between six and eight weeks. No more than that."

We fell silent, each lost in our own thoughts. Had Lilah even known? The thought that perhaps she hadn't struck me as unbearably tragic. A little face took shape in my mind, a baby boy who had sojourned at Gull Manor a year ago, who in a very short time had worked his way deep into our hearts. In the end we'd had to give him up—rightly so and, for him, happily—but the experience had changed all of us who dwelt beneath this roof. Especially me. A tiny yearning had come alive inside me. Not an urgency, but a certainty that someday I would wish to be a mother.

"Poor Lilah," I found myself saying. "Her poor babe. Oh, Jesse . . ." I lowered my head to my hand and pressed my fingertips to my brow. An ache pressed against my throat.

"Emma." Jesse called to me softly. When I looked up I knew he had guessed the train of my thoughts. He, too, had held that baby boy in his arms last summer, and like me he had fought to discover the child's rightful place in the world. Jesse had come to understand the value of a human life, no matter how small, how insignificant it might seem. "Emma," he repeated. "Do you understand how this changes everything? For the Wetmores, I mean."

"Good heavens." I had been so wrapped in my memories I had forgotten that this lost life, Lilah's and her child's, held ramifications far beyond the obvious. "George Wetmore."

"Yes, George Wetmore." Jesse shook his head sadly. "A woman comes to a public arena where she has her best chance of gaining the Wetmores' attention. She demands to speak with Mrs. Wetmore, but isn't given the chance. She then turns up at their home—dead. And she is with child."

With a great effort, I pushed the words past my lips. "You believe the senator is the father, and that he killed her, don't you?"

"I believe there is a good chance the senator is the father. As to whether he killed her . . ." He breathed out harshly. "I don't want to believe it, and to tell the truth, Emma, I cannot. We're speaking of George Wetmore, for heaven's sake. A U.S. senator. A former governor of our state. A man who has lived in Newport all his life and performed countless services for his fellow man. No, Emma, I cannot believe it."

His distress was so evident, I longed to circle the sofa table, sink before him, and take his hand. I resisted the unseemly act, remaining where I was but nonetheless attempting to convey my empathy. "The most obvious conclusion isn't always the correct one. You and I know that only too well. If you cannot believe George Wetmore committed murder—and I do not either—then your instincts are telling you there is more to be learned."

He nodded, but the gloom didn't leave his eyes. "There is more, actually. There are bruises, not all of them caused by the fall. Some are older, in various states of healing. Someone had been abusing her on a regular basis."

"I'm sorry to have to point this out, but for a woman in her circumstances, such bruises are typical. You remember Stella." When he nodded, I went on. "She came to me last summer in wretched condition, but no single individual had been to blame. Although . . ." I looked down at my hands. "She did tell me that most of those injuries were inflicted by her wealthier clients, not working men or sailors. Ironic, isn't it?"

"*Revolting* is the word, I believe. Men preying on women . . ." He spoke so bluntly Patch lifted his head from his paws, his brown ear twitching. Jesse glanced away, brooding, and then smiled. "I'm sorry."

I shook my head. "No need. We both know that not all in Newport shines as it should. At the polo match, I heard some things that, in light of Lilah Buford's death, bear repeating." I leaned forward in my eagerness to impart to Jesse the conversation I'd heard between Harry Lehr, Stanford Whittaker, and Robert Clarkson. "They're angry about this tariff act. Each stands to lose, and Stanford Whittaker in particular seemed anxious that, in his words, George Wetmore not be allowed to get away with it."

Jesse crossed one leg over the other and tilted his head back. "Senator Wetmore isn't the only politician pushing for tariffs on imports. The Panic of Ninety-Three prompted a return to protectionism and economic tightfistedness."

"Which I don't understand. I thought the Panic started as the result of the bankruptcy of the Reading Railroad. What did that have to do with imports?"

"It was much more complicated than that. Such things always are."

I conceded the point with a nod. "That aside, one might argue that George Wetmore has been particularly vocal about the Dingley Act, one of its staunchest supporters."

"The vote, I understand, is a month away. I don't see how Stanford Whittaker or anyone could hope to influence the outcome at this late date. And," he added, "in such a way as I think you are suggesting." He studied me a moment, and I could all but see the speculative wheels turning in his mind.

"You are suggesting, my dear Emma, that Mr. Whittaker and his cohorts conspired to set George Wetmore up as a murderer by planting a deceased woman of the evening at the foot of his stairs, yes?"

"It's possible."

"Is it?" He frowned, not in derision, but in his attempt to see the logic of my theory, or so it appeared to me. "A lot of work would have gone into the simple act of discrediting a senator."

"A senator with an unblemished record? One who is highly esteemed in his hometown, his state, and in the nation's capital? With no transgressions in his past to resurrect, what choice is there but to resort to invention?"

"Perhaps, but Lilah was with child, Emma. Surely such a plan leaves too much up to luck and timing."

I sat back rather suddenly, prompting Patch to his feet. He nuzzled my hand with his nose, his way of asking me if anything was wrong. I scratched behind his ears. "That might merely have been a coincidence and nothing to do with the plot against Mr. Wetmore."

Usually at this point in the conversation Jesse would shake his head, tsk, and tell me I was stretching the facts to suit a scenario assembled by my imagination. At least, up until last autumn that would have been the case. Now he nodded decisively and came to his feet. I stood as well. Patch leaped out from between my faded, slightly threadbare sofa and the table that sported more than a few dings and chips.

"It bears looking into," he said. "You're right that the most obvious solution isn't always the correct one. I must be going."

"Jesse, wait." I came around the table and stood before him. "There is something else I think you should be aware of."

Before I could continue he laughed softly. "Do you mean the fact that Mrs. Wetmore has asked you to intervene? To investigate, perhaps?"

"How did you know?"

"My dear Emma, you and she were holed up in her parlor this morning for how long? And when you came out, you barely spoke a word, but instead sat ruminating beside me as I drove you home."

He knew me all too well. "I haven't agreed to her request. I told her I must think on it first."

"And have you? Thought on it and decided, that is?"

"Yes, I have." I hadn't known I'd reached a decision until that very instant, but it seemed as inevitable as the tides that lapped the edges of my property. No longer did I consider the task purely for the benefit of the Wetmores. But as Mrs. Wetmore had urged, Lilah Buford—and now her child—deserved the truth. I felt I owed it to them both, or how could I possibly pretend to carry on with Great Aunt Sadie's legacy? I owed it to Sadie's memory, too, for all she had taught me about the value of independence and for the home she had given me. I didn't explain all of this to Jesse. I merely said, "I have to help her. I must find the truth of what happened to Lilah Buford."

"I knew you would. I'd admonish you to stay out of it, but I know you won't. Be cautious, then, and keep me informed." He held me in his gaze another moment, and then he left.

Chapter 4

Despite my brave words to Jesse, I didn't contact Mrs. Wetmore for the rest of that day. There might be more to learn from the coroner, who had not finished his examination of the body. I saw no point in rushing headlong into inquiries before all the facts of Lilah's death were known.

At about midmorning the next day, a caller arrived on my doorstep. I heard the carriage coming up the drive and looked out the parlor window at a sleek victoria carriage with brass fittings and pulled by a handsome pair of grays. The oiled canvas top obscured the passenger, but the driver's top hat and tails told me this was no ordinary visitor. I assumed it must be Mrs. Wetmore coming for her answer, and hurried to greet her at the front door.

A high-heeled, patent leather boot emerged onto the footboard, and an ivory-gloved hand reached for the driver's as he helped her down. A wide silk hat covered my visitor's head, but as she turned to descend to the ground it was not auburn hair, but raven curls that gleamed blue-black in the sunlight, framing Lavinia Andrews's beautiful face. I drew a little gasp.

Derrick Andrews's mother. What on earth? I hadn't heard from him for several weeks, and as far as I knew he was still in Italy. My heart thrust up into my throat. Had he met with some ill fortune? An accident?

But no, as Mrs. Andrews approached me she smiled and held out a hand. "Miss Cross, I do hope my sudden arrival is not excessively ill timed. Have you a few moments?"

"Mrs. Andrews." Stupefaction held its grip on my tongue, but as she reached my doorstep I revived sufficiently to shake her hand and invite her inside. "How long have you been back in the country?"

"Not long." She preceded me into the parlor and stopped on the well-used hearth rug. "I see nothing has changed." She whirled about to face me, pulling off her gloves and smiling. "I am glad nothing has changed, Miss Cross. This house became most dear to me last summer, you know."

Mrs. Andrews and her daughter had been my guests at Gull Manor a year ago, when circumstances forced them to abandon their luxurious steamer yacht anchored in the harbor. At the time, I thought she and I had finally come to terms, whereas previously she had resented my place in her son's affections and had taken no pains to hide the fact. She once had done everything in her power to discourage any possibility of an attachment between us. That was, until the events of last summer, when she had warmed toward me, or so I had believed. Our last words before the Andrews family left Newport for Italy had dissuaded me of the notion that Lavinia Andrews would ever truly accept me. She had reached into her purse and drew out money, in order to pay me—*pay* me—for my hospitality.

Even now, the memory had the power to make me wrinkle my nose in distaste.

I asked Katie to bring in tea and bade Mrs. Andrews to make herself comfortable. Despite her claim that she was glad nothing had changed, she noticeably hesitated before choosing a spot on my tired old camelback sofa. I sat beside her at her prompting, and we spent the next quarter hour catching up and sharing all the news of mutual acquaintances. She brought tidings about people who had become dear to me last summer, tidings that touched my heart and squeezed tears into my eyes, though I blinked them away before they could fall. I resisted the urge to ask about Derrick. I trusted that she would bring him up when she was good and ready and not a moment before.

Our tea and cakes arrived and the next several moments were spent in pouring and passing the cream and sugar. Then, quite abruptly, she said, "What do you hear from Derrick?"

My spoon went still in my cup. "I, uh, haven't. Not in several weeks, ma'am. I received a letter from Italy at the beginning of last month."

"Yes, well. He's back. We arrived together in New York, but he went straight up to Providence to see his father. I, on the other hand, came here." Her gaze met my quizzical one. "To see you, Miss Cross."

"You came to Newport to see me?" I had been reduced to inane repetition.

"Indeed, yes. She held her cup and saucer with one hand while pressing her other to my wrist. "Miss Cross, I came to clear the air between us. You and I have a history of being at odds."

To put it mildly.

"This past year has taught me much," she went on, "as you might well imagine. I have learned the value of being more accepting. I have also come to see my children's happiness as the most important thing in the world."

She paused, and since she seemed to expect a reply, I said, "That is well, Mrs. Andrews. Every mother wants the best for her children."

Her gaze traveled over my features in a way that left me bewildered. "I do wish my son to be happy, Miss Cross, and it appears you are key to his happiness. I am here to give you my blessing. I will no longer stand in your way."

Did my mouth hang open? I fear it must have. She had shocked me thoroughly, but she had also arrived on my doorstep under a false assumption. "Mrs. Andrews, have you spoken to Derrick on this matter?"

"No, indeed not." She raised her teacup to her lips, sipped, and then set it back in its saucer with a clink. "I would not be so indelicate as to broach the subject with him. But I know my son's mind, Miss Cross. I know where his sentiments have lain this past year. Do know that you may feel free to accept Derrick, and that I am ready to welcome you into the family."

As I said, a false assumption. While it was true Derrick had once asked me to marry him—a hasty, impulsive proposal—when last we parted we had agreed to begin anew once we found ourselves together again. Even that simple understanding had become vastly complicated, however, for much had changed over the ensuing year. *I* had changed.

"Mrs. Andrews," I began, "I appreciate your visit. Truly. But—"

"Don't say anything, Miss Cross." She set her cup and saucer on the sofa table and came to her feet. "I suppose you think me a meddling old busybody, with nothing better to do than live vicariously through my son." She laughed lightly as she slipped her elegant hands back into her gloves. "And perhaps you are correct. But rest assured, henceforth my meddling will be put toward a good cause—the very best of causes. Now, when you are ready, and I hope it will be soon, you may depend on me to assist in any way I can."

I stood as well. "Assist?"

She laughed again. "In the wedding preparations, my dear

girl. There is much planning to be done. Flowers, menus, your trousseau . . . I expect Derrick to race down to Newport just as soon as he is able. If his father thinks to delay him in Providence, I will send for him myself."

"Please don't, Mrs. Andrews. There is no reason for Derrick to race anywhere."

"Nonsense. These matters mustn't be allowed to linger indefinitely, and it has already been too long."

I saw that I must take a more direct approach to make the woman understand. "Yes, ma'am, but you see, I haven't accepted Derrick. There is no understanding between us."

"My dear girl, play coy for now if it pleases you, but we both know you can do no better. Alice Vanderbilt herself could not hope to make a more advantageous match for you." She stepped closer and raised a gloved hand to my cheek, touching it for an instant. "Well, I am off, but we shall see each other soon, rest assured."

She left me with the disheveled sensation of having opened my door to a whirlwind that blew in, swirled wildly about my parlor, and blew out just as suddenly. I waited in the doorway long enough to be certain her carriage turned onto Ocean Avenue. Then, bemused, I returned to the parlor and sank onto the sofa.

Katie Dylan strode into the room and began collecting the tea things. "Has your guest gone already, miss?"

"Yes, she's gone. My goodness, Katie, what an odd visit that was."

"Aye, miss? And why is that?" My maid's soft brogue helped calm my nerves, as it often did.

"Mrs. Andrews is assuming that her son and I are destined to walk down the aisle together, and soon."

"And are ye not, miss?" Though she ducked her head as she hoisted the tray, she could not quite hide her smile.

"Not to my knowledge, no. I haven't seen Mr. Andrews in over a year."

She blew at a coppery spiral that had escaped her linen cap. "But he did ask ye, didn't he, miss?"

I sighed. "I suppose. But not in the way he should have. He asked in haste. We barely knew each other, and after all this time apart we'll barely know each other again."

"If he comes courting, will you turn him away then?"

I saw that Katie had missed Mrs. Andrews's cake plate. I stood to retrieve it and placed it with the other china on the tray she held. "I don't know that I wish to be courted, Katie. Not just now. But no, I'd never turn Mr. Andrews away from Gull Manor. He's done us too many good services to deserve that."

She turned away and headed into the hall. She murmured her last comment under her breath but I heard it nonetheless. "If a man like Mr. Andrews wished to court me, I'd certainly have no objection. Then again, that Detective Whyte is awfully nice, too."

It was true what people said about house staff. They never missed a thing.

Nanny found me a little while later brooding out past the kitchen garden. I'd visited the barn to water and feed my carriage horse, an aging roan gelding named Barney who knew how to convey my gig at one speed only: slow. I had walked him outside and set him on his lead, and I watched him pensively as he ambled about the yard and nibbled at grass, brome, and tasty tufts of swine cress. Beyond the small peninsula that marked the perimeter of my property, the Atlantic Ocean rolled gently, a leisurely tide that promised there were no storms approaching.

Nanny shuffled across the yard and came to stand beside me. "Was that Mrs. Andrews here?"

She roused me from my thoughts, and one look at her renewed my recent worries that dear Nanny was getting on in years and must not overexert herself, especially not on my account. Though she had come to Gull Manor to serve as my housekeeper, the truth was I had wanted her here because I had leaned on her ample shoulder all my life and couldn't imagine getting on without her support.

"You know good and well it was," I teased in reply to her question. I took her plump hand in my own and regarded her soft blue eyes behind their half-moon spectacles. "And you might have come downstairs to greet her."

"She didn't come to see me, sweetie, I know that for certain." Holding my hand, she gave my arm a little swing, as she used to do when I was little. "What did she want?"

"You weren't listening from the top of the stairs?"

Her chin went up, jiggling the slack skin beneath. "Certainly not." Her expression turned sly. "I tried, but I couldn't hear you well at all."

"She gave me her blessing to marry Derrick."

Nanny released my hand and grasped my shoulders. "Emma, that's wonderful news. I never thought I'd see the day. I suppose you'll be hearing from Derrick any day now."

I was shaking my head before she'd finished her comment. "Derrick and I agreed before he went away that we would begin anew. As I told his mother, there is no understanding between us."

She held me another moment, embraced me, and let me go. "You must do as your heart tells you, sweetie."

I couldn't help laughing. "How terribly sentimental and maudlin, especially coming from you, Nanny."

"I suppose. But I want my lamb to be happy."

I strolled toward Barney, who raised his head from a particularly lush tuft of weeds to greet me. I stroked his velvet nose and leaned my forehead against his warm cheek. "I *am* happy. And I'm luckier than most." I turned so my cheek lay against Barney's and I could peer across the way at Nanny. "I'm going to help Mrs. Wetmore." I had told Nanny everything last night. She had merely listened and not offered advice.

She crossed the distance to me. Her hand came down lightly on my shoulder, prompting me to raise my face from Barney's. "I knew you would, Emma. I understand that you have to. You'll do it for Lilah Buford, won't you?"

"You know me well."

"I used to change your diapers. Do you wish to talk about how you're going to begin?"

"I know how I must begin." I squinted out over the water, glittering in the sun. "With a visit to the Blue Moon."

Nanny gasped. "Emma, you mustn't."

"Where else will I learn anything about Lilah Buford?"

"If you must go, bring Jesse with you."

I shook my head. "I'd wager the quickest way to still those women's tongues is to bring Jesse. Or any police officer. Or any *man*, for that matter. No, I must go alone."

"But . . . what if someone sees you?" Nanny looked crestfallen. "What if Mrs. Andrews finds out? Goodness, Emma, what if *Alice Vanderbilt* finds out?"

I addressed her second two concerns first. "I am not beholden to Mrs. Andrews. And Aunt Alice has enough to occupy her thoughts, taking care of Uncle Cornelius. I cannot imagine anyone being so cruel as to increase her burdens by telling her tales about me. As for anyone seeing me . . ."

I thought a moment. I'd once donned men's clothing in order to follow someone through town at night. The workpants and corduroy jacket had belonged to Aunt Sadie, who used to do her own repairs on Gull Manor and declared such activities impossible in skirts and petticoats. But I couldn't possibly visit the Blue Moon at night, when the establishment would be at its busiest. Good gracious, no, the risk of discovery would be too great with so many people about.

And wearing Aunt Sadie's work clothes in broad daylight would do little to prevent me from being recognized.

"There is nothing for it but to simply go in the daytime. If I arrive too early in the morning the place will be closed and the . . . uh . . . inhabitants likely asleep. I'll go later today. I'll drive to Thames Street and then simply walk straight to the Blue Moon. If I skulk and look over my shoulder, I'll only attract attention. I could have any manner of business at the wharf itself. As long as no one sees me enter the Blue Moon, all will be well."

"Someone you know could very likely see you. Emma, you're a grown woman and usually a sensible one, but I cannot allow you to do this."

I merely set my hands on my hips and tilted my head.

"Emma, please . . . you cannot."

"Is it much more shocking than when we took in Stella, a known lady of the evening?"

"Yes, it most certainly is. It's one thing to have a woman like that *here*. And *that* raised eyebrows. It's quite another for you to go *there*."

Yet go *there*, I did. After attempting to reassure Nanny, I hitched Barney to the carriage and drove over to Chateau sur Mer. I didn't ask to speak with Mrs. Wetmore. I merely handed the butler my calling card with the word *yes* written on the back, and asked him to give it to his mistress. Then I steered Barney west into town, to Lower Thames Street and the offices of the Newport *Observer*. Even from outside, I could hear the rumble of the presses deep inside the building. I watered Barney from a nearby trough and slipped the strap of his feed bag behind his ears. Pedestrians passed me by without a second glance. I blended in with the foot traffic and went about my business, like everyone else.

Quickly I crossed Thames Street and walked the few streets over to Carrington's Wharf. The briny odors of the harbor, always prevalent along Thames Street, became stronger here, borne in with the westerly breezes skimming the water. I decided to avoid the wharf proper, where men would be loading and unloading boats and transferring goods in and out of the warehouses. A walkway plunged between the backs of the buildings on Carrington's Wharf and those on the next wharf. Brady had told me—under some duress—that the entrance to the Blue Moon faced this narrow alley, where patrons could come and go discreetly. Hoping I would enjoy the same anonymity, I slipped down the passage.

At one time, textile mills vied for space along the harbor with shipbuilders and machine shops. Most of these were long gone, unable to compete with similar operations on the mainland. And once the Four Hundred discovered Newport, industries shifted more toward supplying the kinds of goods needed to keep their cottages running and their parties well stocked.

Nowadays, Carrington's Wharf primarily housed the operations of the Lyman Fuel Company, which shipped in, stored, and delivered coal and firewood throughout the city. As I passed the rear of the main warehouse, I wondered how long before times once again changed, and electric companies such as the Newport Illuminating Company rendered coal and wood obsolete.

I also passed a dry goods store that catered to fishermen and dockworkers who lived nearby, and a small carpentry shop. Up until this point I could have, if seen, pretended to be searching for a legitimate business. Perhaps I needed coal delivered to Gull Manor, or wished to engage a carpenter to mend that noisy shutter.

I reached a door above which a sign beckoned with a full moon painted a lurid shade of blue. Beside the door, a mullioned window provided wavering glimpses of the shadowed interior of a public room. Even from outside, the odors of stale tobacco and sharp spirits, and one or two things I didn't wish to contemplate, tweaked my nose and made me want to do an about-face. What on earth was I doing here?

The Blue Moon Tavern appeared closed to business, but not to be so easily deterred, I tried the door latch. It yielded beneath the slight pressure I applied, and the door creaked inward.

"Hello? Is anyone about?" I stepped inside and closed the door behind me. The unsavory aromas outside, I realized, were merely a precursor to those pervading the interior, along with the oppressive addition of perspiration and the heavy perfume of tobacco smoke. Though I could boast no first-hand knowledge of such establishments, I easily guessed this was a far cry from the more fashionable enterprises outside of town, where spacious, shingle-style houses that stood shaded by stately old trees might have been mistaken for respectable homes.

The place seemed unnaturally quiet. Shouldn't the workers be preparing for their evening business? Yet no clanking of pots and pans emerged from the doorway that presumably led into the kitchen, and no charwoman could be seen wielding a mop over the floors, though they sorely needed attention. Attempting to breathe shallowly, I made my way between tables to the bar, beside which a doorway gave way to a stairwell. I poked my head in. "Hello? Can anyone help me? Miss Perry?"

For such was the name I had wheedled out of Brady at the polo grounds—Heidi Perry, who presided over the Blue Moon and its occupants. Apparently she claimed to be a descendant of Oliver Hazard Perry, a onetime Newport resident, a naval commander, and hero of the War of 1812. A lofty connection, indeed, if a dubious one. I chuckled inwardly and called out again.

I had just put my foot on the bottom step when a voice from above shouted down at me.

"Get out. We're not open. Are you completely daft?"

"I'm sorry. The door was unlocked. Are you Miss Perry?"

An oath worthy of a longshoreman rained down on me. "Who's asking?"

I thought better of shouting my name back up at her. I peered up the staircase, and saw, a floor above me, the dim outlines of a female figure in a shapeless dressing gown leaning over the railing. A profusion of spiraling hair spilled over a pair of amply rounded shoulders. "I've come on behalf of Lilah Buford, Miss Perry."

"Lilah? Where's that hussy gotten to? I ain't seen her in . . . how many days it been now?"

"Two, Miss Perry." So Jesse and the police officers hadn't been here yet. The notion made me angry. What were they waiting for? But I already knew. Just as Mrs. Wetmore had predicted, they were hushing up the crime and George Wetmore's possible connection to it. Well, Jesse might be subject to the pressures of city politics, but I was not. "Might you come down? I really do need to speak with you."

Grumbling words accompanied the creaking of steps and a good deal of indignant huffing. "A good thing for you I was already awake, missy," she said, upon reaching the bottom. She secured her dressing gown around her with a satin sash. Even so, her bosom threatened to spill from the frilled neckline. "A happy coincidence for you. Not everyone is in bed with the sunset and up with the roosters." She waved a finger at me. "Not in our line of work, missy. Not here."

"Yes, of course. I'm terribly sorry."

Close up, I could see that Miss Perry was younger than I might have imagined, in her early thirties at most. Blond hair of shocking brightness fell nearly to her waist, though as she descended the stairs she had twisted most of it into a knot at her nape. Her eyes were blue, her skin clear and pale. She possessed a pleasant countenance, one that might aspire to beauty were she not in such a state of dishabille.

Miss Perry possessed the kind of figure I often envied—softly rounded, abundant of bosom, generous in the hips. I easily pictured her making the most of the latest fashions, which oftentimes swallowed those of petite frame, like myself. Nanny was forever taking in leg-o'-mutton sleeves so as not to appear like great sails that would carry me away at the slightest wind. No, if her circumstances were different, Miss Perry would command the latest trends to her best advantage, rather than her clothes commanding her.

She eyed me levelly. I supposed she was sizing me up even as I did her, and her next words confirmed it. "What could such a little slip of a girl possibly have to say to me?"

Her question reminded me of my own words regarding Lilah Buford's demand to speak to Mrs. Wetmore. "May we sit down, please?"

She studied me for another several moments, giving little shakes of her head as if she could not quite make sense of the present circumstances. "Not here," she finally said. "The barkeep will be here soon to go over his books and he doesn't need to know my business. Come upstairs."

Quite unexpectedly, I inwardly panicked at the thought of venturing farther into this den of iniquity, to quote my minister. As Miss Perry didn't wait for my response but started back up the steps, I silently followed her. After passing through another door at the top, she took me only as far as a parlor so comfortably appointed, so utterly at odds with the squalor in the tavern below, that I came to an abrupt halt and stared. With an impatient gesture she bade me sit on a crimson velvet sofa cushioned generously with an array of satin pillows.

"Tea?" she asked, and, at my "No, thank you," settled herself in a wing chair facing me. She folded her hands primly on her lap. "Now then, missy, what is this all about? Why is a respectable young lady like yourself risking ruination by coming to the Blue Moon to see Madam Heidi? I don't expect it's Lilah's job you're after."

After another befuddled glance around the room, I blurted, "Indeed not." I set my purse on my lap and held on to it with both hands—not out of fear of being robbed, but as a sort of anchor in these untried waters. Then I realized what I'd said, and the indignant tone with which I'd said it. I glanced up at Miss Perry. "I *am* sorry. I didn't mean to imply . . ." I trailed off helplessly as she chuckled, her shoulders and bosom heaving with merriment. If nothing else, she apparently found me entertaining.

"Well, don't keep me in suspense," she cried. "Where has our Lilah been? Her customers are getting downright testy and if she doesn't show up soon, they might take their business elsewhere. We can't have that now, can we, missy?"

Heat crawled into my cheeks at the reference. In recent years I'd witnessed all manner of deceit, violence, and death, and had harbored more than one reformed prostitute under my roof. Yet such a blatant reference to the oldest profession still had the power to make me blush. Miss Perry noticed it, too. She must have, for she smiled in a cunning sort of way. Perhaps she enjoyed my discomfort.

"Miss Perry," I began, but she stopped me.

"Madam Heidi. Everybody calls me that."

I frowned. To my chagrin her request renewed the heat in my face. She laughed again. "Never mind, missy. Call me whatever strikes your fancy. What shall I call you?"

I felt tempted to give her a false name. But to what end? I very much doubted any threat to my reputation would come from this woman. "My name is Emma Cross."

Her eyebrows, artificially darkened and elongated, shot up. "The Fancies and Fashions Emma Cross? Well, land's sake."

"You read my column?" I felt a tiny and quite unexpected thrill, a surge of pride.

"Every week. We all do. Is it true what they say, that you're one of them Vanderbilts?"

"I am, but my connection to the family goes back several generations. But that's not why I've come, Miss Perry. Lilah Buford has, well . . ." I drew myself up and took a deep breath. "Lilah's gone missing."

She stared across the space at me, unblinking, while a clock I hadn't previously noticed ticked loudly from somewhere in the corridor. Then her expression blackened and her fist came down on the little brandy table beside her chair, the blow so heavy a bud vase toppled and crashed to the floor. "The hell she has. She was my best girl and what's more, she was thankful to be here. Who killed her?"

Chapter 5

"I didn't say anyone killed her, Miss Perry. Only that—"

"Do you take me for an imbecile, Miss Cross? Would you be here right now if Lilah were alive? A woman like you, here without doggone good cause?" She tilted her head back and regarded me through hooded eyes. "Either you speak the truth, missy, or you can see yourself out."

I blew out a breath. "All right, yes. Lilah is dead, Miss Perry. She was found at the bottom of a staircase in one of the houses on Bellevue Avenue."

"Bellevue? Have you lost your mind? Lilah knows better than to set foot in one of them cottages."

"I saw her myself."

The woman's eyes once more narrowed on me. "Where was she found? Which house?"

"Before I get to that, can you think of anyone who would wish ill on Lilah? Did she have enemies, or a disgruntled . . . customer?"

"Customer? No. Enemies?" She sucked in her cheeks as she considered. "Some or all of the other girls mighta had it in for her. Lilah showed up one day and by the next she'd become a favorite. Knew how to *entertain* a man, she did. Took business away from the others. Even from other establishments. But if one of them did her in, why take her to some house? Why not just dump her in the harbor?" She held out her arm, her wrist dripping ivory lace as she pointed to a window. "It's just a stone's throw."

Her crass indifference made me wince, and made me regret telling her of Lilah's fate. But she did have a point. "Are you sure none of your patrons wanted her out of the way?"

"Missy, if one of them did, my guess is it's the owner of this cottage you won't name." She raised an eyebrow as if to say *touché*.

"Did you know Lilah was with child?"

Her smug expression vanished. "What?"

"She was pregnant," I said, enunciating the last word.

"Land's sake. I had no idea. . . ."

"I need to find out who the father might have been. Was Lilah close to any of the other girls? Someone she might have confided in?" That was, I added silently, if she had been aware of her condition. According to the coroner it had been early enough that Lilah might not have realized it.

Miss Perry stood. "Wait here."

Minutes later her voice traveled down from the upper story. "Get up, all of you. Get up, you lazy things. I want you in the parlor in five minutes."

While she roused the others, I considered what she had said about dumping Lilah's body in the harbor. Logical, unless the culprit wanted Lilah gone *and* wished to punish George Wetmore by framing him for the crime. Perhaps Lilah had taken Mr. Wetmore's business away from one of the other girls. For women such as these, a wealthy client could make the difference between merely subsisting and living well, and possibly retiring sooner rather than later.

It might be possible for a woman to convey another across a lawn and into a house—improbable, but not undoable. What seemed impossible to me was Senator George Wetmore in a place like this, with its seedy location overlooking the Lyman Fuel Company. But perhaps I was being naïve.

Miss Perry returned leading four young women into the parlor. All appeared to have dragged themselves from their beds and were clad in dressing gowns of decent, if not opulent, quality. Two had hastily tied back their hair while the other two peeked at me from beneath untidy fringes of curls. They ranged themselves around the room. One sat at the other end of the sofa from me. I judged them all to be about my own age, give or take a couple of years. They at least seemed well nourished.

Miss Perry began with a blunt question. "What do any of you know about where Lilah took off to the other day?"

The four girls exchanged glances and shrugged. "Nothing," one of them said. "Why? She in trouble?"

"She's dead," Miss Perry replied before I could speak a word.

A couple of the girls gasped. The other two remained silent, watching me. One of them, a brunette whose expression spoke of world-weariness, gestured at me with her chin. "Who's she?"

Would Miss Perry identify me as Miss Cross of the Fancies and Fashions page? I found myself no longer caring and told them the truth myself. This brought on a little barrage of *oohs* and words of praise, until Miss Perry motioned them to be silent.

"This is about Lilah," she said. "And about what any of you might have known before she left."

The individual with whom I shared the couch, a slender, golden-haired girl with large green eyes that held a lost, haunted look, spoke. "She didn't tell me she was leaving, if that's what you mean."

"Did any of you know Lilah was with child?" I asked.

More glances were exchanged, followed by denials. I believed them on that account. Why lie about it?

Deciding to leave that matter for now, I changed the subject. "What can you tell me about the men who come here?"

This only earned me four puzzled expressions. From the other end of the couch came the question, "What do you mean? All kinds of men come here. Sailors, fishermen, workmen—the ones that can afford us that is, and then there's the occasional wealthy cottager—"

"Tell me about those," I interrupted. "The wealthy men."

"*Humph.* Some aren't very nice," the brunette said with a disparaging look. The girl sitting in the chair beside her, a blonde as bright and brassy as Miss Perry, nodded in agreement. The brunette spoke again. "I guess that's why they come here, instead of some o' them fancy houses outside o' town."

"Are you willing to name names?"

This question had them all seeking Miss Perry's authority. She appealed to me. "You're trying to find out who killed Lilah, and you think it might be one of the cottagers?"

"I'm merely trying to piece together what happened to Lilah." I didn't add that Lilah finding her way into Chateau sur Mer certainly suggested a connection between her and members of the Four Hundred, whether one of them killed her or not. But perhaps I was being too broad in my questions. I needed to simplify, be more direct, beginning with the men from the polo match who had appeared to know Lilah, or at least her name. "Do you know men by the names of Robert Clarkson, Stanford Whittaker, or Harry Lehr?"

I held my breath, suddenly realizing that men of quality might use assumed names in a place like this. Would I need to describe them? Could I do so well enough to spark a reliable identification?

"Robert Clarkson," the girl across the sofa from me said. Her golden hair fell forward, nearly obscuring her face from me. She spoke to her lap. "He's only been here a couple of times. But I know him—that is, I . . ." She tossed a glance around at the others. "But the other two you mentioned. They come more often. Especially Mr. Whittaker."

"So they don't attempt to hide their identities when they come," I said.

The brunette, who seemed to be the unofficial spokesman of the group, shrugged. "They don't seem to care who knows they're here. Of course, they know we don't go telling tales. Wouldn't be good for business."

"Except now," the golden-haired one said softly, glancing up with fear growing in her large eyes. "We're telling tales now, aren't we?"

"This conversation is strictly between us," I assured them. "Your confidences are safe with me. Tell me about them. Did Lilah entertain them, or one of you?"

"The older one, Whittaker, he liked me until Lilah came along." The brunette gave a shudder. "He paid handsomely, but I wasn't too sorry to lose him to Lilah. Good riddance, I said."

I leaned toward her in a gesture meant to gain her confidence. "Why was that?"

"He's . . . he's not a nice man. Not that all of them are, mind you. But Whittaker . . . he could be mean. He wanted . . . things other men didn't ask for." She rubbed her forearms up and down. Was she remembering past bruises, like the bruises that marred poor Lilah's body? I thought, too, of Whittaker's wife, Bessie. Did he treat her in kind, or did he spare her and take out his frustrations with women who were unlikely to complain? Did she know of his predilections? Perhaps so. Rumors often circulated about parties at the Whittakers' cottage, the details making their way through the servants' networks straight to Nanny's ears. She never told me specifics, and that in itself spoke volumes about the kinds of things that went on. Shameful things. Word had it Bessie Whittaker would take to her room and not emerge until the last guest had left.

These girls had no such luxury. The coroner had found bruises, new and old, on Lilah's body. Whittaker? I didn't doubt it.

"What about the others, his friends?" I prompted. I turned back to the girl at the opposite end of the sofa. "You said you'd entertained Robert Clarkson."

"Only a time or two, miss."

"Did he prefer Lilah?"

My question produced a wounded expression on her youthful features. "I told you, he doesn't come very often. I don't know if he ever called on Lilah."

"And Harry Lehr?" I kept on.

Chuckles circulated among the girls, and the brunette said, "King Lehr, they call him. Did you know? Anyway, he always spends his time in the smoking room down the hall. Mind you, he pays for the privilege, but he just sits there smoking his cigarettes, drinking our best brandy, and staring into space. If any of us offer our services, he just shrugs and keeps staring."

I sat back. "That's odd. He's never asked for any of you?"

All four shook their heads and exchanged knowing looks I didn't understand.

"He never asked for Lilah either?"

Miss Perry, silent all this time, spoke up. "Never that I know of. Don't know why he bothers coming."

Again, that secretive look passed among Madam Heidi's girls. He must have had some reason. Harry Lehr was a known womanizer. Perhaps he missed the thrill of conquest in a place like this, where the women needed no coaxing to ply their trade. I set the matter aside for now. "Did Lilah entertain other customers of note?"

"Sure, there were other society bucks, but mostly young ones," Miss Perry said. "You know, raw youths in search of wives, but who wanted to learn a few things first. No one as regular as Whittaker, though.

"But there were others?" As they nodded, I noticed disparaging expressions among the girls. "Did any—or perhaps all—of you have reason to resent Lilah?"

"She was taking business away from the rest of us," the brassy blonde said with a scowl. "Good business. Even if it was rough sometimes."

"Did any of you wish her ill?" I bluntly asked.

"Sometimes I did," the brunette said with no hint of apology. "Anyway, I wished she'd go away." With a glare at Miss Perry, she gathered her dressing gown around her as if gathering her dignity.

The others nodded their agreement, except, I noticed, for the one at the other end of the sofa. She'd gone quiet again, drawn in on herself.

"One more question. Do you all know who George Wetmore is?"

"O' course."

My blood ran cold at the eager and unanimous answer, until the brunette continued speaking.

"We do get out upon occasion, you know. Mr. Wetmore presided over this year's July Fourth celebrations in town. Those Wetmores, they're different from the rest of the quality. They're Newporters."

"Yes, they are," I agreed. "And that's how you know of Mr. Wetmore?"

They seemed puzzled by this until Miss Perry chuckled. "Are you suggesting Mr. Wetmore has been *here*? Hardly, though we'd surely not turn him away should he ever come knocking. Don't think he will, though, more's the pity."

Were they telling the truth? Had they been paid or threatened into silence on the matter? I gazed from face to face, detecting no sudden tension that hadn't been there previously. "Have any of you ever known Lilah to behave in a reckless or erratic manner?"

"Gracious, no." Miss Perry whisked strands of hair back from her face. "Lilah, she knew how to act a part. Could be quite the lady when she wanted to be. That's what kept the rich gentlemen coming back, why they paid court to Lilah almost as if she was one of their own. One willing to let them do, you know, what their wives and sweethearts wouldn't. Hell, even their mistresses wouldn't let 'em do what Lilah let 'em do."

I schooled the distaste from my features while the girls agreed with Miss Perry's assessment, albeit begrudgingly. My questions answered for the moment, I prepared to rise. I had one more request. "Might I see Lilah's room?"

"Suit yourself." Miss Perry came to her feet and led the way up another flight of stairs.

A hodgepodge of scents greeted me at the top: rosewater, lavender, and a spicy citrus scent mingled with that of tobacco and a sweet hint of spirits, brandy, I surmised. We had arrived at a rectangular landing covered in a well-worn Turkey carpet. Several doors opened directly onto the landing. I glimpsed unmade beds, clothing tossed over chairs, and dressers covered in a scattering of personal items.

It all seemed so . . . ordinary. These could have been any young women's bedrooms. I don't know what I had expected. Perhaps colorful silks and velvets, as one might find in an exotic harem. Or perhaps insects crawling on the walls, rats scurrying about, and drunken men sprawled across the floors. But this—*this* was somehow worse than anything my imagination could conjure. This brought home to me how easily *any* woman might find herself in such circumstances, forced to work in whatever means she could in order to eat and have a roof over her head. Ordinary young women of decent background, fallen on hard times . . . Ordinary young women like myself, had my life been different. In theory, of course, I had always known this. I had met, housed, fed, and helped women such as these begin anew. But I had never before contemplated how very like me they were.

Oblivious to my revelations, Miss Perry led me to a room on our right. "This is Lilah's."

This could have been my own room at home. Simple furnishings, iron bedstead, and a patchwork quilt that made me wonder if Lilah had made it herself. The homey touch banished what lingered in my mind of the sordidness of such a place, or nearly so.

As I made a circuit of the room, I absently ran my hand over the pine surfaces. Personal effects littered the dresser top. Jars of powder and rouge, hair combs, a brush and mirror, a tattered fan . . . These abandoned items brought an ache to my throat.

What had brought Lilah to the Blue Moon? Had she had plans to leave, or had she given up believing her life could be anything more? Somehow, whatever path she had traveled, and the reasons for it, had led her to the bottom of the Wetmores' staircase.

Coming back around to the dresser, I opened the top drawer. Once again I was struck by the ordinariness of the contents. Linens, handkerchiefs, stockings, gloves, a buttonhook. The other two drawers yielded similar results. I rummaged through them all, uncovering nothing more significant than undergarments, scarves, a string of glass beads, extra buttons. In the night table beside the bed, I found a pair of spectacles.

"Lilah wore glasses?"

"I suppose. Not often." Miss Perry thought a moment, then grinned. "She wore them to read your column out loud to us."

The comment pierced me unexpectedly. It drew a connection, however tenuous, between Lilah and myself. I was about to close the drawer when the edge of something brown and gold caught my eye. I reached in and drew out a leather-bound photograph album, its pages edged in gold leaf.

"I'd forgotten about that." Miss Perry perched one hip against the end of the dresser. "She used to look through it sometimes," she said unnecessarily, for why else did someone keep a photograph album? Though perhaps Heidi Perry found dwelling on the past a fruitless occupation.

I flipped through. That ache returned as a child of about five peered at me through the camera lens. With each turn of the page Lilah aged—a year, perhaps two—but the resemblance remained strong. I'd found some people were like that—features evident in childhood changed little into adulthood.

In some pictures a woman who must have been her mother held her hand, or sat with Lilah in her lap, the two of them still and solemn while the photography worked its magic. Then a man appeared, obviously wearing his Sunday best. Her father, I presumed. And then a second child joined the family circle, a boy, though in the first few pictures he sported the sack-like dresses little boys typically wore until they were old enough for knickers. Here and there, a picture went missing. Had they fallen out, or been removed?

The last couple of pages featured an older Lilah, perhaps thirteen or so, looking sweet and smart in a dress cinched at the waist with a wide sash and a matching ribbon in her long, loose hair. The garment appeared to be of passing good quality, and it struck me that the mere existence of this album, with its many photos, suggested the family had not been poor. Downstairs, Miss Perry had said Lilah knew how to act the part of a lady. Perhaps it was no act, but rather the lessons imparted to her by her own mother.

What had happened to them? Why did Lilah leave her home? In those last pictures, her face held all the fresh, eager promise of any girl of that age. But all too soon, the pages turned blank, and I glimpsed no further insight into Lilah's life during the years prior to her arriving at the Blue Moon.

"Do you know what happened to the family?"

Miss Perry pushed away from the dresser and came to glance over my shoulder. Reaching down, she turned back the pages to ones holding photographs of the whole family. "She told me diphtheria took her parents. I asked about the boy in the pictures and she said he was dead, too. She talked about it once and never spoke of it again."

I had looked for the reason that brought her to the Blue Moon, to this dismal life, and I had found it. It was exactly the sort of thing that could have brought me here, or anyone. What money the family might have had most likely went to paying doctor's bills or debts, or had been stolen from the young girl who had found herself alone in the world.

"And you don't know who raised her afterward?"

"Missy, one of my hard and fast rules here is no questions. If a girl ain't telling, I ain't asking. Lilah never said."

I gazed down at the album. "May I take one of these?"

"Suit yourself. That book's no good to anyone anymore. Take the whole thing, if you like."

I did. Then I not only thanked Miss Perry for her time, I reached into my purse for a few coins, all I could spare. When I held them out to her, she regarded them a moment, and then smirked. "You keep that, missy, I won't have your money. You couldn't afford me if you wanted," she added with a laugh. "Now, that house of yours, out on Ocean Avenue? Yes, I know where you live. You could really do something with it, make yourself quite a showplace. Attract the crème de la crème. You and I together . . ." She laughed again at my wide-eyed look as I gathered her meaning. "Never mind."

My last words to her exacted a promise that neither she nor her girls would divulge any of our conversation. I hurried down the three flights, relieved to emerge into sunlight and fresh air, or what seemed fresh after the oppressive atmosphere of Lilah Buford's bedroom. A voice called my name before I'd taken many steps.

"Miss Cross, wait."

I turned to see the young golden-haired girl standing in the tavern entrance. She approached me with a wary expression. "It's true, then, Lilah is dead."

I couldn't help treating her to an incredulous stare, until I realized the full impact of someone's death often took time to set in. It's not that she hadn't understood me upstairs in the parlor, but that she hadn't truly accepted it until now. "Yes," I said gently. "I'm afraid so."

She had traded her nightgown and robe for a proper cotton day dress and shawl, her slippers for a pair of low-heeled boots. She looked like a child, like the Lilah of the last pages of the album.

"I didn't want to say in front of the others, but Lilah was afraid. She told me she overheard something—men talking. Her last customer had just left, and she'd come down here for a breath of air and to see if there might be anyone loitering about. Lilah was real good at drawing in the ones who hadn't quite made up their minds whether they wanted to come in or not. It was a talent she had. Anyway, there were two men—leastwise she thought there were two—talking just around the corner of the building." She said all this in a rushed whisper.

I drew her farther away from the tavern, up along the walkway that led back to the street and out of sight of the Blue Moon's windows. "What is your name?" My question wasn't simply a means to be friendly. In the event she revealed something vital, I wanted to know whom to ask for should I need to speak with her again.

"I'm Florence, but everyone calls me Flossie."

"Well, then, Flossie, what is it Lilah heard?"

"Like I said, two men talking. About that Mr. Wetmore you mentioned. They were angry about something and wanted to . . . oh, what were the words she used?"

"Take your time," I said patiently, while half wanting to shake it out of her.

"Now I remember. They wanted to see a good bit of mud splattered on the Wetmores' doorstep. A funny way of putting it, I thought, and I laughed. A lot of us hereabouts wouldn't mind seeing a little mud splattered on some of those cottagers. Serve 'em right. But Lilah, she said I shouldn't laugh, it wasn't funny. She said the Wetmores were good people and someone had to warn them."

Those words practically echoed what I'd heard at the polo match. Robert Clarkson, Harry Lehr, and Stanford Whittaker—and the Dingley Tariff Act. Could it all be as simple as that? "Did the men say *why* they wished ill on the Wetmores?"

"I asked the same question, and I think Lilah knew, but she wouldn't tell me. She said I was better off not knowing, and she had already said too much."

Lilah thought she'd heard two men talking, but perhaps there had been three. Had my disgruntled trio discovered that she had eavesdropped, killed her, and brought her to

Chateau sur Mer? If so, then finding justice for both Lilah and George Wetmore lay within reach, for Mr. Wetmore had done no wrong. He had no connection to Lilah Buford, except that she had wished to do the right thing and warn him.

But why had she insisted on speaking with *Mrs.* Wetmore? Did she merely believe another woman would listen to her and take her warning seriously? No, it could *not* be this easy. A piece, or several, still lay hidden. It seemed I needed to speak with Mrs. Wetmore again.

Flossie turned to run back inside, but I stilled her another moment. "I could see upstairs that the others aren't overly distressed about Lilah's passing."

A sadness entered her eyes. "I liked her, Miss Cross. She was like an older sister to me. I didn't care if the customers preferred her. They couldn't help it, and neither could she. The others, well, I suppose they couldn't understand that."

"Had Lilah had words with any of them?"

"All the time. We're always having words. But it doesn't mean anything," she added hastily, looking wary once more. "Like sisters. Do you have any sisters, Miss Cross?"

I shook my head, but said, "I have a brother, and yes, we sometimes argue."

"Then you know. Well, I'd . . . I'd best go back inside. And you, Miss Cross, you shouldn't linger here any longer. It wouldn't do for you to be seen talking with me."

"Thank you for your help, Flossie." Before I'd quite finished expressing my gratitude, she was gone, the tavern door banging behind her. I wished she had lingered another moment, for I had wanted to tell her that if she ever needed help, or perhaps wished to leave this life, the door at Gull Manor would be open to her.

Disappointed but resolved to convey that message at a later date, I turned away, back toward Thames Street. A looming figure blocked my path, and a broad, square face like that of a bulldog leered down at me. I froze, a cold lump of fear growing in my stomach.

The wide mouth stretched in a grin that sent me a step backward. "Well, if it ain't Miss Emmaline Cross."

I drew a steadying breath. "Please step out of my way, Mr. Dobbs." I couldn't walk around him, as the narrowness of the passageway forbade it.

"It's *Detective* Dobbs, or was, until you stuck your prim little nose into my affairs."

I said nothing, but took a quick survey from his toes on up to his slouchy tweed cap. He wore workman's clothes, stiff and thick and none too clean. Coal dust caked his hands and smeared his face.

"That's right," he said with mock cordiality, "I'm shoveling coal brought in from the barges into the warehouse, and then into the delivery wagons. Quite a step down for me. Happy?"

I gathered my courage and looked him in the eye. "Have you forgotten that if not for my intervention, you very likely would have been hanged for a murder you did not commit?"

"Your saving me from the hangman's noose was an unfortunate accident for you, a convenient one for me. Either way, you were out to destroy me. Did it to get even for Brady, didn't you, Miss Cross?"

It was true that I'd long since concluded that Anthony Dobbs, former detective with the Newport Police, was a menace to decent society. He had hounded my brother for years, locking him up for the slightest offenses and more often than not knocking him about in the process. Dobbs had been all too happy to arrest Brady on suspicion of murder two summers ago, but when the tables turned soon after and it was Dobbs accused, I'd fought to prove his innocence. As I would have done for any individual wrongly accused.

No, I didn't like the man, but neither had I ever done him an ill turn. He had done that himself when he decided to extort local businesses. The truth of it came out during his incarceration for suspected murder. He'd supplemented his detective's salary quite nicely in exchange for his "protection" and looking the other way when merchants weighted their scales or blatantly broke laws concerning fair business practices.

"You are delusional, Mr. Dobbs. Now please move aside." I took a step, but was again forced to halt when he stood his ground. I began to consider how loud I'd need to scream to be heard by the workers on the wharf or passersby on the street.

"What are you doing here?" he asked, as if only just realizing the oddity of finding me on Carrington's Wharf.

"That is none of your business."

The heavy steps of feet clad in work boots sounded behind me. "Tony, what are you doing?"

Relief pooled in the pit of my stomach, until it occurred to me this new individual might pose further complications, rather than assistance.

Dobbs glanced beyond my shoulder to the person standing behind me. "Just saying hello to an old friend. Isn't that right, Miss Cross?"

I peered around, and felt a vague sense of recognition. The workman was no one from within my circle of acquaintances, that much was certain, yet something in his face seemed familiar. Quickly I studied the mouth, and the nose that ended with a bit of a hook, as if it had met with the blunt end of a fist on more than one occasion. His eyes, blue, were surrounded by crow's-feet that were not the result of age, for his robust figure spoke of a man in his twenties, but of much time spent in sun and wind. He regarded me almost as curiously as I regarded him.

Then he gazed past me. "Say good-bye to the lady and let's get back to work."

Dobbs stepped around me, nearly bumping my shoulder in the narrow passage and causing me to recoil. He noticed and smirked out of the side of his mouth, and kept going. I hurried to Thames Street, and to Barney, waiting patiently at the roadside.

Chapter 6

The next morning saw me once more at Chateau sur Mer. Another carriage, a dapper little spider phaeton pulled by a sleek black horse, stood parked beneath the porte cochere. I parked behind it. Before I'd alighted from my own gig, the front door opened and a man came striding out. He set his hat on his head as he walked, but even that couldn't hide his scowl. Then he swung his ivory inlaid walking stick in a tight arc and hit it sharply against the ground.

He saw me and stopped, the scowl intensifying as it seemed to find a target on which to focus all its enmity: me.

My hail of "Good morning" didn't ease Harry Lehr's expression in the slightest. Though his feet had been taking him toward his own carriage, he changed course until he stood in front of me. "You warned her, didn't you?"

I shook my head in bafflement. "Warned whom of what?" But the answer came to me even before he huffed out a breath.

"Meddling little busybody. I came here to pay my respects to Miss Wetmore, and she barely blinked an eye before bidding me good morning and dismissing me. Made up some flimsy excuse about supervising the monthly silver inventory, but I could see she must have been on the lookout for me. What did you tell her?"

"I told her nothing, Mr. Lehr." An admonishment bubbled for release: that he should come here so soon after the family's terrible shock. Though no one yet knew the true details, word had leaked out about the police and ambulance coming to Chateau sur Mer three nights ago. In a town as small as Newport, it was bound to happen. The newspapers reported that a guest had fallen down the stairs and broken her neck, but remained vague as to the identity of that guest. My co-reporter at the *Observer* surmised, indelicately, that she had been a spinster friend of one of the Wetmore sisters.

I held my tongue. Either Harry Lehr didn't read the newspapers, or personal tragedy meant little to him in the course of his fortune hunting.

"If you told her nothing, what are you doing here now?"

"It is none of your business, but . . ." I thought quickly. "I am assisting Mrs. Wetmore in recording the history of various items in the house. Now, if you will excuse me."

He raised his walking stick out sideways to bar my way. The confrontation brought back the still-fresh memory of my encounter with Anthony Dobbs outside the Blue Moon yesterday. Yet here, one sharp cry from me would bring a footman or two, and perhaps a groom, hurrying out to see what the matter was.

Oddly though, Mr. Lehr didn't frighten me. I couldn't have said why not, but I simply felt annoyed rather than threatened. Reaching out, I laid my fingers on his walking stick and lowered it. He didn't resist my efforts, and then I simply bid him good day and brushed past him.

Mr. Callajheue, the butler, opened the door when I knocked.

He admitted me immediately and without question, even though I had no appointment to visit Mrs. Wetmore. Upon stepping into the cool, shady interior of the Stair Hall, I dismissed Mr. Lehr from my mind. With no conversation after a perfunctory greeting and inquiry after my general well-being, the butler escorted me up the main double staircase—the side opposite the one on which Lilah had been found dead. At the top, we traversed the gallery that looked down into the Tapestry Hall on the first floor. We passed several closed doors, turned a corner into a smaller hall on which several more doors opened, and stopped outside one of them. The butler knocked, and I was admitted into a sitting room that made me feel as though I'd suddenly been transported to a vibrant, exotic world. From the richly woven carpet to the lush silk draperies and upholsteries to the unique treasures that decorated the room, I might have been standing in a home in faraway Istanbul. French doors, open to the breeze, looked out onto a square terrace above the original entrance. The front lawn and driveway stretched away below us to Bellevue Avenue.

Mrs. Wetmore sat near an unlit marble fireplace. Her loose-fitting morning dress bore many of the colors found in the room; I wondered if she always dressed to match whatever room she would be using at any particular time. It wouldn't have surprised me one bit. Most society women changed their attire upward of nine times each day to suit their various activities.

She looked up from what appeared to be an appointment book open in her lap. "Miss Cross, to what do I owe the pleasure?" Her words, I immediately realized, were for the butler's benefit, for she knew quite well what business had brought me here. Obviously, our arrangement had not been made common knowledge. She smiled up at me. "Might I offer you some tea and refreshment?"

"No, thank you, Mrs. Wetmore. I shan't keep you long."

At that, she signaled to the butler, who backed out of the room and closed the door. Mrs. Wetmore bade me sit near her.

"Mrs. Wetmore, I came to ask if you've been completely honest with me."

Her gaze, lingering on the flower arrangement that occupied the hearth in lieu of coal or firewood, darted to mine. "Whatever do you mean, Miss Cross?"

"It is my understanding that Lilah Buford wished to warn you and Mr. Wetmore of some threat against your husband."

Her hand clutched the sofa arm beside her. The other rose to the lace neckline of her gown. "A threat? Of what sort?"

"That I haven't yet learned. But the first question is why she would specifically want to speak with you, as opposed to your husband."

"I'm sure I don't know."

"Are you certain, Mrs. Wetmore? Can you think of no occasion when you and Lilah Buford met?"

"Met? A . . . woman of that . . . that . . . sort?" She looked scandalized. "Don't misunderstand, Miss Cross. I sympathize with such women and through my philanthropic works I seek to improve their circumstances—as do you, from what I understand."

I nodded.

"But *meet* her? My goodness, no. Besides, since my husband's senatorial duties take us to Washington much of the year, most of my charitable activities in Newport have been from afar. Miss Cross, I do not understand you. I asked you to discover the truth of Lilah Buford's death and how she came to be lying at the foot of our staircase. But here you are, accusing me of . . . I am sure I do not know what." Her voice rose as she spoke, ending in a high-pitched crescendo.

"I'm not accusing you of anything, Mrs. Wetmore," I

replied calmly. "I'm merely attempting to trace whatever link existed between Lilah Buford and this house."

"Oh, this is all too distressing. We sent our boys away. They're with William Vanderbilt and his two sons aboard his yacht. It was the only way we could protect them. Our daughters, on the other hand, refused to—"

A knock sounded at the door, and Maude Wetmore, the younger of the two Wetmore daughters, stepped in. "Mother, I thought I heard you cry out a moment ago." Her gaze shifted to me and lingered warily. "Is everything all right?"

Mrs. Wetmore let out a telling sigh, but said, "Everything is fine, Maude, dear. You remember Miss Cross?"

"Of course. How could I forget?" The young woman's chin jutted slightly as she took my measure, as both she and her sister had done the morning Lilah Buford was found. The gesture spoke of strength of will combined with a fair dose of stubbornness, and I didn't doubt Maude Wetmore, only a year my senior, could make a formidable foe. Harry Lehr wished to marry her? He could not fully understand what that would mean. "I hope you are not upsetting my mother about what occurred here the other day."

Yes, formidable. "It is not my wish to do so, Miss Wetmore, but this is an upsetting business, all the same."

"Then perhaps you should go."

"Maude!" Her mother's tone scolded as if her daughter were a child and not a grown woman. "That is no way to treat a guest in our home."

Miss Maude raised an eyebrow and looked anything but contrite. Again I thought of Harry Lehr and his scheme to marry this woman. She was no green girl and certainly no fool. No wonder she had sent him summarily packing this morning.

"Perhaps your daughter is right, ma'am." Seeing no good

arising from alienating any member of the Wetmore family, I came to my feet. "Should I learn anything new I'll be sure to let you know. Good day to you both. I can see myself out."

"Miss Cross." Mrs. Wetmore jumped up from the settee and met me at the doorway. "Please don't give up. Your question took me off guard, but I meant no offense. And my daughter, please forgive her. She is very protective of me. Do say you'll continue."

I met her gaze levelly. "Of course I will, Mrs. Wetmore." I didn't say my quest had become more about seeking justice for Lilah Buford than removing all potential tarnish from George Wetmore's sterling character. She wouldn't have understood how a woman like Lilah could claim an equal or even greater hold on my conscience than a senator. I merely accepted her thanks, her daughter's somewhat contrite nod, and went on my way.

Later that day, after luncheon and a rest for Barney, I drove into town to see Jesse.

Jesse and I left the police station soon after I arrived. If we were to talk about the case, we must do so where no one would overhear us. We walked together up Marlborough Street, and at the corner, by the long, plain wooden Friends Meeting House, we headed north onto Farewell Street, away from town. The day was fair and warm again, with lovely breezes flowing in from the harbor.

"Chief Rogers has tied my hands once again, though it's not his fault," Jesse told me. "He's merely following orders, as I'm expected to do."

"Which is to do nothing about Lilah Buford's death. Mrs. Wetmore predicted as much." As I could have. This was not the first time Jesse Whyte had been forbidden to pursue possible suspects in a murder investigation. The last time had involved a death at The Breakers, the summer cottage of my relatives Cornelius and Alice Vanderbilt.

"And we must be seen as nothing more than two friends walking on a fine summer's day." Jesse laughed bitterly and swore softly. "This was not why I became a police officer."

"No, you joined the police force because you have an unquenchable thirst for justice."

He laughed in earnest this time. "Yes, very true. So then, what do you have to tell me?"

"Something that in all the excitement I'd forgotten to tell you sooner, something I overheard at the polo match."

"If you mean about the men upset because of the Dingley Tariff Act—"

"No, something else." A carriage rolled by, and though the driver could not have heard me, I nonetheless remained silent until it had passed. "Though it does involve one of those three men. Harry Lehr wishes to marry Maude Wetmore."

"For her money, one would suppose."

"Yes, he admitted as much. But unless he's the worst kind of fool, he knows perfectly well that George Wetmore would never allow his daughter to marry a known fortune hunter like Lehr. Why, one of his friends said as much. And although he attempted to visit Maude today and was turned away, I've no doubt he'll try again. It makes me think Lehr wouldn't be unhappy to see George Wetmore placed permanently out of the way."

"Then Lehr might be doubly happy to see Mr. Wetmore go. For Miss Wetmore's sake and because of the Dingley Act."

I shook my head. "I didn't have the impression that Harry Lehr cared one way or the other about the tariff act. That seemed only to concern the other two, Robert Clarkson and Stanford Whittaker. Most especially Whittaker. I believe

Harry Lehr's sole objective is to win Maude's hand and secure her fortune."

The gates of the Common Burying Ground Cemetery came into view. Jesse and I both had ancestors buried there from as far back as the late seventeenth century. We stopped beside it and gazed through the wrought iron fence.

"So what do we have so far?" Jesse's question was a rhetorical one, for he held up a hand and used his fingers to count off each detail we had learned. "Harry Lehr wants Maude Wetmore's fortune, but her father would never allow them to marry. Meanwhile, his two friends, Robert Clarkson and Stanford Whittaker, are incensed over Wetmore's staunch support of the Dingley Tariff."

"Not only that, but Mr. Whittaker has a penchant, apparently, for brutality against women. And it's come to my attention that Lilah might have overheard Clarkson and Whittaker conspiring against Mr. Wetmore. Their identities can't be confirmed, and it's merely hearsay, but if Lilah overheard something and was discovered, it would certainly be a motive for murder, as well as for leaving her body at Chateau sur Mer."

"Two birds with one stone, eh? Where did you discover this?"

"I did some checking in town yesterday," I replied. "I also learned that Madam Heidi's girls at the Blue Moon were none too pleased that Lilah had become a favorite among the customers. She took business away from the others. Which could also be a motive to be rid of her."

Jesse pivoted to face me, his expression registering horror. "How the devil do you know all this?"

"I went there. Yesterday."

"To the Blue Moon?"

"Yes."

"You went *inside*?"

"Yes, and I asked them if George Wetmore had ever hired their services. They all denied it, but I still wonder if perhaps Lilah stole him away from one of the other girls, and that girl took her revenge on both of them."

Jesse continued to gape at me. "You went inside and *spoke* to them?"

"They would not have spoken to you, would they? I went during the day, when the place was empty of customers. There was no danger."

"Emma, the danger lay in your being there. In being *seen* there. Have you lost your mind?"

"You sound like Nanny." I shook my head and emitted a laugh.

Jesse blew out a breath and turned back toward the cemetery. "Why must you always make me regret involving you in any case?"

His tone and his words stung, for I was being put in my place and all value of my visit to the Blue Moon stripped away. I stared at his rigid profile and wished I could make him understand that the same passion for the truth that drove him drove me as well. I'd thought he had come to terms with it, but apparently I had been wrong. Yes, I took risks, but so did he. He considered them worth it. Why couldn't he accept that I considered them equally worth it, and that they were *my* risks to take?

I reached out and closed my hand around one of the iron bars of the fence. "We have the three men I overheard talking at the polo match, and the women who work at the Blue Moon. Not to mention that George Wetmore himself is not above suspicion." I spoke as if the past several few moments hadn't occurred. "If Lilah came that night to tell him about her pregnancy, he might have killed her to silence her. No matter your orders or how upstanding a man he may seem, he must be considered a suspect, at least for now."

Gradually the ire drained from Jesse's frame. He relaxed his stance and nodded. "Yes, Wetmore is a suspect. Anyone else?"

"You'll think I'm daft."

"I already do." He softened the claim with a small smile.

"Mrs. Wetmore."

With a tilt of his head, he turned to lean his shoulder against the fence. "Surely you don't believe so."

"It must be considered, for the same reasons her husband must be. Because of the child Lilah carried. Because it might have been Mr. Wetmore's. Maybe it wasn't George Wetmore who left his bed first that night. Maybe it was Mrs. Wetmore who went down to hear what Lilah Buford wished to tell her. Such news would have frightened and enraged her. Such news would have meant the destruction of her world, the life she and her family had been living. She might have killed to protect that world, Jesse."

"Then why hire you to investigate? Wouldn't it have been safer for her to allow the police to declare the matter an accident and close the case?"

"She loves her husband. This is just a possibility, mind you. But perhaps fearing he would be accused, whether officially or in the court of public opinion, she hired me to erase all guilt from his name, at the same time believing neither I nor anyone else would ever suspect her of committing the deed. This much is certain. There is some connection between Mrs. Wetmore and Lilah. Else why would Lilah have insisted she speak with Mrs. Wetmore?"

When Jesse and I parted outside the police station, I made the short walk over to Washington Square, and to a small office on the north side. A clerk occupied a stool before a high desk by the front window, his shoulders hunched as he bent low over his work. A blueprint crackled beneath his forearms as he busily took measurements using a compass and made notations in a ledger beside his elbow. He hadn't noticed me entering.

"Excuse me."

He looked up with a start. "Oh, do forgive me, miss. I didn't hear you come in."

"That's quite all right. Is Mr. Whittaker in?"

Although Stanford Whittaker's architectural firm was headquartered in New York, where he employed numerous workers, he also kept this small office for his Newport projects. I was glad of that. I wished to speak with him, but I didn't wish to do so at his home in his wife's hearing. The woman suffered enough indignities simply being his wife. I had no desire to add to Bessie Whittaker's burdens.

"I'm afraid he isn't here presently, miss, but if you care to wait, I expect him back shortly." The clerk gestured to a seat on the opposite wall.

"Thank you, I believe I will." I made myself as comfortable as possible in the straight-backed wooden chair. The clerk went back to his blueprint, while I gazed out the window. This angle afforded me a good view of the square.

Two trolleys rolled past, and from one of them alighted a man in a checked town suit and a derby. A fringe of red hair stuck out from beneath the brim of the hat, and Mr. Whittaker paused as he pulled his watch from his vest pocket and glanced at the time. The watch still in hand, he waited for a carriage to rumble by and resumed walking toward his office.

I made a mistake then by standing up and moving toward the door. Through the window overlooking the street our gazes met. Mr. Whittaker stopped short, and even through the dusty glass between us I saw his displeasure. He made a show of checking his watch again. As if he suddenly remembered he needed to be somewhere else, he pivoted and set off up the square, toward the Colony House.

To the apparent astonishment of the clerk, I bolted outside. "Mr. Whittaker! Mr. Whittaker!"

He neither turned around nor broke his stride. I followed at nearly a run, drawing curious stares from pedestrians. I finally caught up to him outside the National Exchange Bank of Newport, a two-story Federal-style building on the corner of Meeting Street.

I panted to catch my breath. "Mr. Whittaker, a word if you please."

He eyed the building's doorway as if contemplating fleeing inside. It would have made a good escape, for if I'd followed him in and demanded his attention, I'd find myself summarily escorted outside.

With a sigh he slowly turned around to face me. He did not, however, tip his hat. "Miss Cross, is there something I can do for you?"

"I had hoped to speak with you quietly in your office, sir, rather than on a busy, crowded street."

"Is that so?" He smiled suddenly, his eyes lighting with interest. "Perhaps we might arrange to meet somewhere later, then. I believe I could clear my schedule sometime tonight." His gaze shimmied slowly down my length, returning to a point well below my chin, where it lingered for several interminable seconds.

"Now will have to do," I said curtly. "It's about Lilah Buford. How well do you know her?"

He drew himself up. "I fail to see what business it is of yours."

"I'm afraid it's very much my business. She is missing, and I have been hired to discover what happened to her."

"Hired by whom?"

"I'm not at liberty to say."

"What's it got to do with me?"

I reverted to the lie I'd attempted to tell Madam Heidi, not that she had been fooled. "Miss Buford has been missing since the evening following the polo match with the Meadowview Club. You remember that day, don't you, Mr. Whittaker?"

I scrutinized every nuance of his expression as he took in my words. A scowl drew his fiery eyebrows together. His lips pinched so tightly they disappeared beneath his mustache. Did he know where Lilah had disappeared to? Did he know she was found at the bottom of the staircase at Chateau sur Mer?

Raising an arm without quite touching me, he ushered me around the corner onto Meeting Street. There were fewer pedestrians here—fewer people to overhear our conversation.

"Of course I remember that day," he said in a hissing whisper. "What exactly are you getting at, Miss Cross?"

"Lilah turned up at the polo match and raised something of a spectacle. You saw her."

"I saw her, and I heard her insisting she speak with Mrs. Wetmore, of all people. Then I saw her being escorted from the grounds by a pair of policemen. Again, what's it got to do with me?"

I regarded him in silence a moment, considering. Then I decided I had little to lose. "You don't like the Wetmores very much, do you, Mr. Whittaker? Mr. Wetmore in particular."

"Ah, yes. You were eavesdropping that day, weren't you?"

I didn't look away. "It's my job. And if you don't wish to be overheard do not conduct sensitive conversations in public places. I can hardly be blamed. But as for Mr. Wetmore . . ."

He made a grinding noise in his throat. "It's no secret that

I don't agree with the man's politics. It doesn't matter who knows it. Men like Wetmore will ruin the country."

"Your grudge sounded more personal than that."

He scrutinized me, his eyes narrowing with suspicion. "You said you wanted to talk about Lilah Buford. Why are we suddenly discussing George Wetmore?"

I had to think fast to avoid revealing the truth. "Lilah's insistence on speaking with Mrs. Wetmore is highly unusual, and so far it's the only lead we—I—have."

"Maybe the Wetmores are hiding her in their basement."

"Don't be absurd." I decided to come as close to the truth as I dared. "It's highly possible that in Lilah's line of work, she overheard something to do with the Wetmores. Some threat," I added, watching him closely for the slightest reaction. "And perhaps someone decided to silence her."

"Are you saying someone might have—good heavens— *murdered* her?" His voice rose, attracting the attention of two pedestrians on the other side of the street. I hushed him and moved along, out of their hearing range.

"I don't yet know."

"Aren't the police searching for her?"

The question seemed both sincere and spontaneous. Did he really believe her to be missing? Continuing my ruse, I smirked. "Mr. Whittaker, how many city resources do you think will be spent finding a woman of Miss Buford's standing?"

"Humph. 'Good riddance' is what I expect they'd say."

"And what do *you* say, Mr. Whittaker?"

"If you must know, Miss Cross, I hope Lilah returns soon. She's a . . . oh, how shall I put it to your delicate, feminine ears?" He gave a snide laugh. "She's a most talented young lady, and her services shall be greatly missed. Greatly missed indeed."

His lack of empathy for the fate of another human being

was despicable. Loathing filled me until I could hardly bear to look at his smug face. I decided to wipe some of his arrogance away. "I have it on good authority that you aren't a kind man, Mr. Whittaker. That you find enjoyment in . . . oh, how shall *I* put it? In mistreating women. In hurting them. Did you hurt Lilah Buford, Mr. Whittaker?"

His aplomb did indeed fall away, and a tinge of uncertainty, perhaps even fear, entered his eyes. "The last time I saw Lilah—was with her, I mean—she was fine. Perfectly fine. Anything that happened between us happened with her consent."

"As if a woman in Miss Buford's line of work has a choice."

"It's her choice how she lives her life, isn't it? No one forced her. I certainly didn't force her to be what she is."

What she is. He spoke of her in the present tense. I had waited for a slip. According to Jesse, almost all murderers will slip up at some point, usually in the course of conversation, and speak of their victims in past tense. A simple human tendency. Then again, some were more clever than that.

"Are we done here, Miss Cross?"

"You haven't answered my question. Did you hurt Lilah Buford?"

"If you mean am I responsible for her disappearance, the answer is no."

I shook my head at him. "I'm told she often sports bruises, and that you are a frequent patron of hers."

He had the shameless audacity to shrug. "All a game, Miss Cross. One you could never understand."

No. Neither would I wish to. A knot the size of a fist lodged in my gullet, threatening me with nausea. I'd have liked nothing better than to never speak with this man again, or lay eyes on him. "I have one more question for you, Mr.

Whittaker. How did you spend the evening following the polo match?"

"Not that I'm under any obligation to tell you anything, but as it happens, I was at home that evening. All evening. We had guests. You may verify it with my wife if you like." He said this last in a spiteful, defiant tone.

I threw his defiance back in his face. "Did you know about Lilah's pregnancy?"

The color drained from his face.

"Is the child yours, do you think?"

"I . . . that is . . ." He compressed his lips and scowled. "She certainly never told me . . ."

"Perhaps she did, perhaps she didn't, Mr. Whittaker." I let that hang in the air a moment. "You don't seem to be denying it, which means you believe it's possible Lilah's child could be yours."

"I . . . well . . . the child could be mine, or it could be anyone's. Either way, she shouldn't have let it happen. Women in her position are supposed to know . . . you know . . . how to take care of these things. What's she going to do about it?"

Beyond a doubt I had caught him off guard. Unsettled him. And that made his bafflement all the more believable. Had he sneered and made some unpleasant comment, I'd have suspected him of murdering Lilah because of the baby and using the opportunity to smear George Wetmore's name.

I, too, was left unsettled by his last question, for whatever Lilah might have done, whatever decision she might have made concerning the child or whether or not to inform the father, would go forever unanswered. Sadness welled up inside me, leaving me too drained to fashion a reply to his question.

"Good day to you, Mr. Whittaker," I merely said, and turned away.

* * *

My day wasn't over yet. Impulse, more than anything else, sent me back to Carrington's Wharf. I hadn't promised Jesse I wouldn't return there, and neither had he asked me not to. An oversight on his part? Or had he simply given up trying to protect me? I hoped it was the latter—except for a tiny voice inside me that wondered if I had lost a portion of his regard.

At any rate, the Blue Moon was not my destination this time. In a moment of surprise last time, I had let an opportunity slip away, and now I intended to remedy that. Once I parked my carriage on Thames Street and secured Barney's feed bag, I passed by the alleyway and strode directly onto the main area of the wharf. The wide cobbled area teamed with activity as men in shirtsleeves worked to unload a freight steamer piled high with lumber.

My quarry labored near the door of the Lyman Fuel Company's main warehouse, busily shoveling coal from a wheeled coal bin that ran on tracks from inside the building, into the back of a delivery wagon. Sweat dripped from Anthony Dobbs's face and soaked his shirt through. Two other men, roughly clad, toiled along with him. I recognized the young man who had called Mr. Dobbs away when he had detained me in the alleyway.

With a deep breath I continued toward them, aware of gawking eyes and the murmured comments directed at me. My head high, I avoided the stares. The young man from yesterday noticed me before Anthony Dobbs did.

He removed his cap and wiped his sleeve across his brow. "Ma'am. Can we do something for you?"

Mr. Dobbs stilled his shovel and looked up. An ugly sneer twisted his upper lip. "Maybe she's lost. Are you lost, ma'am?"

"No," I said more steadily than I felt. "I wish to speak with you, Mr. Dobbs. Privately, if you would."

Several men close by smirked. Dobbs leered. "Can't imagine what the very proper Miss Emmaline Cross would want with the likes of me."

Laughter and snippets of speculation carried in the breeze. I refused to be cowed. I held up an arm to gesture toward the street. "If you would, please."

Still sporting an insolent grin, he set his shovel down and sauntered after me. I stopped and turned, but he spoke before I could. "You've got a nerve, don't you? Think I owe you any favors?"

"Mr. Dobbs, you would have been hanged without my efforts to clear you of murder. I do not see why you continue to bear a grudge for circumstances you brought upon yourself by your own actions."

His hands fisted at his sides, and for several tense moments I believed that, had I been a man and we were not in full view of dockworkers and pedestrians, he would have leveled me with a blow. Perhaps, if not for our audience, he would have done so anyway.

The best way to proceed, I deduced, was to forge ahead with my questions. "Did you know Lilah Buford?"

"The whore that died the other night? Of course I did. Not that I could afford her."

I clenched my teeth against the admonition that rose like bile inside me. I also stifled my surprise that he knew Lilah was dead, rather than merely missing. Word apparently spread among the wharves in ways that did not extend to Bellevue Avenue. "Did you see anything that night? Anyone unusual coming or going from the Blue Moon?"

"It's not like I'm here all night. I do have a place to live, hovel though it is."

I experienced a wave of disappointment. "So you saw nothing?"

"Didn't say that. I did see someone come to the Blue

Moon early on that night, someone not usually seen in these parts."

He seemed to need coaxing at every turn. "And who might that have been?" I expected him to name Robert Clarkson, Stanford Whittaker, and Harry Lehr. He did not.

"*They* might have been James Bennett and Dominic Ellsworth."

My eyebrows rose. These were names I hadn't been expecting. "They both played polo earlier that day."

"I know. I was there. Saw you, too, during that ruckus with Lilah. Always got your nose in the thick of it, don't you?"

I let that pass and was about to ask another question, but Dobbs had more to add.

"Lilah left the Blue Moon that night. All done up like a lady, or trying. She'd pretend to be respectable and pay her admittance into the Casino at night. Found herself a lot of swanky customers that way. Lilah wasn't stupid. She knew how to make her way."

"Anything else?" I asked.

"Nope." He shoved his hands into his trouser pockets. With mock deference, he asked, "May I go back to work now, Miss Cross?"

Instead of replying, I tersely thanked him and went on my way. With my mind thoroughly occupied with what I had just learned, I turned half blindly onto Thames Street, navigating more by instinct of habit than sight. I didn't at first see the figure standing beside Barney until, as I crossed the street, he hailed.

"Emma."

Derrick. Caught off guard, I halted in my tracks and was very nearly struck by one of the Newport *Observer's* own newsies, leaving the office on his bicycle with a pouch full of papers to deliver. The boy swerved just in time, called out for me to be more careful, and raced away down Thames Street.

"Are you all right?" Derrick met me in the street. He hooked my arm over his and walked me to my gig. "I didn't mean to startle you like that."

"What are you doing here?"

"I had business in the area and thought I'd see if you were at the *Observer*'s office. And then I spotted old Barney here."

My heart thumped as he handed me up onto the carriage seat. As he stood looking up at me, I traced every line and plane and compared it to the memory I had carried since the last time I'd seen him more than a year ago. The same thick, dark hair, midnight eyes, and chiseled features filled my view and put a little jog in my pulse. He remained, as always, trim and tailored and so very masculine.

That last thought nearly made me laugh out loud. Yes, Derrick Andrews had the power to knock the sense right out from beneath my hat.

"How are you?" I asked him once I'd mastered my voice.

"I'm fine, Emma, but I have so much to tell you. And you? Have you been well?"

I nodded. "How is Judith?"

"Thriving, as is Robbie. Italy agrees with them both."

"Oh." I couldn't hide my disappointment. I would sorely have liked to see little Robbie again. "Then I suppose they'll be staying on there."

"They will. That's all part of what I wish to tell you. But first, how is Nanny, and your cousins? And Brady?"

I laughed. "Yes, we do have much to talk about. Will you drive out to Gull Manor with me now? We'll give Nanny such a surprise." I reached for the reins. "And—oh—your mother came to see me not long ago."

"I see you survived the onslaught. What did she have to say?"

"Come home with me and I'll tell you all about it. Will you?"

"I was hoping you would ask." He climbed up beside me.

Nanny greeted Derrick with an unabashed display of joy, while Katie curtsied primly before serving tea, but didn't leave the parlor without tossing me a significant and cunning look. Well, perhaps she knew something I didn't. While thus far my reunion with Derrick had been cordial, even warmly affectionate, I sensed no overtures of deeper feelings. We were as two old friends catching up after a long separation.

"He's grown by leaps and bounds," he said, speaking of Robbie, who had been a guest at Gull Manor for an all too brief time last summer. "Walking, even saying a few words."

"You don't say. But he's only a year old."

"A little over that. He's sharp and clever. Smarter than me, I'll wager."

I smiled down at my tea. "I'm so glad. I want the best for him in life."

"He'll have it, if I have anything to say about it. You can be sure of that. Now, about Mother's visit . . ."

"Yes, that." I sipped my tea and then inhaled a steely breath. "You must speak to her. She all but has us trotting down the aisle together." As soon as I'd spoken, I almost wished I hadn't. This was no light topic of conversation. It involved deep sentiments and the many layers of Derrick's and my acquaintance, which was no simple thing. We had been through a great deal, more than most people even after many years of knowing one another, intimate things no casual acquaintances should ever share. Tears, fright, and life-and-death matters. He knew me possibly better than anyone else did, with the exception of Nanny.

And yet, marriage had always been a sore subject between

us. He had proposed rashly two summers ago, and I—I had turned him down almost as rashly. I had suffered regrets and second thoughts, but I knew in my heart I had been correct in refusing him. He had proposed for the wrong reasons, and had I accepted, it would have been for unsuitable, capricious reasons as well. We both knew it, though he had taken longer to come round to acceptance. When we parted last summer, it was with the understanding that, when we again met, we would begin anew and proceed slowly from there.

Whatever exactly that meant.

But now here I was, talking openly and casually about marriage, even if this time the subject had been instigated by his mother.

He sat quietly for some moments. Patch wandered in, his tail wagging furiously as he explored the potential of this new guest. Patch hadn't yet joined my little family before Derrick went away last year. Now he sought to ascertain whether friend, foe, or indifference occupied the armchair across from me. Derrick obliged his breathy entreaties with a thorough petting, and hadn't quite finished when he glanced over at me again. "Did you tell my mother neither of us is prepared to go ahead with marriage plans?"

"I did. She wouldn't listen."

Derrick's hand stilled. "That sounds like my mother. Once she has a notion in her head, there's almost no dislodging it."

"But we must. She's ready to begin ordering flowers and hiring the caterer."

"I'll be honest." He leaned back in his chair, though continued absently petting Patch behind his floppy ears. "A year ago, I might have encouraged her to order those flowers and everything else that goes along with them." He shook his head. "The events of last summer and everything that has happened since have changed me. Taught me. Rushing into something—anything—can have calamitous results." He held up a hand when I started to reply. "Mind you, I'm not going away. You won't be rid of me that easily. I'm simply . . . waiting."

"Biding your time?" I smiled, though not altogether happily. "I've done some changing as well. But I am no closer to knowing what I want. In fact, such things are murkier to me than ever, and I cannot in good conscience ask you to wait—"

"You didn't."

I only just kept myself from sighing. No matter my feelings for him, and in truth, they were significant, the life he led—and which I would lead as his wife—held little appeal for me. His family's wealth assured them a place among society's Four Hundred, and I had no wish to emulate the lives of my Vanderbilt aunts, Alice and Alva. An endless procession of society events filled their days. The triteness of such an existence would stifle me.

How could I make him understand that one of the things I had realized in his absence was that making no decision concerning marriage was also a choice open to me? Great Aunt Sadie had never married—by choice. She always said she had too much to lose, meaning her life had been rich, filled with purpose, and independent of outside influences.

Did seeing the value of such a life make me hard and heartless? I didn't believe so, for my heart did ache, just a bit, when I contemplated spending the years ahead alone. There must always be a price to pay, no matter one's choices.

"Derrick . . ." I trailed off, deciding to let it go for now. "I am very glad you're back. Will you be staying in Newport long, or returning to Providence?"

"Yes, about that." He shifted his position, crossing one long leg over the other. "I am not returning to Providence anytime soon. You see, there is no longer any reason for me to be there."

"What about the newspaper?" Derrick's father owned the Providence *Sun,* which Derrick would one day inherit.

He shook his head slowly. "I am no longer an employee of the *Sun.* I have been replaced. My punishment, it seems, for taking Judith's side and accompanying her to Italy."

"I don't understand. How can you be replaced? You're your father's only son."

"Apparently, I am no longer that. I have been thoroughly and, according to Father, irrevocably disinherited."

Chapter 7

In an instant, Derrick's announcement changed everything. I entertained no doubts that he would make his own way in life, and quite nicely. My cousin Neily, formerly his father's principal heir at the New York Central Railroad, had been disinherited a year ago. He had been allowed to stay on as an employee, which he had accepted rather than live entirely off his wife's dowry. But he was also continuing his education with a higher degree in engineering as his goal.

No, disinheritance would not hold Derrick back, and might perhaps propel him to a far more rewarding life than otherwise. Perhaps he'd start his own newspaper business, and I—I could work for that paper, and report on real news openly and without restrictions, as I had longed to do. His newly fallen state also, I realized with no small jolt of amazement, set the two of us on far more equal terms, socially speaking. If he and I were to marry, I might not be required to carry on like a typical society matron. Added to that, we now had his mother's permission.

I waited for a sense of joy to take hold of me. It did not,

and the reason became obvious. As I had been telling myself all along, I was not ready to be a wife. Any man's wife. I was still becoming myself, the person I wished to be, the person Aunt Sadie encouraged me to be. The reasons for denying Derrick's proposal, and for holding Jesse at arm's length, had nothing to do with either man or my conflicting feelings for them, and everything to do with myself. Confidence in the decisions I had made thus far in my life rose up in me, along with a kind of serenity.

Until another thought occurred to me.

"You mother doesn't know, does she?"

"I don't believe so. Not yet. She'll be furious. I'm sure she'll rush off to Providence and have the most awful row with my father. I wouldn't be surprised if we heard them from here."

"That isn't all." I couldn't help the ironic smile that curled my lips. "Her enthusiasm for any kind of association between the two of us shall wane as quickly as it waxed."

"Mother isn't as fickle as all that." He frowned. "At least I don't think she is. Besides, you've done nothing wrong. This is between my father and me."

"Don't you see? Once your mother learns the family fortune might not be going to you as planned, she'll be on the hunt for a suitably wealthy daughter-in-law."

He thought that over a moment, and smiled as I had done—ironically and without genuine amusement. "She can try."

After one of Nanny's hearty New England dinners, Derrick and I set off back to town. On the way, I had an idea. I had showed him a photograph I'd taken from Lilah Buford's photograph album, and told him everything that happened from the time of the polo match to my brief interview with Anthony Dobbs on the wharf.

"You should not have approached that man on your own, Emma."

"It was broad daylight and we were surrounded by others."

"Other dockworkers. Not exactly the most savory or trustworthy bunch."

"Perhaps not, but I felt safe enough. Aren't you going to scold me for entering Madam Heidi's brothel, as Jesse did?" Where Ocean Avenue met Bellevue, I turned Barney toward town. We passed Rough Point and soon after Marble House and Beechwood. Carriages heading toward dinner parties and balls traveled up and down the street, their elegantly dressed occupants waving to one another.

"Would it do any good?" Derrick replied to my facetious question. "Did the detective's scolding change anything?"

I grinned, raising one hand from the reins and adjusting my hat. "That photograph is a good likeness of Lilah, even though it was taken long ago. She hadn't changed much since she was a girl. I want to show it around at the Casino and see who reacts to it, and *how* they react. I'd appreciate your coming with me, if you would."

"Ah, so you'll engage ladies of the evening and dockworkers alone, but you require a chaperone to enter the Newport Casino?"

I tilted my chin at him. "Don't be impertinent. I don't fear to approach any Newporter. No matter how unsavory some may appear, I am one of them and not likely to come to harm."

"Dockworkers are not all Newporters," he interrupted before I could make my point. "Many of them come in on boats from who knows where, work here for a while, and then move on."

"Be that as it may. At the Casino I will be dealing with members of your set—"

"I'm not of their set any longer."

"They don't know that yet. Besides, you were born to the Four Hundred. You'll always belong, fortune or no. And what I'll need tonight is someone who belongs, to whom the others are willing to speak. I can manage among my Vanderbilt relatives, but the others? That is where you come in, if you're willing."

He leaned back against the carriage seat, a small smile playing about his lips. "I am."

Carriages lined both sides of Bellevue Avenue outside the Casino, and stretched away into the distance. We passed by the Casino's row of fine shops to our right, while to our left stood Stone Villa, the three-story Italianate mansion owned by James Bennett.

Mr. Bennett had purposely bought property for the Casino directly across from Stone Villa, as a reminder to the Four Hundred that at *this* place of entertainment, his rules would prevail. Seventeen years ago he had been temporarily expelled from the Newport Reading Room, farther down the avenue, for encouraging his friend to ride his horse up from the steps and onto the veranda. The building of the Casino had been his reply.

I guided the carriage onto nearby Bath Road, where I found space to park. A few moments later Derrick and I passed through the entrance arch of the Newport Casino and through the paneled corridor. Like many of the Four Hundred, his family maintained a membership here, and as his guest I need not pay an entry fee. A set of stairs led to the second floor, where reading rooms, card rooms, the billiards room, and gentlemen's accommodations were located. It would have done me little good to go that way, for attempting to break in on card or billiard games, or intrude upon gentlemen renting private rooms, would result in a hasty escort back out to the street. We continued on, emerging into the open air of the courtyard.

Beneath a starry sky, a crowd milled over the main lawn. A covered piazza stretched along the north side of the enclosure while the Horseshoe Pavilion curved around to embrace the courtyard. Beyond the pavilion lay the tennis courts and the Casino Theater. Lively music floated from one of the covered patios on the upper story of the piazza.

I took a moment to savor the lovely shingle-style design of the structure, with its gables and intermingling of English, French, American Colonial, and most surprising, Japanese architectural motifs. Behind us, beside the entryway, the clock tower with its bell-shaped roof emulated the turrets of Loire Valley châteaux. Thanks to the inner Tiffany works, the clock was said to keep perfect time.

In studying the mingling crowd, my confidence flagged. Where would I start? Whom would I question first? I did have a plan, which was to portray Lilah as a missing young woman last seen here. Word of her death, and of her occupation, had not yet become common knowledge. What with the way news traveled in Newport, especially in the summer months, I had limited opportunity in which to work my deception.

Derrick took my arm in his and led me onto the piazza. "Perhaps we should begin with your cousin."

He gestured with his chin, and sure enough, I spotted Neily sitting with his brothers, Alfred and Reggie, at a table overlooking the green in the open air section of the restaurant. All three stood when I called to them. We climbed the few steps up to join them. Reggie was the first to greet me.

"You're not often here, Em. What brings you?" The youngest of Cornelius Vanderbilt's sons, Reggie had passed his seventeenth birthday some months earlier. He had achieved a man's height and filled out in the shoulders, but he remained clean-shaven and youthful but for the weariness lurking beneath his heavy eyelids. He rocked slightly on his feet as he took my hand, and I saw in an instant that he had been drinking, and as usual more than he should have.

Alfred, the middle brother, showed no such signs of inebriation. His eyes were clear, keen like his father's, his clothes crisp and sharp, and he bore himself with the steadiness of a man who saw his future plainly laid out for him, the prince and heir apparent. Apt, for upon Neily's disinheritance, Alfred became his father's primary heir. At only twenty, Alfred had already taken on much of his father's responsibilities, both within the family and at the New York Central Railroad. He took my hand and bowed over it in his very proper way, his gaze sliding sideways at Reggie as he did so. He glanced back at me with a look that apologized, for he knew as well as I that his brother had over-imbibed. Then he bade me good evening and resumed his seat. We had never been close, Alfred and I. Never at odds, but never true friends.

It was Neily who embraced me fully, held me a moment longer, and released me with an observation of his own. Quietly, his words nearly gobbled up by the surrounding chatter, he said, "You're looking somber tonight, Emmaline. What brought you here, and is there anything I can do?"

I could never hide anything from Neily. Of all my Vanderbilt cousins, his was the friendship I valued most, which I could not do without. Though I had applauded his marriage to Grace Wilson despite his parents' objections, I had also secretly mourned the loss of our easy rapport. For though I might enjoy a close camaraderie with my single cousin, I certainly couldn't make claims on the time of a married man.

With Alfred and Reggie engaged in conversation with Derrick, I opened my handbag and slid out the photograph of Lilah. "This is not recent, but the resemblance is strong. Do you know her?"

He studied the print, squinting slightly in the dimness of the gas lighting. When he still hadn't spoken a moment later, but rather swallowed and compressed his lips, I knew that he recognized her and was uncomfortable discussing her with me.

"Were you here after the polo match two days ago? Did you see her here that night? It's important, Neily, so please don't prevaricate in the effort to spare me indelicate details. I know what sort of work Lilah Buford did."

His head snapped up. "Did?"

I immediately realized my mistake. I took him by the arm and moved him farther away from his brothers. "Lilah is dead, Neily, but please, tell no one. Not yet. I've been hired to find out what she did that night, and who last saw her."

"Hired by whom?"

"I can't tell you that. Did you see her here? I know she came sometimes to solicit business. Someone told me when she left her . . . home . . . that night, she appeared to be dressed to fit in here."

"I believe I did see her." He fidgeted with his cuffs, a sure sign the conversation made him uncomfortable. "But where she went, and with whom, I cannot tell you."

"What about your brothers?"

He hesitated, and then called Reggie over. I showed him the picture.

"She looks familiar . . . Is that Lilah Buford?" As soon as he spoke her name, Reggie looked sheepishly at his older brother. "I mean . . . uh . . ."

"I know what you mean, Reg." Neily shook his head in disapproval.

I hadn't time for a brotherly squabble. "Reggie, were you here three nights ago, and if so, did you see Lilah here?"

"Why? What's going on?" Reggie didn't wait for an answer. "Does this have anything to do with her showing up at the polo grounds earlier that same day?"

"You know about that?"

"Sure I do, Em. I was on the hill. I saw the whole thing."

His elder brother asked, "What were you doing up on Morton Hill? Why weren't you on the grandstand?"

Reggie shrugged. "I happened to be escorting a young lady, and I use the term loosely, who preferred the hill." He turned back to me. "What did Lilah want with the Wetmores?"

So Reggie had heard as well as seen. Odd that he had escaped my notice. "Did she arrive on the grounds with anyone?" I asked him. "Did you see her with anyone at all?"

He thought a moment. "She talked with some fellow. A footstool, by the look of him. Up on the hill before she decided to make a scene."

I remained silent a moment. I'd heard the term *footstool* before and I didn't like it. It reduced our local population to mere props that existed for the comfort of the summer set. Then I remembered the man who had come down off Morton Hill to speak to Lilah as the police escorted her from the polo grounds. She had been resisting, but at a few words from him, the fight left her and she went out quietly. Could he be the same individual Reggie had seen her with prior to that? "Was he wearing a workman's straw hat? The kind gardeners often wear to keep the sun off their necks?"

"Now that you mention it, I believe he was. Didn't pay much attention, really."

"And could he have been the same man who intervened as the police escorted her away?"

"That I can't say. By then my, uh, lady friend decided I'd been ignoring her long enough. By the bye, did you know Westchester and Meadowview are scheduled for another match?"

This news took me by surprise.

Reggie seemed excited by the development. "It was decided today. Westchester raised an official protest over the oversight in upgrading Meadowview's skill rating. I'm surprised you didn't hear. The Competition Committee ruled in West-chester's favor." He leaned closer and lowered his voice. "I don't have to tell you I'm relieved. I lost a hefty wager on the first match. I'll make it all back this time."

I couldn't help the skeptical slant of my lips. "I hope you're right, Reggie, but you might employ a bit of pru-dence when making your wagers."

"Same old Em. We can't all be as sensible as you."

"Yes, well, never mind. I'd like to ask another question about Lilah. When she came here to the Casino in the evenings, whom did she typically approach?"

"She didn't typically approach anyone," Reggie replied with a shrug. "They approached *her*. Single fellows, mostly, though not always."

"And two nights ago? Did you see with whom she might have left?"

Reggie absently ran a finger between his collar and his neck as he considered. "The evenings tend to be a little blurry, if you know what I mean. All I can say with certainty is that she didn't leave with me."

"Well, if you remember anything about that day, or about the man Lilah was with, will you let me know, please?"

"You can count on it, Em."

I didn't hold out much hope. As Reggie had said, his memories of social gatherings were blurry more often than not. After taking our leave of my cousins, Derrick and I walked along the piazza. I found Robert Clarkson excusing himself from a group of people, and when he turned away from them I stepped into his path, forcing him to a sudden halt.

"Andrews," he said, speaking to Derrick while ignoring me. "Didn't know you were back in the country."

"Only just arrived. Do you know Miss Cross?"

The young Rhode Island senator turned his small, pale

eyes in my direction and swept them over me once. "Miss Cross. I didn't know the two of you were acquainted."

It was my turn to ignore him, or at least the comment. I slid Lilah's picture from my handbag again. "Mr. Clarkson, this woman has gone missing. It is important that she be found."

He bent over the photograph, sighing as he did so. "She's a child."

"Look closely, Mr. Clarkson." I held the image closer beneath his nose. "She is no longer a child, but the resemblance is there. You know her, Mr. Clarkson. Her name is Lilah."

He stiffened, then raised his head. "Missing, you say? When?"

"Sometime after the polo match. After she tried to make her way to the grandstand." I raised one eyebrow and regarded him without blinking, waiting for his reaction. His complexion deepened. His chin jutted as he drew in a breath. "I know you saw her there," I said. "You and your associates, Mr. Lehr and Mr. Whittaker, seemed to know her."

"What of it? Lilah is on intimate terms with any number of men in this town."

"Including yourself." The words were hardly past my lips when Derrick's hand came up to cup my elbow in a subtle caution. "Did you see her after the match, later that evening? Here?"

"No, I did not. I was not here that night."

"Where were you?"

He balked, his lips turning down as if he'd tasted something sour. "I see no reason why I should answer such a question, especially from the likes of you."

"And what does that—"

Derrick moved forward, half shielding me with his body. "Now see here, Clarkson. There is no need for that. Miss Cross has this woman's best interests at heart."

"I can hardly fathom why. What difference if Newport is short one whore?" With that he pivoted on his heel and strode past us.

Derrick's voice tickled my ear. "Maybe we should leave. I can't see what you're going to learn from any of these people."

I swallowed my disgust with Robert Clarkson and shook my head. "I did just learn something. When he spoke of Lilah being on intimate terms with any number of men, he said *is*, and not *was*. Stanford Whittaker used the present tense as well when I spoke with him. That may indicate they don't know she is dead."

"Not exactly an exonerating detail. Either of them might deliberately have used the word to appear innocent."

"Mr. Clarkson just said it rather briskly, though, without thought. You're right, however. We can't discount him." I gazed about me. Picking a random direction, I stopped several more young men who were not accompanying ladies. Some of them recognized Lilah, or at least knew of her by reputation. Others claimed no knowledge of her. None of them displayed any particular concern when I told them she had gone missing. "Perhaps you're right," I conceded to Derrick. "We seem to be learning nothing here."

"Let's cross over and walk on the other side." Offering his arm, Derrick guided me onto an open walkway. An elderly man approached us before we took very many steps.

"I hear you're looking for Lilah Buford?"

His abruptness startled me and I didn't immediately reply. Thank goodness I had Derrick with me.

"That's right. Do you know her?" he asked as I studied the gentleman. He stood tall and trim but for a slight paunch pressing against his evening coat. A white silk scarf draped around his collar, and he leaned on an ebony cane topped with a silver handle. He didn't seem at all familiar—odd in a town where the wealthy came to see and be seen, and where it was my job to become familiar with all of them.

"I know *of* her," he said with an air of wounded dignity. "What has happened to her?"

"That is what we are trying to find out, sir," I said evasively. "Is there anything you can tell us about her?"

With the help of his cane, he drew himself up taller. He inched his nose higher for good measure. "Certainly not. She came here making trouble, and if you were wise you'd leave her be. Wherever she has gone, let her stay there."

Unsteadily, he made his way around us and kept going until he reached the horseshoe piazza. There he must have been greeted by an acquaintance, for he reached up and grasped an assisting hand as he climbed the steps.

I stared after him another moment. "That was odd."

"Exceedingly. Do you know who he is?"

I shook my head. "I was hoping you did." At his half shrug I retook his arm, and we resumed walking. "It behooves me to find out, doesn't it?"

I'd hoped to make another circuit of the Casino and this time include the upper porches. That plan came to a sudden end as we circled back around to the entry arcade.

"Mr. Andrews and Miss Cross." James Gordon Bennett stepped out from the archway, his arms folded across his chest. "I'm going to ask the pair of you to leave, please."

"Leave?" Derrick's hand moved to cover mine where it rested in the crook of his arm. "I think you'd better explain yourself, Bennett."

"With pleasure." The man smiled and released his arms to his sides. His was an athletic figure, not surprising since in addition to polo he excelled at tennis and golf and was an active yachtsman. His cool eyes assessed us in a way that made Derrick's muscles tense beneath my hand. I longed to cut this encounter short. He and Derrick were already rivals of a sort—in the newspaper business—for James Bennett owned the New York *Herald.* Would Mr. Bennett, known for his irreverent sense of humor, find amusement in haranguing his competitor, even make a scene?

I wouldn't have put it past him. James Bennett was known for neither discretion nor decorum.

"You are harassing my guests." Mr. Bennett's smile didn't waver. "And I cannot have that at my club."

"We're doing no such thing, and technically this is not your club." I kept my voice low, but firm. "You may be responsible for the Casino having been built, but there is a board of governors now, along with patrons and supporters."

His gaze slid to me. "Would you like me to gather them all here right now, Miss Cross? I assure you, they will be no happier than I at the prospect of your asking sordid questions about ladies of the evening."

"Do you know Miss Lilah Buford? Were you aware she visited the Casino regularly?" My implication, that a known prostitute had been suffered to enter the establishment and ply her trade, brought a wash of crimson to Mr. Bennett's face. And something else. Wariness, and if I didn't know better, something akin to remorse.

He recovered swiftly. "No, Miss Cross, I was not aware of that. Now, if you please." He gestured toward the street and added, "Before I send for the police."

I almost laughed and challenged him to do just that, with the proviso that he ask for Jesse specifically. But this being a private establishment, I could easily find myself barred from entering, permanently.

"Is someone here in need of assistance?" A man with an olive complexion and glossy black hair swept neatly back from his forehead came to stand at James Bennett's side. I recognized him as Dominic Ellsworth, who played with Mr. Bennett on the Westchester polo team, and I entertained no doubts to whom he would render his offered assistance. He fixed his dark gaze on Derrick and me, one ebony slash of an eyebrow raised. Mr. Ellsworth's exotic good looks favored his mother, the beautiful Cuban American Lucinda Yznaga. Coincidentally, her sister, Consuelo, was a great friend of my aunt Alva Vanderbilt, and they had named their daughters after each other.

Mr. Bennett emitted a soft laugh. "I think Mr. Andrews, Miss Cross, and I have reached an understanding."

"Have we, Mr. Bennett?" I ran my gaze over both men, allowing my expression to register an amusement I didn't quite feel. "I'm glad Mr. Ellsworth has joined us, for there is one last question I'd like to ask you both."

James Bennett scowled. "Miss Cross, I made no idle threat when I said I'd summon the police."

"Perhaps that is a good idea, sir. For you see, someone witnessed the two of you visiting the Blue Moon several nights ago. The very night Lilah Buford disappeared."

Dominic Ellsworth's dark complexion turned florid. "That's a lie."

It might have been, considering I'd gleaned this bit of information from Anthony Dobbs, but I took care not to let my own doubts show. "Then why do you color so, Mr. Ellsworth? I seem to have struck a nerve. Tell me, how well do you know Lilah?" I made sure to place emphasis on the words *do* and *know*, rather than asking how well he had *known* Lilah.

"That's quite enough." Mr. Bennett reached out an arm, guiding Derrick and me, without quite touching us, through the entryway. "We wouldn't want to cause a scene, now, would we?"

Derrick's eyes narrowed dangerously. "Don't think this is the end of the matter."

"That's quite all right, Derrick," I murmured to him. "I believe we've learned enough for one night."

The strident complaint of alarm bells confronted us moments after we entered the street. My senses instantly alert, I breathed in a deep draft of air. "Fire," Derrick and I said at the same time. I paused to listen. "West of us. Oh, Derrick, heaven help us."

The Newport *Observer*'s offices were west of us. So was the Blue Moon, and a host of other taverns, homes, shops, and businesses.

Chapter 8

Derrick and I set off running along Bath Road toward the harbor. The ringing became louder as we went, and as we approached Thames Street we were swept into a current of individuals, mostly men, hurrying southward. Billows of black smoke poured from a building several streets down. I strained to make out which one it was. A ladder truck pulled by a team of four horses and bearing several firemen barreled along the street. Moments later the steam engine and the hose wagon rumbled past.

The air became thicker, hotter, with each street we crossed. Sparks swirled and crackled; flames leaped above the rooftops. I gasped for breath. My heart thudded in my throat as I strained to peer through the growing crowd, wafting smoke, and my own rising dismay. Relief poured through me as I realized the burning building stood closer to us than the *Observer*'s offices. I could determine little more, for the confusion of flame and smoke, the pooling crowd, the scrambling firemen, and the water, now bursting from hoses connected to the steam engine, left me disoriented.

Derrick placed a firm hand at the back of my waist. "We shouldn't go any farther. They don't need spectators closing in on them."

He was right, of course, generally speaking. "I'm not a spectator. I'm a reporter." I continued forward, but I moved to the opposite side of the street, the side closer to the harbor, from where I could observe without getting in the way.

"It's the cigar shop." I pointed at the half-consumed sign above the shop window.

Beside me, Derrick whistled low through his teeth. "Ellsworth Cigars serves half the population of Newport."

"Half the summer population, you mean. The average Newporter can't afford cigars, much less those." It was true, the establishment catered to the expensive tastes of Bellevue Avenue, importing the finest cigars from around the world, but especially from Cuba. This was but one shop in the Ellsworth empire. There were others in nearly every major East Coast city. Still, this loss would be acutely felt. As families arrived for the summer, men inundated Ellsworth Cigars with orders that would be delivered periodically throughout the season.

"Poor Dominic." Derrick emitted a low whistle through his teeth. "I could almost feel sorry for him, if he hadn't acted the ass along with Bennett back at the Casino. I wonder what happened. There must be a fortune inside, going up in smoke." He looked down at me with a contrite expression. "Sorry. I don't mean to make a joke of it, but it *is* rather ironic."

"Thank goodness the shop was closed for the night." As I spoke, I caught sight of several familiar faces, Madam Heidi's included. Her bright blond hair, though swept back and piled high on her head, flashed like a beacon among the gawking crowd. Beside her, one of the girls, the young, golden-haired Flossie, caught my gaze, her own wide and filled with alarm.

"I'll be right back," I said to Derrick.

He grasped my wrist. "Where do you think you're going?"

"Just there." I pointed to Flossie across the flood of on-lookers. "I'm going to see what I can find out. Wait here, please." He nodded reluctantly and released me. It wasn't until I reached Flossie that I realized he had followed me despite my request.

Flossie reached out and latched onto both my hands. "Isn't it awful, Miss Cross? We feared at first it might be one of the warehouses on Carrington's Wharf, and that the flames might spread to us. The customers went running outside, and the rest of us followed." She raised her voice to be heard above the commotion and the whoosh of the fire hoses. She took a moment to look around her. We stood only a few yards shy of Howard's wharf, and the lumber mill that occupied space there. With a start I realized a single floating spark could ignite the wooden structure and its contents, especially with the sawdust that coated every surface inside. Apparently, Flossie shared my concerns. "Do you think they'll be able to get it under control before it spreads?"

"I hope so, Flossie. I think they will." But what about the businesses flanking the cigar shop? A carpenter's workshop stood to the left; to the right, a spice shop. The proprietors would lose everything should the flames leap through the walls between them.

Derrick moved beside me and eyed Flossie. He couldn't fail to guess her occupation, not with her loose hair, ill-fitting dress devoid of stays beneath, and her comment about customers running outside when the fire started.

I cleared my throat, feeling suddenly awkward. It was my belief that all human beings should be accorded basic respect, no matter their occupation. I hoped Derrick agreed. He had met Stella, a former fallen woman who stayed at Gull Manor last summer, and treated her cordially. But poor

Flossie was still very much a part of the illicit world of the docks. Well, if he didn't like it, he should not have followed me. I cleared my throat again, already feeling raw from the smoke.

"Flossie, this is Mr. Andrews, a good friend of mine. Mr. Andrews, Flossie." I held my breath as I waited for him to respond. Then a notion occurred to me: Was he already acquainted with her? I couldn't help hoping such was not the case.

"A pleasure, miss," he said with a nod. Even in the dark, with the flames reflected on her perspiring face, Flossie blushed prettily and ducked her head. Obviously, she was unused to the politeness of gentlemen.

We went back to observing the efforts of the firemen. Policemen also arrived and pushed the onlookers back to a safe distance. One tried to usher us along the sidewalk until he recognized me.

"The three of you stay clear, Miss Cross."

I promised him we would. Did he notice or recognize Flossie? Perhaps, but he didn't miss a beat as he moved along to break up a small throng growing on the next corner.

"There's someone inside!" The shout came from the doorway of the burning building. The crowd pressed forward again, prompting the police to redouble their efforts. They dispensed with courtesy and roughly pushed several men backward before using their nightsticks, not to strike, but to clear the area as a shepherd would wave his staff to coax his flock in the desired direction. But even as the onlookers moved back, their shouts darted to and fro.

"Who is it? Who's inside?"

"I think it's the manager."

"Styles? Can you see him?"

"Hurry, you've got to get him out!"

Several firemen ran into the building. I stood on tiptoe, bracing myself with one hand on Derrick's shoulder. Beneath my fingers, his shoulder became rocklike and deep lines scored his forehead. I peered ahead and craned my neck to see around the fire wagons and scrambling firemen. "Derrick, do you think he can still be alive?"

He didn't answer. Sparks blasted from the roof of the two-story building, and flaming shingles rained down onto the street. Onlookers shrieked and pulled back, many flush up against the building fronts behind them. Others spilled onto the nearest wharves. A fireman rushed from the cigar shop, his coat sleeve in flames. He cried out for help, but his fellow firemen were too distracted to notice. The man fell to his knees, striking at his arm with his other hand. Derrick uttered a terse "stay here" and ran into the street. As he did, he tugged off his coat. When he reached the fireman he used it to beat at the flames dancing along the man's arm. Within seconds the flames were out, and the fireman collapsed onto his back. Derrick bent over him, speaking, though I could not hear the words.

A crash sounded from inside the cigar shop and another burst of sparks shot up from the roof. Embers rained down, and I ducked my head and raised my hands to shield myself. I needed to move away—we all did. I could no longer see Derrick as fear drove the crowd in confused directions all around me. I also looked for Flossie, but she, too, was nowhere to be seen. Another explosion sent a barrage of burning shingles flying, arcing in my direction. I took a step in the hopes of moving farther along the sidewalk when a shove from behind sent me sprawling into the street, into a suffocating mixture of dust and mud and ash.

I gasped for breath and attempted to slip my hands beneath me and raise myself up. A near paralyzing fear of being trampled overcame me, along with very real pinpricks of heat as embers landed against my back and singed through my clothing.

In the next instant hands closed around my shoulders

and gently turned me. "Emma, good God, are you all right? Emma?"

"Yes, yes. I think so. I was . . ." I had felt a shove, or so I had thought. But surely it had been an accident. The sparks had sent everyone running, and someone merely bumped into me. "I lost my footing," I concluded weakly.

Derrick helped me to my feet. He slipped an arm around my waist and held me firmly to his side. "You might have been killed. I'd never have forgiven myself."

"I'm fine, I promise." But I trembled against him, and my legs felt barely able to support me.

If anyone knew the perils of a fire, I did. My memory conjured scorching heat, the sickening stench of burning flesh, and the sting of smoke inundating my lungs. Yes, in many ways, smoke constituted the gravest danger, for death could come immediately or later, after the illusion of safety set in.

With Derrick guiding me, we made our way back toward Bath Road, though we stopped well within visible range of the cigar shop. The crackling flames of both recollection and the present moment rendered me immobile and nearly breathless—*afraid* to breathe in the noxious haze—though not for myself but for the individual still trapped within, as if my holding my breath would help him hold his own until rescue arrived.

It arrived too late. Moments later two firemen burst from the flaming building. They carried someone between them, brought him into the street, and gently laid him down. I craned to make out who it was. Before I could glimpse much, someone draped a cloth over him.

I let out the breath I'd been holding and turned my face into Derrick's coat front. I had seen death before—of course I had. But that didn't make it any easier. With each lost life, I thought of all that might have been. I thought of the achievements and dreams that would never come to fruition. I thought of the family waiting for their loved one to come home. I thought of the utter tragedy of such a loss.

And then my gaze lit on yet another familiar face. Anthony Dobbs stood with hands in his pockets and his chin lifted, observing the fire through slitted eyes. Beside him was the younger man who worked with him, the one who had called him back to work the day he confronted me on the wharf. It didn't surprise me to see either of them there. They were workmates, after all, and perhaps Dobbs, his means greatly reduced since he left the police force, had taken a room in the area. Still, he appeared too calm, too assessing for my liking, and the sight of him sent a chill across my shoulders and a suspicion, albeit unfounded, to settle in my mind.

I couldn't have said how long Derrick and I stood there, watching, when a sudden onslaught from Bath Road brought shouting and the tramp of running feet. In an instant these latest arrivals shouldered their way through the bystanders until they came face-to-face with the restraining policemen.

The dark-haired Dominic Ellsworth attempted to push his way past. An officer stepped in front of him to block his path, but it was one of his own group, James Bennett, who managed to stop him. Mr. Ellsworth shouted that he must save his building, and James Bennett shouted back that it was already too late. Mr. Bennett locked his arms about his fellow teammate from the Westchester Polo Club and forcibly prevented him from dashing into the blaze.

I stayed up late that night writing my account of the fire, and drove Barney into town early the next morning to deliver the article to my employer.

Mr. Millford let out a sigh when I laid the page on his desk beneath his nose. "Ed was at the fire as well, Emma. Didn't you see him there?"

"Not a sign of him. I suggest you read both accounts and print the one that rings most true." I had no doubt the more authentic article would be mine, though that didn't guarantee me a byline in the evening edition. Neither would arguing, however, so with a little prayer in hopes of fair play, I turned and left his office.

I considered returning to the Blue Moon to once again question Madam Heidi and her girls, but the early hour dissuaded me of the wisdom of that plan. I'd already roused them from their beds once this week. I'd wait until later this afternoon. On my way out, then, I asked Donald Larimer, the *Observer*'s front office clerk, to keep an eye on Barney for me. Then I walked up to Spring Street, where I caught the trolley that took me to the north end of town. I alighted in front of the Newport Hospital on Friendship Street, a once-private house converted to its present purpose.

It was some minutes before Hannah Hanson was able to meet me in the lobby. "I'm sorry to keep you waiting, Emma. I assisted in surgery earlier and needed to change." She gestured to her starched dress and crisp white pinafore.

"Please don't apologize. Thank you for seeing me."

She took my hand. "Come. We can talk in the meeting room. It's not about Brady, is it? He isn't ill, is he?" She stopped short, her face reddening. "I mean . . . oh, dear."

"I'm not here about Brady, and rest assured, I'm delighted you and he have renewed your acquaintance." I added a bit of emphasis on the last word and Hannah's blush deepened, making her blue eyes and blond hair—of a much more natural shade than Madam Heidi's—stand out even brighter. We entered the meeting room, where I had spent unhappy hours last summer waiting with my Vanderbilt relatives to learn the fate of Uncle Cornelius following his stroke. The news had not been good, was still not good, but he had lived and for that we were grateful.

Hannah closed the door behind us and we took seats at the

long table. "It's about the man who died in the fire on Thames Street," I said. "Do you know anything about him?"

"I do." She glanced down at the tabletop and drew a breath. "He managed the cigar shop. His name was Bertrand Styles. Oh, Emma—the burns were dreadful. I'm glad for his sake he didn't live. He would not have been able to bear it."

My insides chilling, I let this information settle a moment. "Was anyone else injured? Any of the firemen?"

"Yes, three came in. Two suffering from smoke inhalation, the other burns."

"On his arm?" I remembered how Derrick used his coat to douse the flames.

"Yes. He was the man who first realized Mr. Styles was inside and went running in first to drag him out. They were all treated and went home. Against doctor's orders."

"Hannah, the fire occurred well into the night. Did anyone wonder what Mr. Styles was doing in the shop at that hour?"

"Not in my hearing, but now that you mention it, it does seem odd. Perhaps a new shipment came in that day and he stayed to do the cataloguing."

"Perhaps. What about the cause of the fire? Have you heard anything about that? Even speculation?"

She darted a glance at the closed door. "I did overhear some of the firemen who came to check on their friends. They were baffled about this fire, Emma. Yes, the contents of the shop were flammable, but that's exactly why both the owner and the manager always took such precautions against accidental fire. They had a strict policy against open flames."

"The place was lit by gas, no?"

"Yes, but with glass-enclosed fixtures, vented to prevent them from overheating. One of the men said the owner ran frequent inspections of the gas lines to ensure against accidents."

"That doesn't mean an accident couldn't happen, but it

does make it less likely." I sat back in my chair, drumming my fingertips on the table. "Did anyone have a theory?"

Hannah shook her head. "Not yet, but the fire inspector is due to examine what's left of the shop today."

"Any idea what time?"

"No, sorry."

I glanced at the locket watch pinned to my bodice. "I should be going and allow you to go back to work. But I do have one last question. Were there any other injuries found on Mr. Styles's body?"

"What do you mean?"

"Anything to suggest he might have been attacked before the flames got to him."

Hannah studied me a moment, her face taut. "You're implying the fire was no accident." At my nod, she pursed her lips and drew a breath. "I'm afraid the burns were severe enough to hide any evidence if he'd been attacked."

I nodded, attempting to hide my frustration. "Thank you, Hannah. Do let me know when you have a day free."

"I will." She smiled her wide, ingenuous smile. "And Emma, be careful."

I grinned as well. "I'm sure I don't know what you mean." Before I left, I asked for a favor, for I had another important errand to accomplish. "Do you think they'd let me use the telephone at the front desk?"

"I believe I can arrange that."

I reboarded the trolley and about a quarter hour later met Derrick in Washington Square. "Are you ready for a bit of a confrontation?"

"Sounds ominous." He raised a corner of his mouth. "Whom are we confronting?"

"I'll take that as a yes. James Bennett, of course. I'd have mentioned it last night, but it left my mind the moment the fire bells went off. When I spoke Lilah's name, Mr. Bennett got a strange look on his face. Did you notice?"

"No, I was too busy seething at him."

"Yes, well, his reaction raises a question or two, as does Dominic Ellsworth's. I thought he'd have an apoplexy when I said someone had seen him and Mr. Bennett at Carrington's Wharf the night Lilah died." I shrugged. "But I don't suppose it's a good idea to confront Mr. Ellsworth after what happened to his building last night and the death of his shop manager."

"No, indeed. To Stone Villa it is, then."

We did not find Mr. Bennett at home. According to his butler, he was spending most of the day at the Reading Room.

"So much for that idea," Derrick said. "We can try again tonight, or tomorrow."

I stood beside him, staring down the length of Bellevue Avenue. The Newport Reading Room was only a few streets away, but the Casino stood directly across the street from Stone Villa.

"Why, that man." I pivoted to face Derrick. "He's deliberately avoiding me."

"Why do you say that? It's hardly unusual for gentlemen to spend the day at the Reading Room."

"It is in Mr. Bennett's case, or have you forgotten he loathes the Reading Room. Why go there when he could simply cross the street to the Casino and make use of the facilities there? Because he knew I'd be back, that's why." I set off along Bellevue, my stride long and resolved.

"Where are you going?"

"To the Reading Room, where else? He is not going to avoid me."

"Emma, wait. What do you think you're going to do once you reach the Reading Room? If Bennett doesn't wish to come out, that will be the end of it." He caught up with me and reached out to cup my elbow. "I suppose you'll want me to go inside to question him. What shall I ask?"

"No, I need to be there. I need to see his face. You'll have to make him come outside."

We reached the Reading Room, a white clapboard house with upper and lower verandas. A fence surrounded the property, though the gate was not locked. As we approached, several ladies coming down Bellevue Avenue in our direction crossed so as not to walk directly in front of the club. Several men sat on the lower veranda, watching the women and chuckling into their hands. Though they would never behave in such a way in mixed company at a social event, the Reading Room was an all-male domain, jealously guarded to the point that yes, a woman walking too close to the front walkway could expect a derisive comment or two.

I had no such qualms about approaching the house. As Derrick let himself in the gate, I merely stood on the sidewalk and faced toward the street, my head up and my shoulders back. Did I hear a murmur or two? I did. But I paid them no heed. It wasn't until I heard footsteps coming back down the walkway that I turned around. Derrick looked none too happy.

"He's not coming."

"What did he say?"

"Nothing much and none of it repeatable." He paused, waiting, I supposed, for me to say something. When I didn't, he said, "Well, that's it for now."

"Is it?" Some impulse propelled me forward, through the gate. With each step I took, horror at what I'd decided to do grew in one part of my mind. However, the determined part of me failed to heed that horror, nor did I heed Derrick's repeated calling of my name. I reached the steps. Above me on the veranda came murmurs of "Surely not," and "She wouldn't dare." Oh, but I would—and I did. One by one I climbed the steps. The front door opened from within and a footman moved onto the threshold to bar my entrance.

"I'm sorry, miss. You must turn around and leave at once."

"Mr. Bennett," I called out. "Do gather your courage and come outside to speak with me."

The footman puffed up his chest. I knew him. He knew me. We both pretended we didn't. "Miss, Mr. Bennett will not come out, and neither shall you set foot inside."

"No?" I kept going, and sure enough when I reached the doorway and showed no sign of halting, the footman wavered and stepped aside. By now the men on the porch were in a furor—a quiet one. They came to their feet and flanked me on either side, though no one reached out to lay a hand on me. Rather than gentlemanly consideration, I believed it was simple shock that held them in check.

I did not, however, continue into the house. Perhaps a modicum of common sense roused itself and held me back. Despite my exasperation, I yet retained a sense of the consequences should I break one of Newport's hard and fast rules. Simply having passed through the front gate would cause enough of a scandal. Besides, James Bennett rendered my intrusion unnecessary. He stepped out from a room off the main hall and came to the doorway. He looked grim, and not unlike a cornered rabbit. "Miss Cross, consider what you are doing."

"Had you not tossed us out of the Casino last night, I would not now be here, Mr. Bennett. Likewise, had you consented to come outside to have a word with me, I would not have found it necessary to tread on such hallowed ground. Though honestly," I added lower, looking past his shoulder into the entry hall, "I do not see what all the fuss is about."

Mr. Bennett scrubbed a hand across his eyes. "All right, Miss Cross. In the interest of facilitating this as quickly as possible, ask your question."

I smiled. "Thank you." I moved closer to him so as not to be heard by our audience. Faces—bearded, mustachioed, bespectacled, curious, shocked, and downright angry—peered out at us from the rooms that opened onto the hall. Murmurs darted through the air, and I thought I heard a suggestion that someone telephone the police. I hadn't much time.

"Last night, when I mentioned a certain name, Mr. Bennett, you reacted strongly. Please do not deny it. I am quite skilled when it comes to reading the expressions of others. Your reaction, along with that of your friend when I asked a further question, certainly belies all attempts at denial. I would state unequivocally that you are acquainted with the person in question, and that you and your friend were also at a certain place at a certain time on the evening following the polo match. I have been hired to trace the whereabouts of that person on that particular evening. And I believe you have information."

Quizzical murmurs reached my ears. "What the devil did she just say?"

"Danged if I know."

"Sounded like gibberish to me."

Mr. Bennett glanced at the staring countenances surrounding us, both on the porch and behind him in the house. I stole only the quickest peek over my shoulder, searching for Derrick but not spotting him, before fixing my gaze inexorably on Mr. Bennett. He stepped closer to me, hunching to bring himself closer to my height. "I have no information for you, Miss Cross, and if you contradict me again it is as good as calling me a liar."

I didn't need to call him a liar, for once again his expression revealed the truth. So did his manner, his utter lack of the caustic wit for which he was known. After all, he had once persuaded a friend to ride his horse up the steps and onto this very porch. I wished to shake him to dislodge whatever he knew about Lilah Buford. But my time had run out.

"This is insufferable." A portly man with a broad, florid face half covered by muttonchop sideburns appeared at Mr.

Bennett's shoulder. "Davis, James, remove this woman at once."

"Uh, yes, Mr. Forsythe." The footman who had intercepted me at the door moved back onto the threshold, while another strode from the farther recesses of the hall. As they reached me they appeared uncertain what to do next, but at the prompting of Mr. Forsythe, they seized me, albeit gently, by each arm.

Footsteps thudded on the steps behind me. "Take your hands off her this instant." Derrick seized the wrists of both footmen and pried them loose—or perhaps they merely released me at his insistence. My resolve, born of instinct and the fervor of the moment, began to drain away, and the reality of what I'd done rose up with prickling, uncomfortable starkness. Still, I used my remaining shred of tenacity to keep my chin level, turn about, and stride purposely down from the porch and to the street. I chose a direction and walked, my button-up boots raising a defiant clatter along the sidewalk.

Derrick caught up to me, not by hurrying, but with his typically long strides. I fully expected a barrage of admonishments when he reached me. But he merely fell in step beside me.

"I'm sorry I did that," I said without looking at him.

"So am I, but not for the reason you probably think. I couldn't give a fig for their precious men's club. But I do give a fig about you and I know the gossipmongers will blow this out of proportion."

We had crossed two streets by now and were out of sight of the Reading Room. "Do you think that's possible? To blow it out of proportion, I mean." I exhaled a sharp breath. "What was I thinking?"

"You were thinking of finding justice for a deceased woman, and for Mr. Wetmore, who will be destroyed by her death once word of it gets out."

I stopped short. "You say that as if it's a foregone conclusion."

"It is. The dockworkers already know she's dead—you said so yourself. I'm astonished that the fact that she was found at the bottom of Wetmore's staircase isn't yet common knowledge." He spoke barely above a whisper, but even so I glanced around to see if he might have been overheard. Though there were others walking in both directions along the avenue, no one gave us a second look.

Except for one man, though he could not have heard Derrick across the distance between us. I drew a small gasp at the sight of James Bennett rapidly approaching us.

Chapter 9

"Miss Cross, hold up there." Somewhat breathless, he stopped before us. "Miss Cross, I truly don't know what happened to Lilah that night. But I do know she is dead."

"How—"

Derrick cut off my question. "Let's hear what Mr. Bennett has to say. But I'm warning you, Bennett, one disrespectful word to Miss Cross and I'll come after you with a buggy whip."

Mr. Bennett's mouth twitched unpleasantly. "Lilah came to the Casino that night after the polo match, but not for the reason you think. True, she quietly plied her trade most nights, but that night she kept to herself and seemed to be keenly observing some of the other guests."

"Who?" I wondered whether George Wetmore was at the Casino that night.

"No one well-known here in Newport. I don't believe the family has made their entry into the Four Hundred yet."

"A family, you say?"

"Yes. By the look of them, parents and two grown children, your age or a bit younger. A son and a daughter."

"Do you know their names?" Derrick asked.

"I do not. I don't believe they are members, so they would simply have paid their admission and entered."

"Did she speak with them?" I asked.

"I don't believe so."

I narrowed my eyes as I scrutinized his face. "And you can't guess why these people held her fascination?"

"Not in the slightest."

"Did Lilah have enemies?" I asked him bluntly.

"Not that I knew of."

"What about an angry family member of one of her clients? Had you ever heard any talk of that nature?" Derrick's questions made me wonder, not for the first time, if the killer might have been a woman. I had already considered one of the other girls from the Blue Moon, but what about a wife?

My mind whispered a name—again, not for the first time. Mrs. Wetmore. I didn't wish to believe it, but I knew I must consider the possibility.

"Not from Lilah, nor from anyone else," Mr. Bennett replied. "She knew her place and she understood discretion. Otherwise I wouldn't have looked the other way when she came to the Casino."

"Mr. Bennett, why didn't you tell us this last night? Why order us to leave? Especially if you already knew of Lilah's fate." My tone clearly scolded, and deepened Mr. Bennett's frown. "And how *did* you learn of it?"

"In a very roundabout way. Lilah rarely disappointed her regular gentlemen, and that in itself became news immediately. Then came a rumor whispered along Thames Street and passed along by the usual means, worker to clerk to servant to employer." He glanced up and down the avenue. "As for why I wanted you gone from the Casino, Miss Cross, your questions are dangerous."

"What about my other question, Mr. Bennett?" I raised an eyebrow in a challenging manner. "You were on Carrington's Wharf the night she died. You and Mr. Ellsworth, who I would also question today if not for the fire at his business last night. Were you there to see Lilah?"

"No," he replied adamantly. "Whoever told you we were there that night had his facts wrong."

Perhaps, but I decided to give Anthony Dobbs the benefit of the doubt. "Mr. Bennett, has it never occurred to you that the quickest way to appear guilty of something is to deny the obvious? Really, I should think the owner of the New York *Herald* would be more astute than that."

"Oh, you think you're clever, don't you?" His upper lip curled as he shook his head in obvious disgust. But disgust with whom, I wondered, me or himself? I believed the latter, based on his next words. "All right. We were at the wharf. But our being there had nothing to do with Lilah. It was business, purely, and no one's concern but our own. We were checking the schedule on a shipment we were expecting."

I eyed him askance. I noticed Derrick doing the same. He spoke first. "You went yourselves to check on a shipment schedule? Why not send your household accounts manager? Or one of Ellsworth's employees—his shop manager, for one?"

Mr. Bennett drew himself up. "See here. I told you our reasons for being on the wharf had nothing to do with Lilah. They are therefore none of your business."

"Mr. Bennett, you wish to expand the Casino, don't you?" This sudden turn in the conversation clearly took him aback, as I had hoped it would. "But you've met with resistance from city officials and powerful residents. Isn't that correct?"

He set a fist on his hip. "What has that to do with Lilah or anything else?"

"It might have a good deal to do with Lilah." I needed to be careful; I didn't wish to drag George Wetmore's name into the conversation. "I can't help but wonder what lengths you might go to in order to have your way."

His expression blackened dangerously, but just as quickly cleared. He whooped with laughter. "As in murder? Really, Miss Cross, you should give up journalism and take up writing Gothic novels. The very idea." He continued to chuckle. "I've dealt with city politics, both here and in New York, all my life. If I decide to go ahead and expand the Casino, I'll find a way, and there'll be no dead bodies to step over in the process. Good day to you, Miss Cross."

"Mr. Bennett, wait—"

"I've had quite enough of you, Miss Cross. Andrews, always a pleasure to see you." He tipped his hat and prepared to leave.

"Don't you think Lilah deserves justice?" I demanded. I braced for a cynical remark.

That stopped him. "As a matter of fact, I do, Miss Cross. Why else do you think I am speaking with you after such an outlandish display at the Reading Room?"

"Easy, Bennett," Derrick murmured. "You're on thin ice."

As Mr. Bennett shrugged off the implied threat, an odd hunch made me grin. "Actually, I think you're speaking to me *because* of my outlandish display. Admit it, Mr. Bennett. While you went to the Reading Room in hopes of avoiding me today, you were rather delighted by my audacity, weren't you?"

"Maybe." He sucked in his cheeks in an effort, I judged, to avoid smiling. "I will admit I didn't expect that level of daring from you. You do know there will be hell to pay for it."

"I expect so," I replied with a shrug. "Now, what about Lilah? What can you tell us?"

"Lilah left the Casino alone and alive that night. What happened after that, where she went or whom she encountered, I cannot say. But I hope you find out, Miss Cross. Despite her profession, Lilah was decent."

With that he set off back toward the Reading Room, or perhaps his home, which lay beyond.

That night I lay awake for hours considering everything I had learned. If the uncomfortable memory of trespassing at the Reading Room also staved off sleep, I tried not to dwell on it. Much more important was the question of whom Lilah had been watching that last night at the Casino. Who was this family? Did they have any connection to the men Lilah overheard plotting against George Wetmore? I would have to return to the Casino and ask Mr. Bennett to point them out to me, if they returned. It seemed likely they would. Not yet being accepted into the Four Hundred meant their invitations would be scarce, and where better to spend a fashionable evening, seeing and being seen, than at the Casino?

But why had Mr. Bennett and Mr. Ellsworth gone to Carrington's Wharf that night? The excuse of checking on a shipment failed to ring true, unless . . .

Unless that shipment consisted of some form of contraband. But what? Two summers ago Derrick and I had nearly gotten ourselves killed when we stumbled upon black market dealings in molasses, which would have been used for distilling illicit rum and bypassing the import tariffs.

Tariff. As in the Dingley Tariff? Perhaps. I would have to question James Bennett again, as well as Robert Clarkson and Stanford Whittaker, and I would need to be blunt. Were they planning to form some kind of black market ring to evade the Dingley import tariffs, a scheme perhaps George Wetmore had learned of?

When I padded in to breakfast that morning, I found Nanny sitting at the table reading a rival newspaper, the Newport *Daily News.* Katie sat across from her, but upon my arrival she set down her fork and sprang to her feet.

"Good mornin', Miss Emma," she said hurriedly in her

gentle brogue. "Coffee? The eggs are nice and hot, and there are sausages with a maple syrup glaze."

"Sit, Katie. I'll help myself."

It had taken me nearly two years to persuade my maid-of-all-work that it was perfectly permissible for her to sit at the table with Nanny and me. Having worked for my Vanderbilt relatives at The Breakers before coming to Gull Manor, she had viewed such familiarity as grounds for immediate dismissal without a reference. She worked for me, yes, but we were a household here at Gull Manor, and I considered Katie as much a part of that household as Nanny or dear little Patch, who had sauntered in behind me and now curled up beneath the table at my feet.

Katie had been a frightened, wounded teenage girl, all alone in this country, when she found her way to Gull Manor one night in the spring of 1895. She was one of my strays, like Patch, like Stella who had decided to change her life, like a child named Robbie who stayed at Gull Manor all too briefly last summer. If only Lilah had made her way to my front door . . .

I pushed the thought from my mind, served myself some sausages and eggs, and went to sit at the table. Only then did I realize Nanny hadn't said good morning.

"Still asleep, are we?" I teased. She didn't smile, but refolded her newspaper until the front page became visible. She slid the publication across to me.

"I debated whether to show it to you or burn it," she said, and then sighed. "You're going to find out anyway."

Puzzled, I glanced at the headline—and very nearly fell off my chair.

SHAME ON THE OBSERVER! it read, immediately followed by the sordid tale of how Mr. Millford, my editor-in-chief, sent a female reporter into a den of iniquity and then to that most exclusive of gentlemen's clubs, the Newport Reading Room, for the sake of sensational journalism. The article didn't mention my name; it didn't have to. Everyone knew of Newport's sole female reporter, and they knew I worked for the *Observer*. Mr. Millford was termed a villain for being willing to sacrifice the well-being and reputation of an innocent young miss.

I gulped and willed the typeface to magically rearrange itself. My blood ran hot and cold and sent a fever of fire and chills up and down my back and into my face. My stomach seemed to fall out from under me. I pushed my plate away and let my head sink into my hands.

"Oh, Nanny."

"The *Reading Room*, Emma? What were you thinking?"

Without raising my head, I peeked at her through parted fingers. Then I glanced at Katie. Her eyes were wide, and if she didn't know the exact contents of the article, she had gleaned enough of the facts from Nanny's simple statement. Katie was no stranger to scandal or to the rules of Newport society.

I raised my chin slightly. "I am attempting to discover how Lilah Buford died."

Nanny shook her head slowly, her plump shoulders rising and falling on a deep breath. "Your ability to continue doing good for this city depends on maintaining your position in society. Your Vanderbilt relatives can only do so much for you. This"—she grasped the newspaper and gave it a shake— "will alienate both the locals *and* the cottagers."

"This," I said with rising dismay, "is likely to end my employment at the *Observer.*"

Not a minute later, the telephone in the alcove beneath the stairs began to jangle.

"Do you want me to answer that?" Nanny started to rise, a testimony to how much she sympathized with me, as she had never grown accustomed to using what she considered an intrusive device.

I came to my feet. "I'll go."

My name practically exploded in my ear when I lifted the receiver from its cradle. "Yes, good morning, Mr. Millford. I can explain . . ."

"Have you taken leave of your senses? Are you attempting to ruin me?"

"No, of course not, Mr. Millford. I—"

"Balls. Picnics. Fashions. *That* was your job, Emma. But, heaven help me, brothels? The *Reading Room*?" I could hear by the emphasis that, in Mr. Millford's mind, the latter of the two constituted the worst of my offenses. And then I realized what he had said just prior to that: *was your job*.

Desperation rose up inside me. "Mr. Millford, please. I'm trying to find justice for a young woman for whom no one else will fight. Please, sir, if you'd just allow me to—"

"Emma, you don't understand. You may march through Washington Square in your petticoats if you wish. But you will not do so as an employee of the Newport *Observer.* As of this moment, you are no longer employed by the paper."

My heart clogged my throat, but I nonetheless choked out the beginnings of a plea. "Mr. Millford, please be reasonable—"

The line went dead. I stood for some moments, listening to the buzzing coming over the wire and staring at the wall above the call box. Then I placed the ear trumpet on its cradle and made my way, as unseeing as a sleepwalker, back to the morning room.

"I gather that was Mr. Millford calling?" Nanny's voice came as a whisper through the roaring in my ears.

I glanced down at the plates on the table and then at the platters and bowls on the sideboard. Great Aunt Sadie had left me enough in her will to keep this house running, but little more. We needed to eat. We needed to make repairs when necessary. I needed to continue her legacy of helping women in need. And I refused to abandon St. Nicholas Orphanage in Providence, where I sent donations of either money or supplies whenever possible.

I would need new employment, and soon.

I spent the rest of the morning brooding over how the *Daily News* had learned of my visit to the Blue Moon. That word of my trespass into the Reading Room had already spread didn't surprise me. There had been plenty of witnesses. But, besides Madam Heidi's girls, I knew of only two other people who saw me in the vicinity of the Blue Moon: Anthony Dobbs and a man he worked with.

Was this Anthony Dobbs's revenge for my perceived crimes? I couldn't deny that a poetic justice must have existed in his mind. I had lost my employment just as he had lost his. Then again, it could have been one of Madam Heidi's girls. I felt confident in ruling out Flossie. Why come to me outside with information if she didn't want me to use it? But one of the others—yes, someone among them could have resented Lilah enough to murder her, and me enough to destroy my career.

In the end, however, it didn't matter how that damning headline came to be splattered across the front page of the *Daily News*. What did matter, very much, was where I was going to find another position as a reporter. The answer presented itself as readily as the congealed eggs I had helped Katie carry back into the kitchen. Nowhere. With such scandal attached to my name, no newspaper in town would take a chance on hiring me. The backlash would be sharp and immediate, and no editor-in-chief would risk it.

Somewhere outside of Newport, then. Suddenly, I had an idea.

About an hour later, I alighted from my carriage in front of James Bennett's Stone Villa. Before I could put my plan in action, however, another carriage, an elegant brougham trimmed in glossy red, came alongside mine and a voice called to me from inside.

"Miss Cross, a word if you please." Through the partly open window I could make out only a wide hat, plumed and flowered and with a nearly opaque netting that obscured the wearer's face. I went closer and was surprised to recognize Lavinia Andrews.

From inside, she opened the door. "Please get in, Miss Cross."

"It's lovely to see you this morning, Mrs. Andrews."

She didn't smile or offer me her hand, though mine hung outstretched between us. I dropped it to my lap, where I held my drawstring bag, and waited.

She knocked once on the ceiling with a kid-gloved hand, and the carriage rolled into motion. Moments passed as she drew a breath and released it audibly. I noticed she sat perfectly upright, preserving several inches between her spine and the velvet squabs behind her. Then she grasped her netted veil between her forefingers and thumbs and raised it from her face. "Miss Cross," she began calmly, "I wish to make this very clear, so that there can be no misunderstandings between us. You are never to see my son again. You are never to seek him out for any reason, write to him, or contact him in any way."

"Mrs. Andrews—"

"And should he contact you, you are not to respond. Any overtures on his part are to be immediately and adamantly rebuffed."

She turned away, facing front again, and a thick silence fell. I contemplated her profile, realizing how like Derrick's it was, but for a softening of the contours. But in the set of her chin, the straight and determined line of her mouth, and the present tightening of her brow, I saw Derrick's tenacity and strength of will. Funny, had she not recognized those same qualities in her own son? Did she truly believe he would be so easily swayed by a mother's meddling? Did she believe she could intimidate me?

I relaxed beside her. "One can assume you saw this morning's headline in the *Daily News.*"

She flinched as if I had struck her, then spoke through gritted teeth. "Indeed, I have, Miss Cross. It is shameful and entirely unforgivable."

"I shan't argue with you, ma'am. I perhaps made a mistake in climbing the front steps to the porch of the Reading Room. However, my motives for doing so were sound, and the same could be said about my visit to the tavern on Carrington's Wharf."

She whipped her head around to pin me with a glare. "How *dare* you mention such an establishment in my hearing?"

"I didn't. I purposely did not mention the place by name, Mrs. Andrews."

"Insolent girl. I don't know what I could have been thinking when I extended my welcome to you as a future daughter-in-law. You clearly can have no place in the Andrews family. My son is on the path to becoming a great man in society. You are not fit to be his wife —aren't fit to polish his boots."

I took this insult with outward calm, noting how Mrs. Andrews's anger flared her nostrils and consumed the greater portion of her beauty until she resembled a bitter and dried-up crone. A certainty struck me. She still didn't know about Derrick's disinheritance. She could not, or she would not have said what she had about his becoming a great man. This new development would only make a woman like Mrs. Andrews more resolved than ever to see her son married to the wealthiest of heiresses.

I folded my hands primly over my handbag. "First of all, Mrs. Andrews, your welcoming me into your family, though kind, was premature. I have not made any decisions concerning whom or when I shall marry."

"Hah." Her lips pinched with cynicism.

"Second of all, Derrick is not a child. I do not believe he will allow you or anyone else to make his choices for him. Nor will I permit you to make mine."

She sputtered, and as she did so, I knocked on the roof of the carriage. The vehicle eased to the side of the avenue and stopped. Without waiting for the footman perched beside the driver, I opened the door and stepped down. "Good day, Mrs. Andrews."

She started to respond but I quickly closed the door. We had reached the corner of Bellevue Avenue and Church Street. I about-faced and set off back the way we had come. I found Barney dozing where I'd left him at the roadside. I ran my hand gently down the length of his neck.

"Just one more errand today, my friend." I gazed up at the three-story fieldstone and granite façade of Stone Villa and questioned the wisdom of what I planned to do. With a shrug—for I had little to lose—I passed through the open gates, its columns on either side topped by owls, symbolic of Mr. Bennett's New York *Herald*. The elderly butler Derrick and I had encountered here yesterday inquired as to my name and ushered me into a receiving room whose furnishings did not invite visitors to make themselves comfortable. I chose to stand, gazing out the open front window, its curtains billowing gently in the breeze, to where Barney patiently awaited my return.

"Miss Cross." James Bennett's greeting came with a lengthy sigh. "What is it now?"

I turned to face him, keeping my shoulders back and my chin level. "Good morning, Mr. Bennett. Thank you for seeing me on short notice."

"If you've come to ask more questions about Lilah, I'm afraid—"

"No, this isn't about Lilah, unless you've remembered or learned something since we talked."

His long mustaches twitched. "No indeed."

"In that case, I am here, Mr. Bennett, because I am seeking new employment. And I thought—that is, I'd hoped—you might consider me for a position with the New York *Herald*."

An eternity of agony passed as Mr. Bennett regarded me with no small amount of surprise, his gaze rising and falling several times as he obviously took in every detail about my attire, my posture, my bearing, everything. Could he see me trembling? For trembling I was; I hadn't realized until this moment how much store I'd set in the notion of joining the *Herald*'s staff of journalists.

Only briefly this morning had I considered going to Derrick with my dilemma. But even if his father hadn't severed Derrick's ties with the Providence *Sun,* appealing to him for help would have been wrong, circumstances between us being what they were. If I could not commit to him, I certainly couldn't run to him and expect him to save me from my own mistakes.

As he considered my entreaty, Mr. Bennett crossed his arms, uncrossed them, stroked his chin, and then crossed his arms once more. "I already have a society reporter, Miss Cross."

An impossible knot formed in my stomach, which I attempted to ignore. "I have no wish to continue as a society reporter, Mr. Bennett. I'd thought perhaps I might . . ." I thought quickly—what words might best persuade him? "I thought I might regale your readers with stories of the real Newport, from an insider's point of view. I was born and raised here on the island, but I am also a cousin of the Vanderbilts. That allows me singular insight into this city."

He smirked, though more with irony than mockery. "So you would wish me to take on the same criticism as your Mr. Millford at the *Observer*."

My bones seemed to turn to melting wax, but I somehow remained standing and pressed on. "I would think, sir, that what is considered unacceptable in Newport would send newspapers flying off the newsstands in New York."

"Perhaps, perhaps." He studied me another moment, the silence stretching until I couldn't keep silent.

"And if necessary, I'd be willing to travel." Would I? One of my foremost reservations concerning the prospect of marrying Derrick had been the necessity of moving from Newport to Providence. Yet I would not be deterred from my present course. "I could explore news stories from a woman's point of view."

"Fancy yourself another Nellie Bly, do you?"

I wanted to sing out that, yes, I'd be elated to consider myself on a par with Nellie Bly. I merely nodded and waited and hoped.

"Why should I hire you?" he demanded bluntly.

I doubted he could be influenced by my desperate need for independence that could only be guaranteed by a steady income. He needed to be convinced of my worth. "Because you already know I would never shrink from any story. Because I don't take no for an answer and I don't stop until all the facts are known. And also, Mr. Bennett, because after yesterday, you can't help admiring my pluck."

He laughed heartily, until mirthful tears formed. He unabashedly flicked them away. "Indeed, yes, heaven help me. Your proposal is an interesting one, Miss Cross." His hand went up when I broke out in a grin. "However, I shall need some time to think it over."

"Take all the time you need, Mr. Bennett." But please, I thought, not so *very* much time. I left Stone Villa, only to find yet another carriage, this one an open, two-seater phaeton, waiting for me when I arrived at home.

"I came as soon as I saw the headline." Derrick hurried into the hall from the parlor, where Nanny had been plying him with tea and cake.

Calmly I removed my hat and unbuttoned my carriage jacket. "How long have you been here? I hope not terribly long."

He pulled up sharp. "Is that your main concern? How long Mrs. O'Neal has been keeping me entertained while you were away? Good heavens, Emma, I've been half sick with worry over you."

"Why? This isn't the first time I've leaped into a boiling kettle." But even as I spoke, I silently admitted I had never quite cloaked myself in a scandal of this nature. "I went to town to seek new employment, and while there I ran into your mother. She also saw the morning's headline. It would seem she is no longer intent on planning our wedding." I smiled halfheartedly.

"Mother sought you out?"

I shrugged and led him back into the parlor. "I can't tell you if she went out searching for me or merely took advantage of the opportunity of crossing paths with me. She invited me into her carriage and delivered a thorough dressing down." I sat on the settee, arranged my skirts, and sighed.

Derrick sat beside me, his expression pained. "I'm sorry."

"Don't be. You can't control your mother's actions, just as she can't control yours. Or am I mistaken about that?" I said this with a playful hint of challenge, to which Derrick smiled lopsidedly.

"Indeed not. What exactly did she say to you?"

"Oh, what one might expect. That you are going to be a great man someday and I'm not fit to be your wife. That sort of thing."

He groaned and pinched the bridge of his nose. "I dearly wish she would return to Providence."

"She doesn't know yet, does she? I mean about your father's threat of disinheriting you."

"It's more than a threat but no, I haven't told her, and I don't believe she's heard it from my father yet, either." He frowned. "You said you went to town to 'seek new employment.' Then Mr. Millford—"

"Has sent me packing, yes. I half expected it."

"Of all the rotten timing. Here you might have worked for the *Sun*, if only I hadn't gone and infuriated my father."

I placed a hand over his. "You did the right thing in accompanying your sister to Italy. What other choice could an honorable brother make? I believe your father will come to see that in time. As for the *Sun* . . ." I trailed off, searching for words to make him understand. "Even if you owned the newspaper outright—no, *especially* if you owned the *Sun*—I could not work for you, Derrick. No," I hastily added when he appeared about to cut me off. "Listen to what I have to say. Accepting employment from you would be tantamount to imposing on our friendship. And it would alter the nature of our friendship as well. We would no longer be equals. I would become your subordinate, and that would place us in an awkward position."

"Do you really suppose I would treat you as a subordinate?"

"If you didn't, I would be receiving special favors denied your other employees. Don't you see it's an untenable situation?"

"Emma, my dear, the only untenable situation is your stubbornness."

I laughed. "Perhaps. My aunt Sadie instilled in me too much of an independent nature to allow me to lean on others when I might make my own way, on my own two feet."

"That's scandalous talk." His lopsided smile reappeared. "For a woman."

"I have a habit of courting scandal, don't I? But it's all a moot point, isn't it? At present, you and I are both unemployed." I waited for him to ask me with whom I sought new employment. I didn't like the thought of telling him; after all, James Bennett was something of a suspect in Lilah's death.

Nanny's footsteps echoed from the hall just as a knock came at the door. "I'll get it," she said.

A sense of foreboding came over me the moment I heard Jesse's voice, especially when obvious irritation took possession of Derrick's features. Jesse came through the parlor doorway, with Nanny right behind him looking nonplussed.

Jesse opened his mouth to greet me but shut it again when he spotted Derrick. He scowled. Derrick scowled back. Nanny stared at me from over Jesse's shoulder and held up her hands as if to say, *What was I to do?*

I pasted on my brightest smile. "Good morning, Jesse. What brings you out to Gull Manor?"

"The headline in the *Daily News*, for one." His gaze pinned Derrick to the cushion behind him. "It was you, wasn't it? You went with Emma to the Reading Room yesterday."

"There is no need for that," I said, but Jesse would not be deterred.

"Were you or were you not with Emma yesterday?"

Derrick stared coldly back and raised an eyebrow. "I was."

"I've a good mind to horsewhip you, sir. How dare you—"

I came to my feet. "That will be enough of that. Whether Derrick came with me or not, my actions would have been the same." Of course, I thought, that wasn't exactly true, for my plan had been for Derrick to persuade James Bennett to speak with me outside. Striding up onto the porch had been an act of rashness on my part. One I felt sure I would hear about for some time to come.

"Emma, gentlemen, why don't you all relax and I'll bring in more tea." Nanny started to back out of the room, but Jesse stopped her.

"I don't care for any tea, thank you, Mrs. O'Neal. At least not while this miscreant inhabits this room."

"Miscreant, am I?" Derrick's body tensed as though he might spring up from the settee and lunge for Jesse's throat.

Though I didn't question Jesse's concerns about what I had done, it was not lost on me that his pique had equally as much to do with finding Derrick here with me. I calmly met Jesse's gaze and attempted to make light. "Is that charge leveled at me or Derrick?"

His expression eased. "You know it's directed at him, Emma. Men like him think they own the world, think they may do as they please when they please without a thought for anyone else. You of all people should know that."

"What I know, Jesse, is that no one controls my actions, however much that seems to be the popular opinion this morning. And you of all people should know *that*." I turned to look at Derrick. "Both of you, stop posturing. What happened cannot be undone. I count you both as my friends, and if you cannot extend that sentiment to each other, the very least you can do is maintain civility while you are under my roof."

Their standoff continued silently for another several seconds. Then both visibly relaxed.

"Certainly," Jesse murmured. He dragged himself to a chair facing Derrick and me and lowered himself into it.

Derrick nodded. Nanny blew out a breath. "I'll have Katie bring in more tea."

When she'd gone, I said to Jesse, "You alluded to more than one matter that brought you here this morning."

"Yes. It's about Lilah Buford. The case is being reopened."

"But I thought the police were being pressured to call her death an accident."

"We were, until the latest coroner's report came in. It appears Lilah's neck didn't break as a result of a fall down the Wetmores' staircase, if indeed she actually fell. All evidence points to the injury, which caused her death, happening beforehand. The coroner determined that someone held Lilah by the head and deliberately snapped her neck."

Chapter 10

At Jesse's news, I sank back against the cushions behind me. "No more pretending otherwise, then."

"No more pretending," he echoed, "and no more having my hands tied behind my back. This case wasn't the first time, but I tell you, it never gets any easier being told to ignore the facts and go about one's business. This *is* my business."

"The question is," Derrick began, then paused when Jesse darted a sharp glance in his direction. He raised that eyebrow again. "That is, if I am permitted to *have* questions concerning the case . . ."

Jesse consented with a wave of his hand.

"Then the question is, which is the foremost crime? Miss Buford's death, or the apparent attempt to frame George Wetmore for it—assuming he's innocent. Was Lilah Buford merely a convenient vehicle, or was she somehow involved with or connected to the scheme against Wetmore?"

"Good questions," Jesse mumbled.

"What was that?" I asked him with a smile, certain he didn't like acknowledging Derrick's logic.

Jesse narrowed his eyes at me and shook his head. "My instincts tell me Lilah was involved. Not necessarily guilty of anything, mind you, but as you say, Mr. Andrews, connected to the people who set this plot in motion."

"Then you do believe there is a plot against the senator," Derrick said.

"However much I would like to, I cannot entirely rule out Mr. Wetmore as Lilah's killer," Jesse replied. "He's under house arrest."

I pressed my hand to my lips at the thought of a man like George Wetmore enduring the humiliation of a house arrest. Such a circumstance could destroy his reputation and his career, just as his wife feared. "Have you stationed men around the house?"

"No, he gave his word he wouldn't go anywhere, and I'm inclined to trust him." Jesse shoved auburn hair off his brow. "Honestly, though, I'm not sure if it's instinct or wishful thinking that makes me lean toward an outside culprit who wants to ruin the Wetmores."

"That certainly concurs with what I learned from Flossie at the Blue Moon, that Lilah overheard men talking about how they'd like to splatter mud on Mr. Wetmore's doorstep."

"It would seem they decided blood would be harder to ignore." Jesse thought a moment, then continued. "You also told me Lilah felt she owed Mrs. Wetmore for something. What can that be? It's doubtful the women ever had any contact with each other."

"Perhaps Mrs. Wetmore funded some service from which Lilah benefited." Derrick waved away my offer of more tea.

"But practically all the wealthy women in this town involve themselves in philanthropy, usually in groups. They're always forming some beneficent society or other." I set the teapot down on the sofa table. "It seems unlikely that Lilah would single out Mrs. Wetmore in particular. That aside for now, I think we should return to the circumstance of Lilah's having overheard a scheme against Mr. Wetmore."

"We can't use it as evidence, I'm afraid." Jesse angled his head at me. "Since you came by the information thirdhand, it would be considered hearsay."

"True," I conceded, "but it coincides with what I overheard at the polo match between Robert Clarkson, Stanford Whittaker, and Harry Lehr. And all three men are known to visit the Blue Moon. It seems possible they were the men Lilah heard talking."

"Perhaps." Jesse nodded thoughtfully. "But beyond that, there is no evidence linking them to Chateau sur Mer that night." His jaw suddenly dropped. "I just remembered something. Those black marks on the veranda—we assumed they were made by Lilah's boots."

"Yes, by the leather polish she used," I said.

Derrick sat up straighter. "Detective Whyte, you just informed us Lilah's neck had been snapped prior to her having fallen—or being placed—inside the house. If so, she could not have left marks of any sort on the veranda."

"Unless George Wetmore is guilty and killed Lilah inside the house, she could not have walked in on her own volition." Jesse fisted his hands and struck them against the arms of his chair. "She would have been carried. I need to see those marks again."

Alarmed, I asked, "But won't they have been cleaned away by now?"

"I won't know until I return to Chateau sur Mer."

I convinced Jesse to allow Derrick and me to accompany him to the Wetmore estate. When we arrived, the butler summarily sent us around to the service entrance. We descended to a long hallway where we were tersely greeted by the housekeeper, a broad woman with sharp eyes and jet-black hair parted severely down the middle and drawn back into a tight bun.

"May I help you?" The coldness of her tone spoke of dismissal.

She obviously didn't intimidate Jesse. "I have police business here. I must have access to the veranda. There was no need to bring us into the house."

"Mrs. Wetmore's orders," the woman said, her lips forming a thin, flat line. "The police are no longer to have the run of the house. If you need something, you are to make your request through me."

Though Derrick and I had waited quietly behind Jesse, I now stepped forward to stand beside him. "Are you quite certain of that? I find it difficult to believe Mrs. Wetmore would not wish us to explore every possibility."

"Those were Mrs. Wetmore's express words, miss."

"The case has been reopened, but I'm not asking for run of the house," Jesse snapped. "If I must, I shall return with a warrant."

The housekeeper paled. She started to speak again but the butler entered the hallway from the adjoining kitchen. "Mrs. Wetmore asks that the visitors be shown upstairs."

Puzzled, we followed him up the service stairs, past the butler's pantry and china room and across the ground floor to the Green Salon, where I had spoken privately to Mrs. Wetmore that first day. She stood before one of the windows, staring out with her back to us as we were shown into the room. Her shoulders were raised with apparent tension, her bearing stiffly upright. Though she must have heard us coming, she waited until the butler announced us before turning around.

Nearly as brusquely as the housekeeper had spoken to us, she asked, "Why have you returned? Why will you not leave us in peace?"

"I assure you, ma'am, I had no intention of disturbing you or your husband with my visit today. I wish only access to the veranda, and may I point out that I might simply have circled the house to the veranda unannounced. It was merely a matter of courtesy that prompted me to knock at your door."

She visibly relaxed on a long exhalation. "Then you haven't come to hound my husband with more questions?"

"At present, no, ma'am. But if you or your husband can think of anything that might assist with the case, you will be doing yourselves a great favor to convey that information to me."

"There is nothing, I give you my word." Mrs. Wetmore's hand, long and pale, went to her bosom. "Oh, dear. Oh, my husband . . ." Her eyes misted, but several blinks banished all sign of impending tears.

I stepped toward her. "We'll discover the truth, Mrs. Wetmore." Nodding, she allowed her gaze to drift to Derrick, as if she only just noticed his presence. "This is Mr. Andrews," I said. "He and I are assisting Detective Whyte, as you asked me to do, ma'am."

She continued scrutinizing Derrick; her hand lowered to her side as a furrow formed between her eyebrows. "Are you Lavinia Andrews's son?"

"I am, Mrs. Wetmore."

She took a step backward, coming up against the open casement behind her. "A newspaper man . . ."

"No, ma'am," he said evenly, "I'm not here in that capacity. I assure you of that."

Mrs. Wetmore didn't look convinced, but she nodded and turned her attention back to Jesse. "Please, do what you came to do and then leave us in peace."

Both Jesse and Derrick took their leave of Mrs. Wetmore with polite bobs of their heads, and exited the room through one of the French doors that led onto the veranda. Though I had every intention of examining the veranda for myself, I lingered in the Green Salon.

"Ma'am, I don't understand your reticence with the police. You told me you wish to know the truth. Then why not cooperate with Detective Whyte and his men?"

"Because I don't trust them, Miss Cross. I asked *you* to discover the truth, yet my husband is now a prisoner in his own home, all but accused of murdering that girl."

"Mrs. Wetmore, has it occurred to you that were your husband any other man, he would not be under house arrest, but occupying a cell on Marlborough Street?"

She flinched at my reference to the police station and turned crimson.

"I don't mean any disrespect, ma'am. I am merely pointing out that Detective Whyte believes in your husband's inno cence and has advocated for Mr. Wetmore with his superiors. I trust him, and you can as well."

She closed the distance between us. Taking me by the hand, she drew me down beside her on the sofa. "But what have you learned, Miss Cross? I can't bear to be left in the dark. What evidence is there against my husband? What evi dence that he is innocent?"

"I do have news for you, and it's important that you carefully consider what I'm about to say. I have learned that Lilah Buford may have overheard two or more men talking outside the Blue—outside her place of employment. According to someone Lilah confided in, those men were angry with your husband and sought some form of revenge."

The dismay cleared from Mrs. Wetmore's face. "There it is, then. They must have realized she overheard and decided to silence her. Find these men, and you'll find who murdered Miss Buford and left her in our home."

"I'm afraid it's not as easy as that. First, we have no identification, not even a clue as to who those men might be, or why they resented your husband." The names Harry Lehr, Stanford Whittaker, and Robert Clarkson entered my mind. There were also now James Bennett and Dominic Ellsworth. I didn't dare mention any of those names to Mrs. Wetmore. I needed more evidence, though I had yet to devise a means of obtaining it. "You must *think*, Mrs. Wetmore. Think of your husband's recent dealings, whether here or in Washington. Whom might he have angered?"

"My dear, my husband is a politician. He is *always* angering someone. And the police have already asked him that very same question. He can think of nothing out of the ordinary."

"What about recent pieces of legislation he might be sponsoring?" A leading question, but I couldn't help myself. Could opposition to the Dingley Tariff Act lead to the death of a prostitute and the incrimination of an innocent man? In my mind, it didn't quite make sense, for surely George Wetmore couldn't be the only senator supporting the bill. And I found the notion of Misters Lehr, Clarkson, and Whittaker going about the country and having their revenge on every such senator ludicrous.

But what about the other two? If Mr. Bennett and Mr. Ellsworth were involved in illegal trade here in Newport, to what lengths might they go to protect their interests?

"Something to warrant destroying our family, Miss Cross? Certainly not. Not everyone agrees with my husband's political views. That is to be expected. But everyone who knows my husband can be sure of one thing, and that is his integrity."

"Yes, I can believe that to be true, ma'am. Please, if you or Mr. Wetmore think of anything, no matter how trivial it might seem, contact me."

"I will, Miss Cross. And I do apologize for doubting both you and the police. I'm sure you can understand how very distressing this is for us." For the first time since I'd properly met her, Mrs. Wetmore's façade of calm and gentility slipped.

Her eyes filled and she lowered her face to her hands as a sob broke. "Forgive me, Miss Cross."

"There is nothing to forgive, ma'am." I gently touched her forearm. That slight contact seemed to steady her and restore her equilibrium, for she lifted her head, let out a breath, and dabbed at her eyes with the backs of her knuckles.

"Yes, well. What are Detective Whyte and Mr. Andrews looking for on the veranda?"

"Evidence that Lilah didn't enter the house alone that night, that perhaps she was brought here by whoever killed her."

"Oh! I do hope they find such evidence." Her shoulders slumped. "But I believe one of the maids mopped up after the police left the other day. Oh, Miss Cross, it's likely they'll find nothing."

"I'll go see, Mrs. Wetmore. I'll let you know."

Outside, I found Jesse and Derrick in a corner of the veranda, near where the edge stepped down to the grass. They were both leaning low, appearing to study something. Jesse went down on his knee and reached down to draw his fingertip across the flooring.

I went quickly to join them. "What have you found? Mrs. Wetmore just told me the veranda had been mopped."

Derrick turned to me. "That's true, but some of those black marks have proved stubborn. Look here."

Jesse spoke without looking up. "Shoe polish would certainly resist attempts to mop it away. But I don't believe shoe polish left the marks, most of which are gone or substantially faded."

I glanced down over his shoulder. "What then?"

"Being so close to the edge, this mark is lightly smeared, as if it had escaped the maid's notice and she merely wiped her mop over this area with no real enthusiasm. I can think of only two substances besides boot polish that resist water without a good scrub."

"What?" Derrick and I said as one.

"Soot." He came to his feet and faced us, his face grim. "Or coal."

I gasped. "Jesse, coal is brought onto Carrington's Wharf, unloaded, and stored there. So that means—"

"That means," Derrick said, "that anyone who had been on Carrington's Wharf—or anywhere else coal is stored— the night of Lilah's death may be considered a suspect. *All* of them."

"Gracious, you're right," I said, feeling deflated.

Jesse nodded his concurrence. "Even if we assume the source of the coal to be Carrington's Wharf, which is highly likely since Lilah lived and worked there, given the nature of the businesses to be found in the immediate area, we're talking about a wide number of possible suspects. This is a clue, but a frustratingly vague one."

Chapter 11

After leaving Chateau sur Mer, Derrick and I accompanied Jesse to the police station in town. We sat around his desk, reviewing the newly reopened case.

"We still have no idea why Lilah felt beholden to Mrs. Wetmore, and I'm certain that's the key to unraveling the rest of these events."

"How do you propose we discover this fact, Emma?" Jesse tapped a pencil on the desktop. "We've already questioned Mrs. Wetmore, and she can think of nothing that links her with Lilah. Unless she's lying—"

"No, I don't think Mrs. Wetmore is lying. But it's possible she simply doesn't see the connection between her philanthropy and Lilah's gratitude. Perhaps it's not as direct as we might wish. Lilah might simply have admired Mrs. Wetmore for her public service."

"In which case," Derrick said, "it might not have any bearing on Lilah's death."

"Perhaps not. But Carrington's Wharf, and the Blue Moon in particular, remain at the center of events. Even the fire at Ellsworth Cigars."

"How do you reach that conclusion?" Derrick wanted to know.

"She's right," Jesse said. "At least in that the recent robberies and the fire have all been within a small area surrounding the wharf. It could be a coincidence, but perhaps not. I hadn't thought of it before, but there could be a connection between the break-ins and Lilah's death."

"Perhaps she saw something. Perhaps when she overheard those men talking outside the Blue Moon, she learned something about the robberies."

"Even if that's true, the connection to the Wetmores is still unclear." Jesse stared across the room to a map of the city that hung on the wall. "To my knowledge, they don't own any property in that part of town. At any rate, they don't own any of the properties that were robbed and vandalized."

"Then we can dismiss the robberies as irrelevant to the case," Derrick said. "Why would Lilah need to warn the Wetmores if the crimes weren't directed at them?"

I hadn't thought much about the robberies in light of recent events, but Jesse's mentioning them in the same breath as the fire started me wondering. "What have the police discovered about the break-ins? Are they connected? And could they be connected to the fire?"

"They haven't learned much, from what I understand." Jesse tossed his pencil down, and it rolled across the desk. Derrick reached out and stopped it from falling to the floor. "The proprietors and the property owners have all been questioned, and none of them have offered any insight into why they might have been targeted."

"So then, a random crime spree," Derrick murmured, more as a comment than a question. "What about the perpetrators? Does the department suspect the same individuals in each case?"

"Not necessarily, although the accompanying vandalism

does point to the crimes being related." Jesse pressed his right temple, as if he felt the onslaught of a headache. "If we only had a witness, but apparently the uniforms have asked up and down Thames Street and everyone claims they didn't see a thing."

"And now the fire . . ." I mused.

Derrick sat back in his chair. "We're becoming sidetracked here. We're supposed to be focusing on Lilah's death."

"Are we?" I gazed at each man in turn. "Think about it. There is a rash of burglaries and vandalism and no one sees a thing? That's highly unlikely in an area like Lower Thames Street, with its boardinghouses and apartments, not to mention cargo coming in day and night."

"Then how would you explain it?" Derrick asked.

I saw by the keen light entering Jesse's eyes that he already comprehended my point. It was not an alien concept for either of us. "These were likely not ordinary burglaries, but very clear messages meant to frighten. That's why no one will speak up."

Derrick looked from one to the other of us. "Extortion?"

Jesse nodded. "Someone is browbeating our business owners. Anonymously."

I glanced past Jesse to the desk behind his own. A new detective used that desk now, but it had once belonged to Jesse's former partner, Anthony Dobbs. Jesse followed my line of vision and peered briefly over his shoulder.

He turned back to me with a stern expression. "We can't assume Tony has anything to do with this, Emma."

"Who are you talking about?" Derrick nodded as he answered his own question. "Ah, yes. Anthony Dobbs."

"How can we not, Jesse?" In my eagerness, I perched at the edge of my chair. "He's done this before."

"And paid a heavy price for it," he reminded me, unnecessarily.

"He did, and now he's shoveling coal at Carrington's Wharf. He's bitter, Jesse. And he's mean," I added, remembering the day he detained me in the narrow alley. "Would you put this past him, knowing his history and his temperament?"

Jesse was shaking his head. "Without some form of evidence I can't go accusing the man."

"If proof exists we'll find it." Derrick reached over and covered my hand where it rested on the arm of the chair, then removed it just as quickly with a glance at Jesse.

"I believe another trip to the Blue Moon is in order." I started to rise, but Derrick's hand shot out, this time to grasp my wrist. The two men spoke at once.

"Oh, no you don't." They both fell silent, staring at each other. Derrick released me.

I couldn't help laughing. "While it's heartening to see the two of you agreeing on something, it doesn't change the fact that I should speak with Madam Heidi again. I can't believe the woman doesn't have her finger on the pulse of everything that happens on Carrington's Wharf and the surrounding area. I'll just need to phrase my questions carefully."

Jesse ran his fingers through his hair. "If anyone should question Madam Heidi, it will be me."

"And what kind of replies do you think you'll receive?" I shook my head. "Your arrival at the Blue Moon is the one sure way to seal mouths. Madam Heidi and the others already know me. I believe they trust me, or as close to trust as women in their position can manage. Besides, my reputation is already destroyed. What further harm can come?"

"Physical harm." Derrick sounded exasperated. "It isn't safe for you to be on the docks alone."

"Pooh. I'll go now, while it's light out."

"Then I'll come with you." Derrick stood. "No argument."

A uniformed policeman strode to Jesse's desk, spoke in his

ear, and laid a sheet of paper in front of him. Jesse perused
the contents and blew out a breath. "It seems there's been
another burglary on Thames, not far from Carrington's
Wharf. Happened earlier this morning, but the proprietor
only just opened the shop. Come on. We'll all head down
there. For now, I'll leave you two to make the inquiries at
the Blue Moon."

We took the trolley along Spring Street and walked together down to Thames. There Jesse parted ways with us
and Derrick and I continued to Carrington's Wharf. When
we reached the walkway that stretched between the buildings, I placed a hand on Derrick's forearm.

"Wait outside while I speak with Madam Heidi and the
others."

"That isn't what we agreed to."

"They'll be more willing to talk if I go in alone. Please don't
argue. I won't be long and should I need you, I promise you'll
hear me."

He reluctantly agreed, and I went inside. This time, a
woman who identified herself as the Blue Moon's maid-of-
all-work met me at the bottom of the stairs. With a huff and
a shrug she brought me upstairs to the parlor and bade me
wait while she inquired whether Madam Heidi was receiving
or no.

"You again, eh?" Madam Heidi appeared in the doorway
but didn't linger to scrutinize me as she had upon our first
meeting. Her hair fell loose down her back and over her
shoulders today, and with her head partially down a spiraling lock fell forward to hide her face from me. She walked
past me to a window overlooking the wharf and the harbor.
"What is it this time, Miss Cross?"

"Won't you please sit with me, Miss Perry, so we might
talk?" I found I couldn't bring myself to address her by her

working title, Madam Heidi, to her face, even though I'd come to think of her by that name. The woman herself had told me to call her that, yet the appellation seemed to stick in my throat as perhaps too blatant a reminder of what went on here.

"Go ahead and talk, Miss Cross."

I shifted on the sofa to face her without craning my neck. "Miss Perry, I believe you are well aware of the events that take place on and around this wharf. Is that a fair assumption?"

She hesitated. "Go on."

Since she hadn't denied it, I assumed my guess to be correct. "I believe there may be connections between several recent occurrences. The burglaries on Thames Street, the fire at Ellsworth Cigars, and Lilah's death. And I believe the connection has something to do with this wharf."

"I don't know anything about Lilah's death, Miss Cross."

The sun coming through the window gilded her outlines, lending her the fanciful appearance of an angel in a medieval painting. I wished she would turn around. I didn't like speaking to her back. "Have you seen any suspicious comings or goings in recent days or weeks?"

"I don't know what you mean." She swept the lock of hair away from her face.

"Men who shouldn't ordinarily have business on the wharf, and who weren't here to conduct business with your girls. Especially wealthy gentlemen. Have you or any of the girls overheard any odd conversations? Seen exchanges of money?"

"This is a wharf, Miss Cross. There are always all manner of men about and money exchanging hands."

My exasperation building, I suppressed a sigh. "What about fear, Miss Perry? Are people—shopkeepers in particular—becoming wary of a growing situation along Thames Street?"

"What kind of situation?" The beginnings of boredom entered her voice, and I suspected my time here would soon be cut short.

"Specifically, Miss Perry, have you heard of demands being made, along with threats if people don't comply?"

"No, I have not." Yet as she spoke, her back stiffened. She tossed her head in an attempt, I believed, to distract my attention away from her reaction to my question, but I hadn't imagined it.

I rose from the sofa and went to the window. As I faced her, I turned her toward me with a firm hand on her shoulder. "Miss Perry—"

I broke off, staring. Shock and dismay held me immobile for several long moments. A black-and-purple bruise surrounded her left eye, nearly sealing it shut, and a weal stood out red against her cheek. She had tried, unsuccessfully, to conceal her injuries with a thick dusting of powder, which caked in the creases of her swollen flesh.

"Whoever it is," I said, reaching my fingertips toward but not quite touching her bruises, "has been here. Has threatened you to keep silent. Miss Perry, I am so sorry this happened to you. I can help you if you'll trust me."

"Trust you?" She pulled away, taking a backward step. "What I trust, Miss Cross, is that you will ask troublesome questions until someone else gets hurt. Go away. Go back to wherever you came from—to those Vanderbilts of yours. You're not one of us. You can have no inkling what it's like to survive on little but your wits."

"That isn't true. I assure you I am not a Vanderbilt. I rely on myself and am proud to do so." Her skeptical glare silenced me, and I saw my claim for what it was: all but a lie. Yes, I made my own way in the world as much as was possible, but I also had the security of knowing my Vanderbilt relatives would never allow me to be thrown out of my house and into the street. They would never suffer me to resort to such desperate means as those to be found at the Blue Moon. And surely if anyone ever laid their hands on me in such a way, my cousins would stop at nothing to see that that person paid dearly for his efforts.

I did not know what it was to be a woman such as those who worked for Madam Heidi, nor did I know the path Heidi Perry had trodden to reach her present circumstances. To claim otherwise made a mockery of their struggles. Yet I could not leave without some form of answer.

"Please tell me this much. Have you been threatened?"

She thrust her face close to mine. "Do you think this is a lover's touch?"

"What demands were made? Did this individual want money? Your silence on some matter? What?"

Her lips compressed. She turned back toward the window.

"The truth will come out, you know," I murmured.

"Then let it. It shan't come from my lips."

I grasped her wrist, expecting to be shaken off. Madam Heidi merely stiffened again. "Don't you realize that by remaining silent, you're allowing this person to go on hurting not only you, but others as well?"

Her face snapped back toward me. "Don't *you* realize that by keeping silent, I'm staying alive?"

I released her. "For how much longer? A man is dead, or had you forgotten? The manager of Ellsworth Cigars, Miss Perry. He died in a fire that in all likelihood was no accident. My guess is he refused whatever demands were made, and his life became forfeit as a message to every other business owner along Lower Thames Street."

"He was not the owner of the shop."

"No, but he might as well have been. He had been in the Ellsworth family's employ for nearly a decade. The day-to-day running of the business was left to him. I very much doubt he consulted with the Ellsworths on anything more

than the monthly profits." Even as I made the claim, I resolved to speak with Dominic Ellsworth as soon as possible.
The man might still be distraught over the fate of his business, his building, and his manager, but he would surely wish
to aid in apprehending the person responsible.

"Madam Heidi," I said, forgetting my aversion to using her
professional name, "who did this to you? I promise you can
trust me to be discreet." I inched closer to her and moved my
hand to her shoulder, hoping to inspire confidence through
physical, and gentle, contact. "Was it Anthony Dobbs?"

She blinked and darted a glance at me before gazing back
out the window. "Tony Dobbs? He wouldn't dare."

I followed her gaze to the wharf below us. Anthony
Dobbs and several other men labored with shovels unloading
coal from a steamer ferry onto the wheeled bins that ran on
tracks into the warehouse, where it would await pickup by the
many drays that would disperse the deliveries throughout the
city. It was heavy, filthy work that left the men as covered in
coal dust as a miner.

"And Anthony Dobbs has never demanded money from
you for any reason?"

She gave a laugh. "Oh, he's asked. Even demanded it back
when he worked for the cops. But he's never gotten a cent
from me."

"What about Stanford Whittaker?" I asked on a sudden
hunch based on what I knew of the man. With all of his money,
robbery seemed out of his realm of interest, but violence? Even
against women? Not difficult to envision.

Stanford Whittaker might not have needed the money, but
what about his friend, Harry Lehr? Mr. Lehr was always no-
toriously short of funds.

"Mr. Whittaker didn't do this," she replied, her voice flat
as if she answered by rote. "Nor anyone else you're going to
ask me about."

"How do you know whom I'm going to ask you about?"

"Miss Cross, it's time for you to—"

Ordering me from the house would have to wait, for another voice from the doorway spoke over hers. "I'm back, Madam Heidi. Would you let—Em, what are you doing here?"

I spun about to face my half brother, standing in the doorway. "I might ask you the very same thing, Brady Gale." A blush of combined anger and chagrin suffused my face, and I plunked my hands on my hips. "What are *you* doing here?"

"It's not what you think."

"I've heard *that* before."

"Yes, well, this time it's true." In gentlemanly fashion, he removed his boater and held it in both hands before his chest. "I'm here with Hannah."

"*What?*" My mouth dropped open and then snapped shut. A vein lashed in my temple. "Of all the dastardly, contemptible stunts you've ever pulled—"

"Good grief, Em. Hannah is here as a nurse, and I accompanied her to make sure she was safe on the docks. This isn't our only stop for the day."

Beside me, Madam Heidi stood nodding her consensus with Brady's claims. "She comes every few weeks to check on the girls, make sure they're fit. She's upstairs now."

"Oh . . . I . . . You didn't tell me anyone else was here," I said to Madam Heidi.

"You didn't ask."

I turned back to Brady. "I'm sorry. I should have known better."

"Yes, you should have." He crossed the room to me and grasped my shoulders. He grinned. "Although for the life of me, I don't know why. Now, why are *you* here?"

"I'm here because it's occurred to me that recent events might not be random. Lilah Buford's death. The burglaries. The fire at Ellsworth Cigars." I gestured at Madam Heidi. "Didn't you notice her left eye?"

"I didn't come all the way upstairs earlier." Brady gently turned Madam Heidi's chin with his fingertips. He let out an oath. "What kind of devil did that to you? Who was it?"

"Let me go. It doesn't matter. This sort of thing comes with my line of work."

"That's ridiculous." Brady turned to me. "Em, we've got to make her tell us."

"I've tried, Brady."

"Then we'll call Jesse in."

Madam Heidi lurched away and then rounded on us. "Jesse? Do you mean that policeman?"

Brady nodded. "Detective, yes."

"Out! Both of you." She strode from the room and to the foot of the stairs that led to the third floor. "Miss Hanson, time for you to be going. *Now*, Miss Hanson." She whirled to face us again. "You'll wait for her downstairs. And don't come back. If you send that detective, I'll have my girls tell him I'm not here."

"All right, we'll go." I held out my hands as if that could magically calm the woman. With a look at Brady, I led the way past her to the staircase and down to the tavern. She hovered above us on the second-floor landing and watched us until we disappeared from her view, into the pub room.

Brady rolled his eyes and then raised a hand to his nose as the pub's odors surrounded us. "I think it's best if we wait outside for Hannah."

"Let's. Derrick will be waiting to hear what happened. I suppose you saw him on your way inside."

Brady shook his head as he reached for the latch and opened the outer door. "Not a sign of him. And I don't see him now, either."

A burst of panic propelled me outside and, after glancing up and down the alley, around the corner of the building. I knew Derrick to be a man who could take care of himself, but once he had been caught off guard, injured, and left in a garden shed where he might have died.

I didn't stop until I found myself on the wharf proper, surrounded by workers. At first few of them noticed me. Anthony Dobbs and his fellow coal workers continued with their shoveling. Across the way from them, another group unloaded a shipment of firewood from a barge. Several others stood outside the dry goods store haggling over prices. I searched for Derrick among them. Little by little, activity ceased. Chatter ebbed until the only sounds were the cawing of gulls and the slap of water against the pilings and boat hulls. Faces turned in my direction. Shovel in hand, Anthony Dobbs began making his way toward me.

"Can't stay away, eh, Miss Cross? If you aren't careful, people will begin to talk." He didn't stop until he stood nearly toe-to-toe with me. "What brings your meddling self back so soon?"

"I . . ." I cast my glance quickly around me, once more searching for Derrick. "I'm looking for someone."

"Who? Me?" Sniggering meanly, he set the tip of his shovel on the ground and leaned on its handle.

The image of Madam Heidi's blackened eye formed in my mind, along with the possibility that her assailant presently stood before me, her denial notwithstanding. Experience, or rather Brady's experiences with the man, had revealed his violent streak clearly enough.

"No, Mr. Dobbs, not you. Never you." I met his gaze without blinking. "Not if I can help it." Abhorrence radiated back and forth between us. I believed mine to be justified; I didn't understand where his originated, for his disregard for my family began long before our encounters of two summers ago. He was simply mean-spirited, loathsome. Again the image of Madam Heidi's bruised face flashed behind my eyes. I pushed out a breath. "Did you hit her?"

He scoffed. "Who?"

"If you must ask that, the accusation can't be a foreign one to you." For some reason, I lowered my voice. "Heidi Perry. Did you strike her?"

He hesitated, his eyes narrowing a fraction. "No. It wasn't me."

"I don't believe you." I started to turn away but he caught my arm.

"One of these days, Miss Cross, you're going to walk into a situation you can't control. And you're going to get hurt. Very hurt."

"Release me at once and don't you dare threaten me."

"Let her go, Dobbs." Brady was suddenly there. I hadn't heard his approach, hadn't seen him coming. He seized Anthony Dobbs's wrist and spoke through gritted teeth. "Let my sister go or I swear, I'll break your arm."

Dobbs's fingers relaxed a fraction and I whisked my arm away from him, cradling it with my other hand. Brady had yet to let go, and his knuckles stood out bone white, his hand locked so fiercely around Dobbs's wrist that I believed, in that moment, he had the ability to make good on his threat.

But then, I didn't doubt Anthony Dobbs possessed the same ability.

I darted a glance around at the others surrounding us. Some faces were familiar, other not. I remembered what Derrick had said, that not all dockworkers were Newporters, and we could not count on help from that quarter. "Brady, let's go."

He started to move, but without warning Dobbs swung his shovel and struck Brady square in the gut. The flat of the head caught him rather than the edge, or the implement might have sliced into him. As it was, Brady doubled over, his hat tumbling to the ground, and Dobbs prepared to swing again. I cried out, even made a grab to stay his arm.

His workmate, the man who had defused our encounter in the alley that first day, hurried over to us.

"Let it go, Tony. It isn't worth it. You told me this lady is a friend of your old partner's. Do you really think you can win this round?"

Dobbs stood frozen, a debate clearly being waged in his mind. Then he slowly lowered his makeshift weapon. "A pity you didn't hang two summers ago, Gale. Would have been good riddance."

Brady scooped up his boater and straightened with a groan. He exchanged a chilling glare with Dobbs. "We'll see who hangs."

"Let's go." I grabbed Brady's forearm and tugged him along. As we circled the Blue Moon back to the alley, I looked up to see Madam Heidi still at the window, staring down on us. She spotted me and our gazes met. As if I were a complete stranger, she turned away and disappeared into the room.

Chapter 12

We reunited with Derrick and Hannah in the alley. "Where were you?" I demanded in lieu of a more civil greeting.

"I was upstairs, with the girls," Hannah replied, looking baffled. "Where were the two of you?"

"No, Hannah, I'm sorry." I gestured at Derrick none too gently. "Where were *you*? You said you'd wait for me. You have no idea what almost just happened. Brady might have been killed." I very nearly shouted the charge. Fear of what almost happened to Brady and what might have happened to Derrick ruled my actions.

"Em, it's all right," Brady murmured, but he continued to hold an arm against his stomach. "It was better Derrick wasn't there, or it might have become a brawl."

"What brawl?" Derrick surveyed Brady. "What happened to you?"

"Anthony Dobbs struck him in the stomach with a shovel, that's what happened." I drew a sharp breath. At my words, Hannah gasped and moved to Brady's side, ready to catch him should he fall over. "Would you mind telling us what happened to you? Why did you suddenly disappear?"

"I didn't disappear. I happened to notice Dominic Ellsworth driving by in his cabriolet. I assumed he was going to his building down the way so I followed him. I thought you'd be inside longer, and I didn't want to lose the opportunity." Derrick's explanation drained the wind from my sails, for I couldn't but admit I would have done the same.

"Oh," I said feebly. "In that case . . . I'm sorry. I'd thought . . ."

Derrick showed me a wounded look. "You thought I abandoned you?"

"Of course not. I thought something had happened to you. That's why I went around to the main wharf."

"And that's where she met up with Anthony Dobbs wielding a shovel," Brady put in. Speaking cost him a visible effort, and Hannah wrapped an arm around his waist when he doubled over again. "Sorry. I'm fine. Just hurts a bit."

"Mr. Dobbs hit you with a shovel?" Hannah ran a hand over Brady's coat front. "Why would he do such a thing?"

"Because I wouldn't tolerate him putting his hands on Emma."

Derrick lurched toward me. "On Emma? That man put his hands on you? That's the last thing he'll ever do." He started to move past me.

I seized him by the sleeve. He tried to pull away but I stepped into his path. "It's over, Derrick, and I'm fine. He frightened me and he hurt Brady, but it won't do any good for you to go attacking him."

"A sound thrashing is what he needs." Despite his words, Derrick's posture eased and I released him.

"I agree, but not here and not now. And not by you." I turned to Brady and Hannah. "How did you two get here?"

"We rode the trolley from the hospital," Hannah said.

Only now that I'd calmed did I notice her nurse's uniform

and the crisp white kerchief holding her blond curls away from her face. "The hospital sends you to places like the Blue Moon?"

"No. I come on my own time." Dimples flashed in her plump, rosy cheeks. "Although with the hospital's sanction."

"We can discuss whatever we wish once we're gone from here." Brady unclasped his middle in order to use both arms to herd us back toward the street. "There's no telling when Dobbs might take it into his head to come after us."

"Thank goodness for his friend," I said. "That's twice now that man has defused his friend's anger." A vague sensation had me looking over my shoulder toward the wharf as I walked. "I should have thanked him."

"Never mind." Derrick linked my arm through his and hurried me along. On our way up to Spring Street, Brady and I described in greater detail what occurred on the wharf. Derrick turned ruddy with ire and his eyes blazed, but he said little. Hannah expressed her dismay with gasps of outrage.

"Never mind that for now," I said when we reached the trolley stop. "Did you have a chance to speak to Mr. Ellsworth?"

Derrick nodded. "He was meeting with Stanford Whittaker at the burned-out hull of his shop, but I had a few minutes alone with him first. I asked him if he knew of any threats made against him or his manager, and whether the exact source of the fire had been discovered. He cited a gas leak and denied all knowledge of threats."

"Did you believe him?" I asked.

"I saw no reason not to."

"I asked Madam Heidi the same question, and she denied it as well. But Derrick, her eye had been blackened. She wouldn't tell me who did it, nor much of anything else, but I know she's hiding the truth because she's frightened. What's more, I believe it was Anthony Dobbs who hit her. He denies it, of course."

"Is that what you were saying to him when he grabbed you, Em?"

I nodded in reply to Brady's question. "More and more, events seem to have Anthony Dobbs written all over them. Once a bully, always a bully, and extortion is nothing new to him either. Perhaps Mr. Ellsworth denied being threatened out of fear, just like Madam Heidi." I turned back to Derrick. "Did he say why he was meeting with Mr. Whittaker?"

"To discuss rebuilding."

"A gas leak in a cigar shop seems so unlikely."

Derrick shrugged. "Ellsworth said the fire brigade discovered a faulty gas jet."

"In a shop that handled easily inflammable goods, wouldn't the fittings have been inspected fairly often?" My question met with more shrugs and shakes of the head. I turned to Hannah. "Have you heard anything from the women at the Blue Moon about threats or demands for money?"

"Nothing, but when I'm there I keep the conversation focused on their health."

A notion prompted me to ask, "Did you know Lilah Buford?"

"I did, but not well. She hadn't been there as long as the others."

"Did you know she was with child? And for that matter, did she?"

Hannah hesitated, then nodded. "We both suspected she was. The signs were there, but not enough time had passed for me to be able to confirm it for her." She ducked her head and said more quietly, "The coroner did that."

"Hannah, did she give you any indication who the father might have been?"

"I never asked. You must understand, Emma, I don't attempt to discuss personal matters. I can't, or I might alienate the very women I'm there to help."

"But Lilah might have known," I said, "and she might have told the man in question."

"And he might not have taken the news happily," Derrick added, prompting me to shake my head sadly.

"We're learning nothing." I glanced up the street, searching for the trolley. "It's horribly frustrating."

"I didn't say I learned nothing," Derrick said. "Ellsworth seemed willing enough to speak with me at first, but as soon as Whittaker arrived he practically pushed me into the street."

"So it's possible he's hiding something, too." Brady thought a moment. Then his sandy blond eyebrows rose. "I wonder how much insurance Ellsworth had on the place."

While Brady and Hannah continued on to the hospital, Derrick and I exited the trolley on Mary Street and walked up to the firehouse, situated on the narrow corner where the road merged onto Touro Street. The engine bay stood open, and inside a pair of firemen were busy washing down the steam engine. I hailed one of them.

"Mr. Dwyer, may we speak with you a moment?"

From the shadowy interior, the man squinted into the bright sunlight outside. "Is that Emma Cross? Yes, come in." He tossed the wet rag he held into a bucket of sudsy water at his feet. "How are you? And how is Mrs. O'Neal?"

Mr. Dwyer was another longtime Point resident whom I had known all my life. About Jesse's age, he sported the physique of a sportsman with his broad shoulders and trim torso. He towered over me, was even taller than Derrick, but his eyes were kindly and he was known for his gentle ways with children and animals.

"Nanny is fine, thank you for asking. Shall I send her your regards?"

"Do, indeed." He eyed Derrick, and I hastened to make the introductions. The Andrews name didn't seem at all familiar to Mr. Dwyer; he merely shook Derrick's hand and asked what he could do for us.

"We witnessed the fire at Ellsworth Cigars the other night."

"Ah, terrible thing, that. I knew the manager. Bertrand Styles. Good man. Honest and good at his job. Very dedicated. Such a shame. His wife is distraught."

"I'm so sorry to hear that." I waited a respectful moment before continuing. "We've been told the fire started as a result of a faulty gas fitting. Is that true?"

Mr. Dwyer tilted his head and regarded me. Without suspicion or judgment he asked, "Are you here as a reporter?"

"I would like to be able to follow up," I said evasively. Mr. Dwyer didn't need to know that the *Observer* no longer employed me. Besides, with any luck I might be writing for the New York *Herald* soon enough. "But I'm also concerned that such a thing could happen. My own Gull Manor is fitted out for gas, of course, and I foresee no conversion to electricity in the near future. I'd like to be aware of the danger signs."

He nodded his understanding. "Smelling gas is an immediate warning, as I'm sure you know. But you should have the system inspected regularly, at least once a year."

"Was the shop inspected regularly?" Derrick asked.

"It was, although not by the city. Not in recent times, anyway."

I frowned. "What do you mean?"

"Mr. Ellsworth typically hired city inspectors, but lately he went with a private company. More's the pity. Someone missed something, is all I can say."

Derrick and I exchanged a glance, and I asked, "Did he give any reason for the change?"

Mr. Dwyer shrugged. "Not that I know of. But in my experience folks hire private inspectors for either of two reasons. It costs less, *or* . . . He emphasized that last word and held up a forefinger. "They're paying extra for shoddy work to be passed off as acceptable. Not that I'm saying that's what happened in this case," he added quickly. "Could be Mr. Ellsworth knew someone he thought he could trust to do the job."

As Mr. Dwyer himself had indicated, his speculation was merely that, nothing conclusive. Still, Brady's question about how much Mr. Ellsworth had insured his building for lingered in my mind.

We chatted for a few more minutes, but I had the information I'd come for. Derrick and I walked up to Washington Square and found a vacant bench beneath a poplar tree in the park at the east end of the square, near the Colony House. Two elderly men occupied a bench on the other side of the fountain, and off to our right a woman sat alone, a bag on her lap, tossing bread crumbs to an assortment of birds warbling at her feet. Derrick and I remained silent for a time, lost in our own thoughts. My gaze drifted to the bronze statue, high on its granite plinth, facing Long Wharf and the harbor. The monument to Commodore Oliver Hazard Perry depicted him commanding his men during the battle of Lake Erie during the War of 1812. He was a Navy hero, born in Rhode Island, who had chosen Newport as his home, and Newporters hailed him as one of their own.

"Do you believe a family can fall so entirely," I murmured out loud, my gaze still pinned on the statue, "as to never rise again?"

Beside me, his shoulder nearly touching mine, Derrick tilted his head in my direction. "I'm not sure I know what you mean, but yes, once-proud families do sometimes fall into obscurity. War, bad harvests, poor investments, disease—there are so many circumstances that can change the fortunes of a family. Disinheritance," he added in an undertone.

I slipped my hand into his, just for a moment, before sliding it back to my lap. "That won't happen in your case. If anything, you'll achieve greater things on your own than your father can imagine. You only need time." I sighed, looking up at the statue again. "I was thinking of Madam Heidi."

"What about her?"

"Don't you know? She styles herself Heidi Perry, and claims to be Commodore Perry's descendant." I gestured to the bronze figure standing so proudly, his right hand raised toward the sky.

Derrick laughed softly. "I see."

"I know it's unbelievable, but it's possible, isn't it? Take me, for instance. My great-great-grandmother was Phoebe Vanderbilt Cross, daughter of the first Cornelius Vanderbilt himself, yet I'm no one other than a poor relation."

"I'd hardly call you no one, Miss Cross."

"But don't you see how easily a woman in my circumstances can fall into dire straits? If not for my great aunt Sadie's generosity in taking me under her wing and leaving me her home and assets, I might—"

"No." He silenced me with a fierce look. "Not you. You'd have found another way."

I couldn't fault him for wanting to believe that. But a man couldn't possibly understand how limited a woman's choices were. I let it go.

"So far, we have a number of suspects and motives but no clear lead." I raised my face to the salty breeze that traveled up Long Wharf to wash over Washington Square. "Stanford Whittaker resented Mr. Wetmore because of the Dingley

Act, frequented the Blue Moon to be with Lilah, and is known to be abusive."

Derrick nodded. "And his friends who visited the Blue Moon with him? Robert Clarkson and Harry Lehr?"

"Robert Clarkson was also unhappy about the Dingley Act, but that alone creates a rather weak link to the crime. The same for Harry Lehr. He would like nothing better than to marry Maude Wetmore for her money, but there is no shortage of marriageable heiresses. He can always find another. It doesn't seem reason enough to commit murder and attempt to frame George Wetmore for it."

"James Bennett and Dominic Ellsworth," Derrick said, prompting me to consider again.

"Despite Mr. Bennett's protests that he'll expand his Casino with or without the city's approval, the fact remains that Mr. Wetmore has been vocal in persuading the city council against granting the permits. This is also a financial loss for Stanford Whittaker, whose company would have been awarded the contract for the design and construction of the new buildings. But I couldn't help believing Mr. Bennett when he said he hoped we'd find justice for Lilah." I didn't add that I also *wanted* him to be innocent so I could be employed by the *Herald*.

"Dominic?" Derrick pressed.

"There is nothing against him except for having been at Carrington's Wharf the night Lilah died."

"Ah, yes. In all the excitement earlier, I'd forgotten. I also asked him what he and Bennett were doing at the wharf that night. I used the excuse we devised, of Lilah being missing. I asked him if he might have seen anything."

"And?"

"And . . . he denied being there. Flat out denied it, and said whoever thought he saw him and Bennett was mistaken.

Just as Bennett tried to deny it when we asked him the other day."

"They need to get their stories straight."

"What about Brady's theory that Dominic Ellsworth might have had his own building burned down in order to collect the insurance?"

Derrick said nothing, instead staring across the way, where a squirrel attempted to intrude upon the feeding birds and steal their breadcrumbs. The woman on the bench tried to wave him away, but the squirrel would dart off, then slink back and pounce when he saw his chance, resulting in a ruckus of outraged squawking.

"I know what Mr. Dwyer said about using a private inspector," I persisted. "But *why* would Mr. Ellsworth set fire to his own business? What could he possibly gain?" I paused, considering and not liking the possible conclusion I reached. "Unless he had something to hide in that shop. Or worse, his manager knew something, and Mr. Ellsworth had to silence him. Oh, Derrick, I don't want that to be true. It's too dreadful."

He touched my arm briefly. "What now?"

"I want to return to the Casino tonight. Mr. Bennett said the last time Lilah went to the Casino, she spent her time observing a family. I'd like to know more about who these people are. Perhaps Mr. Bennett could point them out to us."

Derrick nodded his agreement. "And someone needs to have a talk with Mr. Ellsworth. In the meantime, I think we should tell Jesse everything that's happened since we parted. He'll need to know." He stood and held out a hand to help me up.

I couldn't hide my grin. "You're voluntarily suggesting we go speak with Jesse."

He led the way off the green and toward Marlborough Street. "Do stop smirking."

*   *   *

That evening brought Derrick and me back to the Casino, although we weren't alone. Jesse had arrived a half hour before us, dressed like any Newporter out for an evening's entertainment. As Derrick and I entered the courtyard, I saw him along the promenade. Our gazes met for a brief instant before sliding away. We made no acknowledging signs.

Such was not the case, however, with James Bennett. Speaking to guests on the restaurant veranda, he excused himself upon spotting us and stepped down to the green. The sigh with which he greeted us conveyed his sentiments better than any words could. But to be certain Derrick and I fully understood, he said, "Back to make trouble?"

"You said you hoped for justice for Lilah," I reminded him. Beside me, Derrick tensed. I placed my hand into the crook of his elbow and applied just enough pressure to prevent him from speaking out, as I knew he wished to do. "Has that changed?"

"It hasn't, Miss Cross. But I'm not going to allow you to chase off Casino guests, either."

Derrick let go a rumbling murmur which I couldn't make out, but judging by how Mr. Bennett's jaw squared, a threat to his person had been implied. "We have no intention of chasing off anyone," I assured him. "And if you'll agree to assist us, our business will be concluded sooner rather than later."

His eyebrows lowered like gathering storm clouds. "Assist you how?"

"The family that so interested Lilah. Will you point them out to us?"

He sucked in his cheeks and his nose flared slightly. When no answer seemed forthcoming, Derrick intervened. "This family could prove important. The police initially called Lilah's death an accident, but they've since reopened the case. You don't want to be seen as hampering an investigation, do you?"

"I can't be hampering an investigation if the police haven't approached me for information, now, can I?"

Derrick smiled mildly. "And what if the police are here tonight, waiting for Miss Cross and me to discover the identity of this family—this family you seem so reluctant to identify?"

"The police are here? Where?" Mr. Bennett scanned the well-dressed diners and the couples and small groups strolling the piazzas beneath glowing gas lanterns. From a distance, it was no easy task to pick out specific individuals amid the glitter of jewels and the sheen of fine silks. Elaborate hand fans and the shadows of beaver hats obscured faces, while the constant chatter prevented any one voice from being identified.

"Here, milling about." An odd sense of authority, and of confidence, filled me, and I felt somehow triumphant. "Watching and waiting."

Mr. Bennett hesitated for another moment. Then he gestured for us to follow him. "Come with me."

On the restaurant's veranda, he spoke some words to the maître d', who then sat us at a table near a corner. Mr. Bennett leaned over the small table and spoke in an undertone. "Three tables over, to the right. That's the family."

Derrick and I glanced past Mr. Bennett's shoulder. The table was larger than our own, big enough for several diners. A man and a woman about my parents' age sat beside each other, and I assumed these to be the parents of the young man, about twenty years old, and the teenage girl who occupied the table with them. They were a handsome family, dressed in the very latest from Paris, but it was the fifth person at the table who most drew my regard. He was quite tall for an older man; even sitting, the others at the table had to look up at him when he spoke. He wore his silver hair slicked back against his head, and a white silk scarf draped loosely around his collar. I was certain an ebony cane with a silver handle rested somewhere against the table close to him.

"Derrick," I whispered, "that's the elderly man who confronted us the last time we were here. Do you remember? He said Lilah came here making trouble, and that we'd be wise to leave her be."

"I remember," Derrick replied low, barely moving his lips. He glanced at Mr. Bennett. "What's the main entertainment for tonight?"

"There's a cotillion at the theater as soon as the dinner hour is over." He tipped his head back in a gesture indicating the mysterious family. "I can practically guarantee they'll attend."

"I agree," I said, scanning the flouncy ball gown the daughter wore. I guessed her age to be about seventeen. Almost an adult, but not quite. She still bore that wide-eyed naïveté of a girl who had yet to experience her first season. She fidgeted with her napkin, the edge of the tablecloth, the frills on her little puffed sleeves. Had her family formally brought her out? I didn't think so. "Something about them—I can't quite explain it—speaks of a fairly recent entrée into polite society."

"New money, undoubtedly," Mr. Bennett said with a sniff of disdain.

Derrick pinned him with a glare. "Why don't you run along now, Bennett? Miss Cross and I can handle things from here."

Again that squaring of the jaw, the sucking in of his cheeks. "I don't like being dismissed in my own club, Andrews."

"Then perhaps you shouldn't overstay your welcome."

At Derrick's retort, Mr. Bennett turned his anger on me. "Perhaps you should be more careful about whom you choose to spend your time with, Miss Cross. Especially if you are still counting on a certain bit of good news."

He stormed off across the veranda and disappeared into the inner dining room. Derrick immediately turned to me. "What did he mean by that? What certain bit of good news?"

A wave of heat had enveloped my face at Mr. Bennett's words, and now I pulled back in my seat, hoping to avoid the light of the candle in the middle of our table. "I don't know," I said quickly. "It must have something to do with Lilah, though I cannot imagine what."

I was lying, and not liking myself one bit for it. But I hadn't yet told Derrick of my bid for employment at the New York *Herald.* I hadn't told anyone. And with the way Derrick obviously felt about Mr. Bennett, I would do myself no favors revealing my would-be plan to him before I knew whether or not I'd be offered a position.

We ordered a light supper of consommé and lobster croquettes. As we ate, we made certain to keep pace with the family that had so interested Lilah. We also kept our voices and our heads low to avoid attracting their notice.

Their voices reached us upon occasion, during rare lulls in the surrounding conversations. The daughter's name was Nanette, the son's Gerald. They addressed the younger of the adults as Mother and Father, the elderly man as Grandfather. They all seemed to dote on Nanette, even the brother. I noted a marked difference in the siblings' coloring, with her being fair, her cheekbones high, and her chin pointed, while he had dark hair and eyes and heavier facial features. In truth they didn't look at all alike, but then neither did many siblings. Brady and I hardly favored each other in looks, though if one observed closely enough, the similarity in the shape of our eyes and the curve of our chins became evident.

My fork was halfway to my mouth when Derrick tossed down his napkin. The family had evidently finished their dinner, for they were coming to their feet. The brother held his sister's chair as she rose, chattering in excitement. "My first cotillion," she said with unconcealed delight. Her brother offered her his arm. Derrick and I watched them until they stepped out into the courtyard. Then we, too, vacated our seats.

Chapter 13

The assembly was being held in the Casino's theater, where the seats had been removed to create a spacious dance floor. Above, the wraparound balcony with its glorious arches became a gallery where those who chose not to dance could gaze down upon the proceedings. A chamber orchestra occupied a corner of the stage, rather than being hidden beneath in the pit.

We spotted the family gathered near the seating along the south wall. Nanette practically bounced on her toes in her eagerness, while the brother, Gerald, seemed rather less enamored of the occasion. Their mother observed their surroundings with a sharp eye, keeping close watch on every passerby, especially families with sons in tow.

"There's no doubt they're here hoping to be noticed by society," I murmured to Derrick.

"You mean hoping society notices their daughter," he replied. He glanced about the room. "I don't see the old man. Dare we hope he's gone home for the evening?"

"We need to meet them before he returns." Easier said

than done, for Derrick and I could hardly walk up to complete strangers, with whom we had no acquaintances in common, and merely introduce ourselves. At least, not without causing awkwardness, and that was something I wished to avoid. Luck came my way in the form of a waltzing pair not far from where we stood. I nudged Derrick. "Look, there are Grace and Neily."

He nodded vaguely, apparently not catching my meaning. As we had planned, we moved away from each other. As soon as the music paused I strolled onto the dance floor. "Neily, Grace. How lovely to see you again."

Grace turned to me with a delighted smile. She looked stunning in gold silk with a jeweled bodice, a design I did not doubt came from House of Worth. "Emma!" she exclaimed. We embraced lightly. Then she gasped with obvious delight and leaned closer to me. "Isn't that Mr. Andrews I saw you walk in with? Where has he gone?"

I decided not to put up a pretense. This was Neily and Grace, after all. Both were familiar with the intrigue in which I typically found myself, and moreover, they had helped in the past. "I need an introduction to someone, Grace. Do you think you could manage it for me?"

She let out a peal of laughter, as if I'd told the funniest of jokes. "I believe this can be accomplished. Who is the party in question?"

"If you'll both excuse me." Neily kissed my hand and his wife's cheek. "I'll leave you two to your machinations." With a rather long-suffering sigh, he moved off the dance floor.

That was twice now I had detected a sentiment of discontent in Neily's manner. Was he unhappy in his marriage? I dearly, fervently hoped not. But it was certainly not for me to interfere in his and Grace's life, nor to become distracted from my present purpose. I pointed out the family I wished to meet.

"Hmm, I don't believe I've had the pleasure." Delicate furrows formed above Grace's nose, and I began to lose hope. "But never mind. I am not Mrs. Vanderbilt for nothing, am I?"

She certainly looked every inch the part of a Vanderbilt wife with her exquisite ball gown and the tiara glittering among the piled curls of her coif. With a mischievous grin, she raised an eyebrow as she set off across the room. She walked straight up to Nanette's mother and extended a satin-gloved hand that shone with an emerald on the ring finger, a diamond on the forefinger, and a cuff of diamonds and pearls encircling her wrist.

"My goodness, how are you?" Grace's voice rang with believable surprise. "It is such a pleasure to see you here."

"Oh, I . . ." A tide of scarlet engulfed the mother's face. "I'm so sorry, I . . . I'm afraid I've forgotten where it was we met. I . . . how are you?"

"I'm delightful, thank you. And, dear me, yes, that last time was such a crush, wasn't it? I could barely hear myself think, and I'm quite sure you couldn't hear a word either. I'm Mrs. Vanderbilt, of course."

"Yes, of course," the woman replied weakly. I wondered if she had the faintest idea which Mrs. Vanderbilt stood before her. Besides Grace, there were three others with ties to Newport: Alice, Alva, and Louise. Meanwhile, her husband looked on with no small measure of astonishment, while her children appeared dumbfounded. "You remember my husband, Mr. Hartwell. And our children, Gerald and Nanette."

"I do indeed. Mr. Hartwell, lovely to see you again. I hope you have all been well?"

"Oh, yes, well. Quite, quite well," Mrs. Hartwell said with a bit of a stammer.

"May I introduce my cousin by marriage, Miss Emmaline Cross." Grace turned to me and stretched out a slender arm to draw me closer. "Miss Cross, these are the Hartwells I was telling you about."

I experienced a moment of panic, realizing they might have heard about me as the woman who so brazenly visited a brothel and the Reading Room. True, the *Daily News* hadn't mentioned me by name in the article, but people could easily guess and word had surely spread by now. Yet I could detect nothing but interest and eagerness in their expressions. I might have been Lizzy Borden herself and they would not have cared, being introduced to them as I was by a member of the Vanderbilt family. "I'm so pleased to make your acquaintance." I shook hands with each of them, letting my fingers linger a moment longer than necessary against Gerald's. I attempted to mimic something of Nanette's wide-eyed innocence. It wouldn't hurt for them to believe I was younger than my twenty-three years.

Grace led us in small talk while I continued to subtly show my interest in Gerald. I wanted him to ask me to dance, for I thought what better way to strike up a conversation? I needn't have worried about my plan working, for Mrs. Hartwell soon discreetly nudged her son and, having gotten his attention, gestured to me with her gaze. It took Gerald looking back and forth several times between his mother and me before he understood her meaning, but at a lull in the conversation he finally held out his hand to me. "Miss Cross, may I have the pleasure of this next dance?"

Soon we were whirling among other couples across the dance floor. Gerald Hartwell made a passing fair partner; he had obviously been well schooled in ballroom skills. He swept me so effortlessly in his arms that I became slightly breathless and made an effort to slow our momentum enough to allow conversation. He must have noticed, and perhaps believed he was overwhelming me, for it didn't take long for him to adjust his stride to a more leisurely pace.

"From where do you hail, Mr. Hartwell?"

"New York, Miss Cross. Long Island."

"Indeed? Is your family in business there?"

"We are. Our company provides support structures for the construction industry."

"Scaffolding?"

"Just so, Miss Cross. It is quite lucrative."

"One might imagine so, Mr. Hartwell." I tipped my head back in a show of pleasure as we glided in smooth, triple-meter rhythm around another couple. "Much of Long Island is horse country, I understand. Are you here for the polo, then? Do you support the Meadowview Club?"

"Polo, among the other diversions Newport has to offer. But yes, my father is a Meadowview patron."

"How extraordinary." I confess I found nothing particularly extraordinary about his father's patronage, but it seemed the sort of thing a young debutant would say. "How long do you intend to visit our seaside metropolis?"

"I couldn't say. And you, Miss Cross? Will you remain for the rest of the Season?"

"I live here."

"Year round?" He said it as if he found something distasteful about remaining in Newport once the Season ended.

"I'm of Newport born and raised, Mr. Hartwell. But tell me, other than my cousin Mrs. Vanderbilt, with whom else are you acquainted here in town?"

"Very few others, I'm afraid. We're rather new to . . ." He trailed off, but I detected the beginnings of the word *society.* Such an admission was just the thing to ensure one's curt dismissal from society, and he must have known it. As his mother had blushed at Grace's insistence that they knew each other, Gerald turned ruddy now.

Apparently, Gerald Hartwell was not altogether comfortable with his parents' social ambitions. I quickly changed the
subject. "Have you heard the latest news? It's quite unset-
tling."

"Which news is that, Miss Cross?"

"There is a woman who has gone missing. Vanished into
thin air, they say. It's positively frightening that such a thing
can happen here in Newport. Oh, what is her name?" I pretended to consider as Gerald swept me past several other
couples. I waited for him to supply an answer, but he did
not. "Buford, I believe. Yes, that's it: Lilah Buford. Have you
heard?"

His expression never changed, never registered anything
beyond polite interest. "I'm sorry, Miss Cross, but I cannot
say I have heard this unfortunate story. I do hope the woman
is found soon, and in good health."

He talked on, but my attention wandered over heads and
across the room. Derrick had made his way over to the
Hartwell family, and now he stood talking with the three remaining members. He seemed to be paying special attention
to Nanette. Gerald turned me, and I craned my neck to keep
Derrick and Nanette in my sights. She was smiling in a sim-
pering fashion and looking utterly entranced, while he bent
subtly closer to her, ostensibly, of course, to be heard without having to raise his voice or force Miss Hartwell to strain
her ears. I knew he was merely doing as we had agreed
upon—asking questions, as I was doing with Gerald. Still, a
wave of something cold, harsh, and unwelcome swept over
me, making me wish to cut this waltz short and reclaim . . .
good heavens, what I had no right to claim.

I tore my gaze away from Derrick and forced my attention back to Gerald. Still, with that cold sensation lodged in
my breast, I remarked, rather abruptly, that Gerald and his
sister did not look much alike.

His smooth stride faltered and then resumed as if nothing had happened. After a hesitation he said, "No, I suppose we don't. Nanette takes after our mother's side of the family, while I favor my father's."

"I see," I said, but in truth I could find little evidence of either claim. The siblings didn't much resemble each other or their parents. Could they be adopted? With a start, I drew my attention back to Gerald. Images from Lilah's photograph album popped into my mind. Lilah had had a younger brother. Madam Heidi seemed to believe he had died, but how could she be certain? Could the man presently leading me on the dance floor be that same boy? Is that why Lilah took such an interest in this family?

Only one thing felt certain: The family was hiding something. Was it merely the fact of their social climbing ambitions? Or something more?

"You there, step away from her."

The angry command rang out above the music and the chatter. Gerald brought me to an abrupt halt, his gaze riveted upon his family. My hand held by his rigid one, I also turned to face them. The elderly man had returned and now stood with his cane raised in a threatening manner.

Mr. Hartwell attempted to intercede. "Father, please. Mr. Andrews is merely—"

The old man didn't listen. He waved his cane and then poked the air with its tip as if to run Derrick through with a lance. "She is too young for the likes of you, sir. Step away from her immediately."

An awkward silence had fallen over the assembly and the dancing ceased. One by one the musicians stopped playing, until only the reedy notes of an oboe faded into nothing. All attention converged on Derrick and the fiercely blushing Nanette. The poor girl looked as if she wished to melt into the floor.

Derrick barely blinked. Calmly stepping in front of Nanette, he bowed to his adversary. "My apologies, sir. I meant no harm. Good evening."

Immediately the music started up again, a lively mazurka that encouraged the dancing to resume. Still holding my hand, Gerald started us walking toward his family. Derrick had attempted to take his leave, but the cane swerved outward to block his way.

Before we reached them, Jesse appeared, having strode decisively through the crush. He held out his detective's badge and thrust it close to the old man's face. Gerald sped his pace, hauling me along behind him. I trotted to keep up, to keep from being dragged. Anger rolled off him in heated waves. I doubted he even realized he held onto me.

"I'm Detective Whyte of the Newport Police," Jesse was calmly saying. "Sir, I must ask you to lower your cane and allow this gentleman to pass."

"He's a troublemaker. He's been following my son's family, prying and . . ." He broke off as Gerald and I reached him. Then he pointed a finger at me. "And *her* along with him. The pair of them, they've been at it before."

Gerald whirled to face me. "Is this true? Are you trying to make some kind of trouble for my family? Is that why you asked me all those questions? And that woman you asked about, Lilah? Has she something to do with this?"

The old man shushed him, his gaze darting to Nanette and back again. Mrs. Hartwell came forward. "Father, dearest, you're making a dreadful scene," she said in a stage whisper. "Do leave off, please. I'm sure Miss Cross and Mr. Andrews meant no harm. After all, they were introduced to us by Mrs. Vanderbilt. Surely you're not going to accuse Mrs. Vanderbilt of some sort of ill-meant mischief. The very idea."

"I don't know about Mrs. Vanderbilt," the old man said, "but these two will bring this family nothing good."

"Grandfather, whatever are you saying?" Nanette swept to him and wrapped a pale hand around his coat sleeve.

He turned to her suddenly, as if startled—as if he'd forgotten her presence there. The anger faded from his eyes. "Never you mind, my girl. Everything is . . . is all right."

"I think you'd better go," Gerald murmured to me, but while his tone may have lacked force, his expression granted no quarter.

Jesse gave me a slight nod. Derrick and I moved away, but we hadn't gotten far when Mrs. Hartwell called out to us. We turned to discover she'd followed us, and she was flushed and out of breath. "Miss Cross, Mr. Andrews, please accept my apologies." Her gaze darted back and forth between us, the whites of her eyes wide around the irises. "I don't know what could have gotten into my father-in-law. Do forgive us."

"It's quite all right, Mrs. Hartwell," I said, and Derrick and I continued on our way. When I felt assured she could not overhear us, I said, "She says one thing, but her eyes tell another story. There is something strange going on with this family, and I believe it has to do with either or both of the siblings."

Derrick sighed as he opened the outside door for me. "Nanette seems exactly what she should be: an innocent and cheerful young lady. Perhaps a bit empty-headed, but that's to be expected at her age."

I slapped playfully at his arm. "We're not *all* empty-headed—at any age. But I believe you about the girl. I didn't say either of them was at fault, necessarily. But there is something . . ." I left off as a sensation stole over me—a sense of something amiss . . . or missing. My thoughts took a sharp turn. "Where is Mr. Bennett?"

"Somewhere on the premises, one would assume."

I shook my head. "He'd want to make sure we didn't start what he would consider trouble again. He knew we were here to observe the Hartwells. Why wasn't he in the theater? Why didn't he intercede when Mr. Hartwell Senior came at you with his cane?"

"I don't know what you're getting at."

I halted our pace and turned to face him. "I am getting at the fact that Mr. Bennett must have left the Casino, or he would right now be escorting us out. But tell me, considering his view that you and I tend to make trouble, what could be so important as to take him away while we're still here?"

There was no apparent answer. We proceeded to the entryway, where Derrick asked the man at the general admission booth if he had seen Mr. Bennett leave.

"Indeed, sir. He left with Mr. Ellsworth about a quarter hour ago."

"Mr. Ellsworth?" I murmured with no small surprise.

"Indeed, miss. A message came and the two hurried off. Would you like to leave a message for Mr. Bennett?"

"No, thank you," I said. Derrick and I hurried out to the street. "It would seem Mr. Ellsworth is over his anguish concerning the burning of his property and the death of his shop manager."

"So it would," Derrick agreed.

"Are you thinking what I'm thinking?"

During our rush to reach Thames Street, Derrick and I admitted we could be very far off the mark in our suspicions. But I didn't think so.

By all appearances, Lower Thames Street, cloaked in a fine ocean fog that formed golden halos around the gas lanterns, was quiet and fairly deserted. But looks could be deceiving. From rooms above and behind shops came the sounds of muffled laughter and music, a crash of glass, a loud thud as though someone had been thrown against a wall. As we came around the corner from Bath Road, a figure darted from the landward side across the street to the closest wharf. Farther down, two men and a woman staggered along the sidewalk. Instinctively I set my hand in the crook of Derrick's arm. I had professed not to fear any Newporter, but Derrick's reminder that not everyone in the dock area hailed from Newport sent a chill across my shoulders.

Quickly and without speaking we traveled the several blocks to Carrington's Wharf. Along the way we passed the burned-out hull of Ellsworth Cigars. Although the wreckage had been cleared from the street, the stench of the fire assaulted my senses. I looked away as the horrific memories of the fire and the man who died raised gooseflesh on my arms. We reached Carrington's Wharf and had barely set foot onto the entrance when a noise sent us lurching back into the shadow of the warehouse overlooking the street. Derrick pulled me farther along until we reached the recess of a doorway, and there he pressed me behind him as a clip-clopping and rumbling wheels identified the sound we'd heard. A vehicle pulled away from the wharf and turned southward on Thames Street. Derrick peered around the corner of the doorway.

"A delivery wagon of some kind," he whispered. His body eased away from mine and he stepped slowly back out onto the sidewalk. I followed, craning to see the wagon over his shoulder. It stood low to the ground, its bed enclosed in wooden walls, with double doors at the rear. The driver was not in much of a hurry, for the dray kept to a slow and steady—almost careful—pace.

"Did you see who's driving it?"

He shook his head. "Stay here. I'll be right back."

Before I could respond he crept past the wharf and then into the street, where he hurried to catch up. With a sharp gaze I followed his progress until both he and the wagon turned onto Lee Avenue and headed away from the harbor.

I suddenly felt very much alone. The surrounding noises became amplified; the muted voices now seemed to surround me, and the laughter from open windows took on a mocking and sinister note. I pressed closer to the mist-dampened building beside me—cowering, I suppose—but at the same time gave myself a shake. Derrick hadn't gone far. He'd be back soon enough, before anything could possibly happen to me. If I had to, I could run to the Blue Moon and seek help there. A little voice inside me reminded me, however, that I would have to make it past numerous drunken men in the downstairs tavern before I would reach the safety of Madam Heidi's domain.

Once again, I became aware of the odor of soot and charred wood mingling with the salty, fishy scents from the harbor. It drew my gaze northward, to the blackened hole where Ellsworth Cigars had once stood a few streets down. Through the darkness I detected motion, silent and stealthy, a shadow moving through the blacker shadows. I should have stayed put, but I moved closer, easing along the sidewalk, staying close to the buildings beside me and hoping the fog muffled my form and my footsteps.

The shadow picked its way across the rubble where the shop's street façade once stood, and as the figure stepped onto the sidewalk the nearby street lamp illuminated a balding head and grim profile. Just before he jammed a flat crowned hat over that receding hairline, familiarity struck me. With a stifled gasp I drew into a gap between buildings, sucking in my breath to fit between them, feeling both my back and my front slide along the damp, none-too-clean shingles.

Had Robert Clarkson seen me? Heard me? I waited, my heart suspended in my chest. His footsteps receded along the street, and I exhaled.

What business could the Rhode Island senator have at the

blackened ruins of another man's property, and in the dark, no less? He carried no lantern, so what could he have been looking for? Had he been present during the fire, when so many others crowded Thames Street to view the destruction? I couldn't remember. His footsteps echoed along the street toward Bath Road. Leaning, I peeked out from my hiding place and saw his coattails swing out behind him as he turned a corner and disappeared.

Gratefully, I slid out from between the buildings. I brushed halfheartedly at my clothing and hurried back the way I'd come. Surely Derrick should have returned by now. Was he searching the wharf for me? I could have called out his name, but some instinct prevented me from doing so. I had every right to be here, walking along a Newport street, yet the notion no longer held any sense of safety for me. I reached the entrance to Carrington's Wharf and saw no sign of Derrick. Foreboding slithered up my spine, and at the sound of a footstep behind me, I whirled.

Chapter 14

The startled gasp that escaped my lips might have become a scream had I not instantly recognized the face before me. My heart gradually slowed. "Oh, it's you. Good heavens, you gave me such a fright."

"What are you doing here—uh—Miss Cross, is it?" The fair-haired young man I'd previously encountered on Carrington's Wharf offered me a look of both concern and curiosity. Twice now he had intervened between me and Anthony Dobbs, and because of that I believed I had nothing to fear from him.

"Yes, I'm Miss Cross. And you are—?"

"You can call me Jonas."

I wondered briefly if that was his given name or surname, but I merely nodded.

"You shouldn't be here alone, Miss Cross. The wharves aren't safe at night." As if to prove his point, a shriek tumbled from the upper windows of the Blue Moon, followed by a burst of male laughter. We both waited to hear what might follow. Someone began pounding on a piano. "Are you looking for someone?"

I regarded Jonas. Never before had I heard him speak so many words, and now I identified his accent as originating in Providence. Despite his towheaded youthfulness, he had a rough look about him, like most dockworkers. He was bareheaded and wore ill-fitting work clothes, his shirtsleeves rolled to the elbows.

"No, I'm here with someone."

He smiled. "An imaginary friend?"

"No, he . . . he went to check on something." My chin inched higher. For some reason I felt a need to justify my being there, until I realized I might ask him the same thing. "Why are you on the wharf at night?"

"I have a room just over there." He pointed down the street to a ramshackle house with a ROOMS FOR RENT sign hanging crooked on its hinges.

Yes, I wanted to say, *but why here? And why now, at this particular time?* Did he have anything to do with the wagon that pulled away from the wharf? And had he seen Robert Clarkson leaving Ellsworth Cigars?

"Did you . . . see anything strange just now?"

"Strange? Like what, miss? Thames Street can be a strange place at night." He flashed a smile that mocked slightly, yet not without kindness.

I decided to take the opportunity to ask an entirely different question. "Do you know Lilah Buford? From the Blue Moon?"

Clearly taken aback, he coughed lightly. "I'm surprised *you* know of Lilah Buford, or the Blue Moon, miss."

"Then you do know her?"

"Well, not in the biblical sense, no indeed, miss. But yes, I know of her. I've seen her hereabouts."

"And do you know anything about what's happened to her?"

"Some folks say she disappeared. Others say she's dead." He shrugged. "That's about all I know."

Footsteps approached from the south, echoing along the building fronts. I turned to see Derrick striding toward me. Upon seeing me he broke into a run, a fierce expression on his handsome features. I held up a hand to signal that all was well. Even so, he came to stand possessively close to me.

"Derrick, this is Jonas. Brady and I have him to thank for calling off Anthony Dobbs the other day. And a time before that as well. Jonas, this is my friend Mr. Andrews."

Jonas didn't extend his hand, but merely nodded and murmured, "Mr. Andrews." Then he hooked his thumbs into his suspenders. "Now that Miss Cross isn't alone anymore, I'll be going."

Was there something slightly accusatory in that statement? Derrick apparently thought so, for he scowled and said, "Tell me, Jonas. Is it common for deliveries to be made at this wharf at this time of night?"

Jonas had half turned away. Without quite turning back, he offered that playful smile again. "Depends on what kind of deliveries you mean."

"So anything brought in now would be of the black market variety?"

Jonas rubbed at his chin as he considered Derrick's question. "Could be. Or could be something someone doesn't want generally known."

"Such as?" I prompted.

He shrugged. "Such as whatever goods some of them cottagers don't want their neighbors knowing about. Heard a story about one of those Vanderbilts, that when she had her house built everything was delivered in secret so the neighbors wouldn't know what she was up to until she was good and ready to show them."

Ah, yes, my aunt Alva. She had enclosed her Bellevue Avenue property within high walls for four years until Marble House was completed in 1892 and ready to be unveiled to the world.

"And you had nothing to do with a delivery that came in just tonight?" Derrick persisted.

Jonas's head tilted. "Mr. Andrews, sounds like you're accusing me of something. And here I was, just out for some air when I happened upon Miss Cross, standing very much alone where she shouldn't be."

Derrick rested his gaze on Jonas a long moment. I could sense his ruminations, and I wanted to remind him that thus far, Jonas had only been of help to me, never a threat.

And yet . . . a sensation nagged, perhaps because I had learned to trust Derrick's instincts as much as my own. Jonas did seem always to be on hand at opportune moments. Coincidence? Or did he make a habit of following trouble?

"I'm not accusing you," Derrick said calmly, more so than he felt, judging by the tension in his stance. "I'm asking if you happened to see a delivery here tonight. A vehicle drove away only minutes ago."

"I hadn't come out yet, because I didn't see anything or anyone until I happened upon Miss Cross."

Derrick nodded and bade the man good evening. I did likewise, and we set off the way we came, toward Bath Road.

"I think he's lying," Derrick murmured.

"I don't see why."

"The delivery was picked up at the wharf, and there he was, on the very same wharf. I cannot believe he had nothing to do with it."

I sighed. "Never mind Jonas for now. Were you able to see who drove the wagon?"

He ignored my question. "I shouldn't have left you alone."

"That doesn't matter now."

"Doesn't it? I understand this man, Jonas, has done you a good turn or two, but why was he loitering about like that?"

"Derrick, he lives in the area. He's allowed to walk in his neighborhood."

"At this time of night?"

"We're out walking at this time of night," I reminded him.

"Exactly, and with good reason. What's his reason?"

The question reminded me of another nighttime loiterer, whom I'd nearly forgotten about in the interim. "Jonas wasn't the only person out and about. I believe I saw Robert Clarkson prowling through Ellsworth's Cigars."

Derrick stopped us short. "Clarkson? When?"

"While you were following the wagon. I heard noises from the building, so I moved down the street—"

"I asked you to stay where you were."

I shrugged. "The question is what brought Robert Clarkson to the neighborhood?"

"I should never have left you."

"You already said that. Come." We reached the remnants of the cigar shop, and I crossed the street to it. Derrick followed close at my heels. "What do you suppose Mr. Clarkson was doing here? Searching for something? Something he might have dropped the night of the fire? You do realize he may have already been searching when we first walked by."

"Are you suggesting a Rhode Island senator set fire to a commercial property?"

My shoulders drooped as I reached the scorched pavement outside the shop. The bitter odors knifed at my throat and clogged my nose. I turned away. "I don't know what I'm suggesting. There are so many unclear connections to Lilah and to the Wetmores."

Derrick's hand alighted gently on my shoulder. "Even if Robert Clarkson had something to do with Lilah's death and wished ill on the Wetmores, I can think of no reason why he would commit arson on Dominic Ellsworth's property."

"Then why was he here?" I snapped, then shook my head contritely. "I'm sorry. I have no reason to be tetchy with you."

"Are you certain it was Clarkson?"

"Fairly certain." Frowning, I turned back to view the shop. "It's terribly dark inside. He didn't have a lantern, at least not that I saw."

"Then perhaps he wasn't searching. Perhaps he was . . ." Derrick sighed. "Perhaps as a state official he felt a responsibility to view the scene." He held up a hand before I could comment. "I know, I know. In the dark?" He shook his head.

"Come." I slipped my hand onto his forearm and we set off walking again. "Tell me, what did you learn when you followed the wagon? Did you see the driver?"

"I most certainly did. When they rounded the corner onto Spring Street, I was able to get up alongside the wagon without being seen, and the sounds of the horse and the wagon wheels covered my footsteps." He turned a severe face toward me. "It was Bennett and Ellsworth, all right."

"What do you suppose they were hauling?"

"That I don't know. I'd have followed them longer to see where they took their cargo, except I couldn't leave you alone indefinitely."

"Oh, dear." A wash of guilt swept over me. "I ought not have come. I'm sorry. I was a liability tonight."

"Never." He covered my hand where it rested in the crook of his elbow. "We'll discover what they're up to."

"I don't see how. It's not as if they're going to store whatever they just drove away with in Mr. Bennett's driveway."

"Isn't the next leg of the polo match between the Westchester and Meadowview clubs tomorrow?"

"As long as it doesn't rain. Why?" We turned onto Bath Road.

"Ellsworth and Bennett are teammates, aren't they?" Without waiting for my reply, Derrick flashed me a knowing look. "You and I must make a point of being there."

*   *   *

The next day dawned cloudy, and I worried the match might not take place. I didn't know what I expected to find there, but Derrick had been so certain the night before that we would learn something. But if that something involved Mr. Bennett and Mr. Ellsworth, would it have anything to do with Lilah and the Wetmores?

A few drops splattered the windows by the time I descended to the morning room. Nanny noticed my pained look. "It's just a sprinkle, Emma. Are you planning some kind of outing today?"

"Today is the second match between Westchester and Meadowview, and I don't wish it to be canceled due to rain."

Katie, who had laid out breakfast on the sideboard, took her seat at the table. She glanced up at me from beneath her lashes. I saw her hopeful look and smiled. "If the match goes on as planned, yes, you may attend," I told her. "Nanny? Would you care to go?"

"Not me. All those horses galloping after a ball. Men waving sticks about. Someone is likely to be hurt."

"I suppose you could say that about any sport."

"Perhaps, but the horses don't have much say in the matter, do they?" She shuddered. "I haven't been to polo since your great uncle William Henry Vanderbilt had to put down one of his ponies after a mishap on the field. Such a lamentable thing."

I filled my coffee cup and returned to the table. Patch wandered in from the kitchen corridor. He circled the table, accepting pettings from Katie and Nanny before offering me his ears to be scratched. Amid a wave of affection I gazed down at his floppy ears and dark velvet eyes, which mirrored my own sentiments back up at me. Would I attend any sport that put innocent dogs at risk? Such pastimes existed, and I considered them cruel. Was a game like polo any different? "Point taken, Nanny. But it isn't for the sake of a diversion that I wish to attend."

Before I could explain, Katie blurted, "I won't be going either, then."

"Nonsense, Katie." I reached across to her and patted her hand. "We all know it isn't for the games that you go. It's sitting up on Morton Hill in a pretty dress and watching all the other people, isn't it?"

She blushed over her porridge. "That's true, miss. Still and all . . ."

"Actually, Katie, you might be able to assist me." I sipped my coffee and swallowed a forkful of eggs to calm my rumbling stomach. "As I was saying, it isn't for the polo I'm going. Katie, you remember Anthony Dobbs, don't you?"

She cringed. "I do, miss."

"If you see him, keep an eye on him for me. And his workmate, too, if they are together. He's younger than Mr. Dobbs, with dark blondish hair and blue eyes, not that I expect you to get close enough to see his eyes. The man's name is Jonas, and thus far he seems a decent fellow, but one can never be too careful. If you see them at the match, I only want you to note where they go. Specifically, whether they leave Morton Hill."

Nanny gave a harrumph. "That's terribly vague, don't you think?"

A splash of wind-borne rain struck the windows. I sagged in my chair. "It might not matter after all, at least not today."

Nanny followed my gaze to the garden outside the rain-dotted window. "It'll blow over soon."

I hoped she was right.

A knocking at the front door brought me to my feet. I found Jesse outside with his collar turned up and his hat pulled low against the drizzle and cool breeze. "Good morning, Emma. I thought you might be interested to hear what happened after you and Derrick left the Casino last night."

"And I have things to tell you, as well," I said, frowning at the clouds. "Come in."

We settled in the parlor, and I bade him share his news first.

"The Hartwells claim to have no knowledge whatsoever about Lilah Buford," he began. "But they were wary, Emma. I'd go so far as to say afraid."

"Did you talk to the brother and sister?"

"The son, yes, but not the daughter. The parents flat-out refused to allow it, and I couldn't demand otherwise, not without due cause."

"I suppose I can understand. She's very young." I couldn't help wondering if they feared that Nanette, in her innocence, might divulge something they didn't want known. "What about the grandfather?"

Jesse nodded and tapped a finger at the air. "Now he's another story. I got him to admit he'd become aware of Lilah following the family around at the Casino, and on one occasion through town during the day. She kept her distance, but he claimed it didn't take him long to realize she might be an unsavory character. Says he feared she might make some kind of trouble, or demand money."

"How did you persuade him to admit all that?"

"I threatened him with incarceration for disorderly conduct and threatening Derrick."

My eyes narrowed as a possibility occurred to me. "Could the old man have killed Lilah? He's got a temper and violent tendencies. And he admits he thought Lilah posed some kind of threat to his family."

"But what connection to the Wetmores? So far I haven't discovered any, but I'm going over to Chateau sur Mer later today to ask them what they might know of the Hartwells."

I angled my chin in skepticism. "I hope they'll speak with you. You remember what happened last time. We were practically thrown off the premises."

"You convinced Mrs. Wetmore to see reason." Jesse said this with a tinge of pride. He pushed out of his chair and came to join me on the sofa, sitting close. "Tell me your news."

I repeated what had occurred on Thames Street the previous night—the delivery wagon, Robert Clarkson, all of it. Too late did I notice the storm clouds gathering in his expression, or I might have edited my version of events.

His nose became pinched, his hands clenched. Finally, he blew out a breath between his teeth. "The man brings you down to Lower Thames in the middle of the night and then leaves you standing on a street corner? What in Sam Hill could he be thinking?"

I winced as his voice rose. "Don't shout. We needed to know who drove that wagon. Derrick never went so far that he wouldn't have heard me if I'd needed him." This might not have been strictly true, but Jesse didn't need to know that.

"And who is this Jonas character?"

"I've told you. He works at Carrington's Wharf, and probably anywhere else that will hire him."

"What was he doing prowling around the wharf after hours like that?"

"You sound like Derrick." That comment earned me a warning look, so I hastened on. "He said merely that he needed some air. Perhaps he had just come from the Blue Moon and didn't wish to say. Considering that he did me the favor of waiting with me until Derrick returned, I certainly had no reason to interrogate him. But what about Robert Clarkson? His actions seem highly suspicious."

"It's strange, I'll admit, but then so is James Bennett and

Dominic Ellsworth driving away with a delivery. Why didn't they send servants?"

"Obviously, they're hiding something, and that's why Derrick and I want to be at that polo match today. If nothing else, we might overhear something during the breaks." I glanced out the parlor windows at the front of my property. The drizzle continued, yet a hint of sunlight brightened my lawn. I felt a ray of hope. "I should go up and prepare."

He stilled me with a hand on mine. "Have you forgotten? You won't have access to the club areas without your reporter's credentials."

I smiled. "I haven't told anyone I was let go. Have you?" At the shake of his head, I grinned. "Then unless I run into Ed Billings, whom I'm fairly certain I can avoid, no one will be the wiser."

The clouds persisted, but broke into luminous swaths that scuttled across the sky, thrusting light and shadow over the polo grounds. I should have trusted in Nanny's prediction, for she always had been able to read the weather as keenly as a sailor.

Though Derrick and I drove together in my carriage, we parted as we entered the grounds proper. Hearing no objections, I took my typical place along the sidelines with pad and pencil at the ready. He entered the grandstand, not to sit but to circulate. I scanned the milling spectators, decked out as usual in top hats or boaters and cutaways for the men, gay silks and cottons and wide plumed hats for the women. Pavilions fluttered in the breeze, while footmen carried drinks and delicacies brought here in service carriages.

In the colorful confusion, familiar faces took shape. The Hartwells occupied seats around a table beneath a striped pavilion. Unlike many of the other groups, they sat alone in their shaded haven, with no guests around them. It struck me as rather sad, and I found myself wishing Grace would introduce some of her acquaintances to them—in earnest this time. Perhaps what Jesse had interpreted as wary behavior was instead the result of their constantly dashed hopes of being accepted into society.

My gaze traveled until I spotted Grace and Neily's bright blue pavilion. As last time, several friends lounged alongside them, enjoying cool drinks and luncheon fare kept chilled on ice. They were chatting, laughing, and appeared entirely carefree. All except Neily. He sat slightly apart from the others and stared into space. The worry I'd first experienced at seeing him days ago set in once more. I so wanted my cousin to be happy.

I dismissed those thoughts. The referees had entered the field, and behind them came the riders. The handicaps had been reassigned, resulting in Westchester being granted a slight advantage. It only made sense, considering the Meadowview Club's players were considered some of the best in the world. I wondered about the debate that must have raged between the two teams, and the deliberations among the Competition and Handicap Committees.

The two teams made a circuit of the field, riding close to the rails near the grandstand. A roar went up, and I used the distraction to continue studying the crowd. No one would notice whether or not I followed the progress of the players. Most in the audience would scarcely notice me at all, except for those ladies who stood and twirled about, allowing me generous views of their daytime finery for my Fashions and Fancies page. If they only knew such a page no longer existed.

Present, too, were the players of another sort. The first familiar face I spotted was that of Harry Lehr, on the second tier of the grandstand. Far from being thwarted by Maude Wetmore's lack of interest, he appeared happy enough, one might say elated, to be ensconced in the shaded box presided over by Mrs. Astor. Seated along with them were Mamie Fish, Tessie Oelrichs, and my aunt Alva, who two years ago had become Mrs. Oliver Belmont. Together they made up what society termed the Big Four—New York's, and therefore Newport's, most powerful doyennes. As I watched, another impeccably dressed matriarch joined them—Mrs. Lavinia Andrews. She moved through the box accepting greetings from the others. Mr. Lehr sprang to his feet at her approach and kissed both her cheeks. For some reason, these leaders of society had adopted Mr. Lehr into their circle. They found him charming and amusing, or so I'd been told. Certainly one of them would find him a suitable wife, and he'd forget all about the indifferent Miss Wetmore.

Robert Clarkson, I was surprised to discover, had joined Neily and Grace and the rest of their party, which again included Brady and Hannah. I was glad for that. Stanford Whittaker hovered in the grandstand among a group of men that included two husbands of the Big Four—Mr. Belmont and Mr. Stuyvesant Fish. Also present were Frederick Jones and Joseph Drexel. And Derrick. He had made his way to them. They and several other men of the Four Hundred stood along the rail of the second tier, talking rapidly, waving their hands about, and shouting. Meanwhile, a clerk in their midst frantically scribbled in a ledger he balanced on one hand. I understood. Wagers, high ones, were being set before the match began.

Ogden Goelet, who owned nearby Ochre Court, tossed out the first ball. The Wetmores, of course, were not present. I glanced back into the stands until I caught Derrick's eye. He nodded slightly and continued his conversation with the other men without missing a beat. For appearances' sake I observed the action for the first few minutes, following along the sidelines and pretending to take notes. Then I hurried beyond the grandstand with the intention of making my way over to Morton Hill.

My brother's voice hailed me from behind.

When I stopped, he ran to catch up to me, arriving slightly out of breath. "I have something interesting to tell you about your sojourn down Thames Street last night."

With a slight wave of annoyance, I demanded, "How did you know about that?"

"Derrick asked me to strike up a conversation with Robert Clarkson and pretend it was I who saw him, rather than you."

My annoyance persisted, rather irrationally, I will admit. Of course Derrick would want to shield me from unnecessary unpleasantness, or worse, a direct threat resulting from our investigation. I appreciated his thoughtfulness, yet at the same time it irked me that such precautions were deemed necessary only due to my being a woman. These were the same considerations that resulted in my losing my employment at the *Observer*.

With a start I realized Brady didn't yet know I'd been dismissed. Now was not the time to enlighten him. I therefore swallowed my notions of inequity, for the time being. "Did Mr. Clarkson tell you anything?"

"As a matter of fact, he did. I told him I was down on Thames Street last night and said I could have sworn I saw him coming out of the Ellsworth property. I added that I found this exceedingly odd."

"The direct approach. What excuse did you give for being in the area?"

"I didn't." Brady drew himself up. "He may think what he likes, just as you did, Em, when we met at the Blue Moon."

The irony of his cavalier attitude continued to chafe, but I chose to ignore it. "Tell me what he said."

"Something surprising. Seems the manager, Bertrand

Styles, was a fellow councilman in Tiverton earlier in Clarkson's political career. Styles was something of a mentor to Clarkson, even after he retired from politics. Clarkson claims he was at the shop last night in remembrance of his friend, that he was out walking and simply felt compelled to go down there, and . . . I don't know, he didn't quite make it clear."

"Sentimental reasons," I supplied, and Brady nodded. "Did you believe him?"

"I do believe the two men were well acquainted. It would be easy enough to verify and Clarkson would know that. It would also be easy to verify whether they were political allies or enemies. Again, Clarkson would be taking quite a chance in lying about something like that. As to whether he might have had anything to do with the fire . . ." Brady shook his head. "That I can't say, Em."

"All right, thank you, Brady."

"Where are you off to?"

"Only to Morton Hill. I've got Katie on the lookout for Anthony Dobbs and his workmate Jonas, who also happened to be near the wharf last night."

Brady's brows drew tight. "You're not going up there alone. I'll come with you."

"Don't be silly. Go back to Hannah. You and I together will only attract more attention and likely end in trouble with Mr. Dobbs. I'm merely going to ask Katie if she's seen them."

Brady hesitated, shuffling his feet and shoving his hands in his coat pockets. "I don't like it."

"Nothing is going to happen to me in a crowd of this size," I assured him, and gave him a little push. "Now go back to Hannah."

He grinned rather crookedly and went on his way.

I had made a point of not dressing as fashionably as at the

last match. I wanted to be able to mix with the ordinary Newporters this time without attracting attention, and now I did just that, wandering in and among families and groups seated on blankets and enjoying the day. For the hardworking, local Newporters, a sporting event such as this presented as much of an opportunity for a picnic as to follow the progress of horses and riders.

A completely different atmosphere than that to be found on the grandstand enveloped me. If the wagering gentlemen of the Four Hundred had seemed lively, here an almost carnival mood prevailed. Hawkers wove paths throughout the hill, enticing the crowd with such treats as steamed oysters and clam fritters, jellied eels, johnnycakes, pickles, and roasted nuts. The myriad aromas made me long to simply join my fellow Newporters and forget about the troubles that had brought me here.

I found Katie sitting on a blanket with a couple of housemaids she knew from when she worked at The Breakers. All three wore bright summer frocks of cotton lawn and wide straw hats secured with ribbons beneath their chins—their very best. And why not? Being out in public, especially in a crowd of this size, happened rarely in the life of a maid.

Before the other two recognized me, I signaled for Katie to follow me. I led the way over the crest of the hill to the slope facing Coggeshall Avenue and, beyond that, Bellevue Avenue. I wasted no time in getting to the point. "Have you seen Mr. Dobbs and his friend?"

"I have, miss. They're sitting near the north end of the hill, with a passel of rough types. Dockworkers, no doubt." She gave a disapproving lift of her pale eyebrows. "They're not drinking lemonade, that I can tell you. Some of the things I heard coming out of their mouths . . . If I were you, miss, I'd steer well clear."

"I intend to, Katie. I only wish to keep an eye on them.

There may be something untoward going on at this match."
Though Derrick's suspicions had turned to the match and
the men we'd seen driving away in the delivery wagon last
night, I couldn't dismiss the fact that Jonas had been right
there at the wharf as well. And I'd learned that where Jonas
was, Mr. Dobbs wasn't far behind.

"What do you mean, miss? Fighting or suchlike?"

"I'm not sure, really. Perhaps something to do with the
match itself."

Katie looked doubtful. "I don't see how the likes of Mr.
Dobbs could muddle the match, Miss Emma, nor anyone
else sitting on Morton Hill. We only come to watch, and
there's some who'll lay a wager or two. If there is mischief
afoot on the field, it's the fine gentlemen you should be
looking to."

I nodded, seeing no reason to enlighten Katie about the
odd and intricate connections that emanated from Carrington's Wharf. It would only have burdened her mind and
thrown a shadow over her day. I told her to return to her
friends and asked her to continue keeping watch. Then I
made my way to the north end of the hill. Sure enough, an
unruly knot of unkempt laborers lounged on the grass,
propped on their elbows with their legs sprawled. I kept my
distance, but the lyrics of a bawdy song reached my ears, and
I noticed then that families had given the group a wide berth.
A couple of the men appeared to be dozing under their hats,
or could they have passed out from drink so early in the
day? The idea appalled me, yet I had no doubts as to the contents of the hip flasks being passed around.

I moved farther back but kept my eyes on Dobbs and Jonas,
sitting among the group but not beside each other. Jonas appeared engaged in a game of cards, while Dobbs sipped slowly
from the bottle passed to him before wiping his lips on his
sleeve. A bearded fellow stretched out his hand, and when

Mr. Dobbs failed to comply, he delivered an impatient blow to Dobbs's elbow, prompting him to reluctantly pass the bottle. They exchanged words that rivaled the worst bawdy song in its coarseness.

In short, I learned that neither man was doing anything suspicious, or anything one wouldn't expect from them. The first chukker ended. The riders walked their horses off the field and the spectators both on Morton Hill and the grand-stand seemed to expand slightly, as if with a collective breath. People stretched their legs, others laid back against the hillside to look at the sky, while still others foraged into their picnic baskets. Jonas and Anthony Dobbs seemed disinclined to move, so with a final glance I started down the hill.

About halfway down I froze. From here I had a full, un-obstructed view of the grounds, including the shaded pad-dock. The horses used during the first chukker were unsaddled, and grooms set about brushing them down. Meanwhile, two fresh sets of horses were saddled and readied for the next chukker. Suddenly I realized what might have sent James Bennett and Dominic Ellsworth to the wharf last night.

Chapter 15

The second chukker proceeded without controversy, and I detected nothing suspicious about the horses or the match itself. When the chukker ended, the stomping of the divots commenced, a privilege reserved for those on the grandstand. Beyond the field, the players gathered beneath two tents beside the paddock, one for each team. Tired, perspiring horses were led to the shaded side of the enclosed circle, while those that would play next were saddled and walked by their grooms. To my untrained eye, the animals all looked very much the same. To the riders, grooms, and Competition Committee, the differences would be evident, but only upon close scrutiny.

I watched as Derrick made his way down to the grass and headed in his direction. After the shade of the grandstand, he squinted in the more direct sunlight. He removed his top hat when he reached me. "Brady told me about his conversation with Robert Clarkson."

"Never mind that for the moment." I glanced about, ensuring we would not be overheard. I needn't have worried.

The activity on the field proved far too entertaining for anyone to be concerned with a pair strolling and talking.

"Mr. Bennett and Mr. Ellsworth may have conspired to cheat in today's match. I believe that wagon last night contained what Brady would call a 'ringer.'" At Derrick's blank expression, I clarified, "Like bringing in a highly skilled player but not revealing the extent of his talents."

"Yes, I know what a ringer is. But—" His mouth opened on an *O*, and he nodded slowly. "A horse brought in to replace one of either James Bennett's or Dominic Ellsworth's."

"No one will be expecting an animal of greater power or agility than they had seen previously. Is it against the rules to do so?"

"It's certainly against the rules of gentlemanly fair play. But yes, a replacement horse, unannounced, would skew the odds wildly in favor of those betting on Westchester, assuming the team won. The Meadowview losses would be considerable."

"No wonder they picked up the horse in secret. If indeed it was a horse."

A bell sounded, and the stomping of the divots ceased. The people on the field shook their feet to dislodge any remaining bit of earth on their costly shoes and boots, and began filing back onto the grandstand. An eager roar went up from Morton Hill. Players, refreshed from their quarter-hour intermission, exited the tents. In the distance Dominic Ellsworth hoisted himself onto the paddock rail and swung himself over. James Bennett entered with the others through the main gate. Which one of them would ride the unauthorized horse?

"Derrick, George Wetmore is on the Competition Committee. Do you suppose Mr. Bennett and Mr. Ellsworth wanted him out of the way so they could carry out their deception?"

"While that part seems feasible, murdering Lilah is rather extreme, don't you think?"

I saw his point, but I didn't quite nod in agreement. "Perhaps not, considering the amount of the wagers that could be at stake. And if Lilah overheard something . . ." My heart pattered. Is *this* what Lilah overheard at the wharf, and wished to warn Mr. Wetmore about? Did she lose her life over a sporting event?

Derrick and I were about to make our way to the paddocks to see what we could learn, when the shadow of a plumed hat fell across our path. Derrick lurched to a halt and stepped partway in front of me, as if to shield me from impending harm.

"Hello, Mother. What are you doing back in Newport?"

Lavinia Andrews expelled a harsh breath and swept closer. "Yes, I am back in Newport. *Why* didn't you tell me about this ridiculous decision of your father's? I was caught entirely unawares when I went home. Why, I could barely form a coherent argument about why your father must immediately rescind this change to his will. The very idea—you're his son. His *only* son."

"Would it be more palatable if you and Father had another son with which to replace me?" Derrick spoke in a kindly tone; I don't believe he meant to upset his mother further, but his jest was ill-timed.

Mrs. Andrews shuddered, and the dignified beauty I'd come to associate with her hardened to a cold, crystalline hostility that found its mark—with me. "My son should be at home, proving to his father that he is a loyal member of this family. But no. He lingers here, and why does he do so, Miss Cross?"

"Mother . . ." Derrick's tone took on a subtle warning. I stood frozen, locked within Mrs. Andrews's anger, both shocked and appalled to have become her target. Yes, I had been the recipient of her censure in the past, on more than one occasion. Yet for all the world, I could not have defended myself just then. I was too bewildered by this latest onslaught—by this woman's utter loss of self-possession.

Her nose flared until two sharp white lines stood out on either side. Her lips were pinched, her eyes small and narrow within their lashes. Loathing poured from her person. "He remains because of you. Because you have ensnared him in your web of lies and deceptions . . ."

Derrick stepped fully in front of me, effectively placing himself between me and his mother's wrath. "Mother, you don't know what you're saying. I am here of my own volition and no one else's—not even Emma's. Just as I went to Italy last summer of my own free will. I went because it was the right thing to do, just as being here now is the right thing to do. I'm sorry you can't accept that, but when you think about it, you'll see that you're being as stubborn as Father. That is your right, of course, just as it's Father's right to bar me from the family business and cut me from his will. I assure you, neither circumstance will have the slightest bearing on my actions."

As I watched over Derrick's shoulder, his mother gaped in obvious horror. I derived no pleasure from the sight. She was his mother, and she believed her argument to be in her son's best interests. I didn't have to like her, but I couldn't fault her for her fiercely protective instincts.

I stepped out from behind her son and lightly touched his forearm. "Derrick, please, this isn't right," I whispered. His mother's gaze slid to me, and her mouth jerked open.

Derrick didn't give her the chance to speak. "I'm sorry, Mother, but I cannot allow you to continue speaking unkindly to Miss Cross. If you'll excuse us—"

I was about to protest when from the field came a frenzied

whinny and a shout, taken up by others. Dominic Ellsworth's horse danced wildly on its hind legs. It came down hard on all fours, kicked up with its back legs, came down again, and circled sharply. Cries came from the grandstand, and shouts of "Help him!" The animal shied away from the other horses and repeatedly kicked out with his hind legs while Mr. Ellsworth struggled to bring him under control. I waited for the referees to call a halt to the chukker, but neither did. The Westchester team might have been playing with only three men, for all the good Mr. Ellsworth was doing them now. Was this horse the cargo delivered last night?

Another jarring kick sent Mr. Ellsworth tumbling headfirst over the horse's withers and landing with a teeth-shaking thud on his back on the grass. He tried to roll out of the way but the horse, in its agitation, bucked forward. A hoof struck Mr. Ellsworth in the ribs. He curled onto his side, drew up his knees, and tucked his head to shield himself as much as possible.

This all happened in a matter of seconds. Then Mr. Bennett and two other players, one from the Meadowview team, sprang from their saddles and closed in around the frantic animal. Their movements were not rushed, but steady and decisive. Mr. Bennett appeared to be speaking to the horse. I couldn't hear the words but I saw his lips moving in a calm oration meant to soothe and reassure.

The grandstand seemed to be holding its combined breath. Even Morton Hill had gone silent but for a low murmur of speculation. Mrs. Andrews had moved away from us to view the activity, one hand pressed to her breastbone. Young girls and matrons alike stood craning their necks with hands pressed to their lips or clutching one another's hands for support.

James Bennett's equine skills proved invaluable. The horse came to a tense standstill, its flanks twitching, watching with one wide-open eye as the human crept closer. A groom walked out as well, but Mr. Bennett signaled with one hand without taking his gaze off the horse. Finally, he came up beside the animal, reached out slowly, and grasped the reins. He signaled again for the groom, who proceeded with similar caution and relieved Mr. Bennett of the horse.

Dr. Kennison, a local physician who tended to my family and many others here in town, hurried onto the field. By now the rest of the players had dismounted. I saw no movement from Mr. Ellsworth and, fearing the worst, I found myself mouthing a silent prayer for his well-being.

Derrick, who had gone to stand beside his mother, glanced back at me. I nodded and gestured for him to escort Mrs. Andrews back to the grandstand or wherever she wished to go. With another destination in mind, I hurried around the rear of the grandstand. My intention was to circle to the paddock, wait for the groom to return with his recalcitrant charge, and attempt to discover whether this was indeed a replacement horse. If so, Dominic Ellsworth's plan had backfired badly. Polo ponies must be trained gradually and carefully. This one had obviously been rushed onto the playing field.

Curiosity drove me. Perhaps this had nothing to do with Lilah Buford's death . . . but perhaps it did.

The back of the grandstand formed a wall that soared high above my head. The paddocks were just coming into view when I reached a stand of beech trees whose trailing branches swept the ground. Without warning an arm reached out to part the foliage, revealing silver hair slicked back beneath a top hat. A man's voice said, "About time you—" Mr. Hartwell Senior left off abruptly. He leaned on his cane, blinking at me, clearly startled. The surprise faded from his features, replaced by an almost feral anger. "You again. Why do you follow me? Why do you plague my family?"

"I'm not, sir. I didn't know you were—" It was my turn to break off as a suspicion took root. What was he doing out here, hidden by the grandstand and the giant beech? Had he just come from the paddocks? "Did you have something to do with Dominic Ellsworth's horse running wild just now? Have you done something to it?"

"You foolish girl." He waved his cane before my face and came toward me. I attempted to retreat, but my back came up against the grandstand wall. With nowhere to escape, I shut my eyes and braced for the blow.

"You there. Leave her be." The distinctive Providence intonations identified Jonas even before he rushed through the branches, appearing like an avenging angel from the shadows beneath the tree. From behind he gripped Mr. Hartwell's shoulder and spun him about, then pried the cane from the elderly man's fingers. Jonas brandished it at him in the same threatening manner Mr. Hartwell had taken with me. "Go on with you, old man. You'll do no mischief here. I've a mind to raise the alarm and hand you over to the police."

Pale and shaken, Mr. Hartwell turned back around and seized my wrist, tugging as if attempting to drag me along with him. Before I could so much as cry out, I heard a clunk and glimpsed a flash of silver beside the man's head. His top hat tumbled to the ground, followed by Mr. Hartwell himself. He crumpled to a heap at my feet. I stood over him, my heart pounding in my throat, my hands trembling.

"Good heavens" was all I could manage.

"I didn't want to do that. He forced my hand." Jonas shook his head sadly. "Poor, deranged man."

I exhaled a long, tremulous breath and attempted to calm my racing heart. "Where could he have intended to take me?"

"I can't say, miss." Still holding the cane, he looked me up and down. "Are you all right?"

I nodded. "Quite all right, thanks to you." I gazed down

at the unconscious man lying in the dirt. He'd plainly shown violent tendencies, not once but several times now. Could he have killed Lilah? Had he noticed her interest in his family and, wishing to maintain whatever secret they harbored, snapped her neck to silence her? "He's hurt. We'll need to get help."

Jonas moved beside me. "He doesn't deserve your kindness."

"You ought not to have struck him." I crouched beside Mr. Hartwell, feeling the side of his head for a lump. "He's an old man, he could be seriously injured."

"What choice did I have?"

"Go and get help. I'll stay with him."

"I can't leave you alone with him, miss."

"Jonas, please." I came to my feet. "Oh, very well. I'll go."

An uneasy sensation held me in place. I studied Jonas a moment, taking in his work clothes, his hands that were permanently blackened beneath the nails from shoveling coal, his bright blue eyes. The last time I had seen him, he was up on Morton Hill engaged in a card game with another dockworker, drinking, singing lurid songs, and paying little attention to the activity on and around the field. "What brought you down here, Jonas, and at such an opportune moment?"

He prodded the cane into the dirt as he spoke. "I saw the old man out here, and then I saw you coming along. I feared you might come to some harm, miss."

"But ... you couldn't have seen me here from Morton Hill. Nor Mr. Hartwell." I didn't like the doubt creeping over me. This man had intervened on my behalf twice before, but it seemed to me that his presence, at this precise moment, suggested he had some prior business here that had nothing to do with me. Could he have come to meet Mr. Hartwell by some prearranged agreement? But then ...

I gazed into his eyes, so clear and blue ... except for an

unusual flaw in one of them, an odd streak of amber that splashed across the iris of the left eye. I had seen that before . . . once before.

My mouth dropped open. "Lilah," I exclaimed, and then pain exploded inside my head and everything went black.

I woke to an incessant tapping at my cheeks and voices calling my name. I wanted it to stop, wanted to be left alone. My head pounded and I could feel my arms and legs akimbo in a most uncomfortable manner. I turned my face from side to side in hopes of avoiding whatever kept pattering against my cheeks. My efforts were in vain.

My eyes fluttered open. When daylight hit them I shut them again. The voices became louder.

"Emma, stay with us now."

"You must wake up, Emma. We're here, and you're safe."

The summons echoed like a hail from a dream, and I shook my head to clear it of a lingering fog. I forced my eyes open despite the sharpness of the light angling through the branches above my head. Derrick's and Jesse's worried faces hovered above me.

I struggled to sit up. One of them, I could not say which, slipped an arm beneath me to help me upright. Dizziness swarmed my brain and roiled in my stomach. I took deep breaths and focused on my lap to stop the world from spinning.

"What happened?" I managed breathlessly. I braved a glance around me. We were between a trailing beech and a high wall. "Where—where am I?"

"We're at the polo grounds," Derrick said. "Do you remember anything?"

"Polo? How . . ." I pressed a hand to the top of my head, which throbbed against my palm. "How did you find me?"

"Lucky for you, your maid, Katie, found you and alerted us," Jesse said.

At first that made no sense. "Katie?"

"I'm here, Miss Emma," my maid called from a short distance away. She stood hugging herself tightly beside the sweeping beech branches. She wore her best summer dress, and her straw sunhat had fallen off and hung from its ribbons down her back. Katie, enjoying a day off. At the polo grounds, watching from Morton Hill. Watching . . . as I had asked her to do . . .

My memory came hurtling back. "Mr. Hartwell, Jonas . . . they were here . . . and—" I pushed myself up higher, craning my neck. "Where is Mr. Hartwell? Jonas struck him. And he . . . he struck me."

It wasn't until I cast a look behind me that I saw the blanket—someone's ordinary picnic blanket from Morton Hill—covering what could only have been a body beneath. A pair of leather-clad feet stuck out from the bottom edge. Jesse placed a hand on my shoulder.

"Mr. Hartwell is dead," he said gently.

My hand went to my lips to catch my horrified gasp. "He was trying to *help* me. I thought he'd gone mad, thought he was trying to hurt me, that he even murdered Lilah, but—" I broke off, aghast, and met Jesse's and then Derrick's gazes. "It was Jonas. He's Lilah's brother. I'm sure of it. Madam Heidi thought he had died as a child, but he didn't. He couldn't have. And the missing photographs are of—"

"Slow down," Derrick said, pressing his hand to mine. "Missing photos?"

"From Lilah's album. It's her family photograph album, of her, her parents, her brother—and some are missing. I think there was another sibling. I think it was—*is*—Nanette Hartwell. Her grandfather was trying to protect her."

"This is crazy," Derrick murmured.

At that moment, two policemen came down along the grandstand wall carrying yet another blanket. Jesse gestured toward the body, then turned back to me. "It isn't crazy," he said. "It makes a darned lot of sense. Tell us exactly what happened, everything you can remember."

"If you *can* remember, that is," Derrick put in.

"I remember it all," I said evenly, and told them everything from my encounter with Mr. Hartwell, to Jonas appearing, to my sudden awareness of his relation to Lilah. Then I called to Katie. She hurried over and sank beside me. Tenderly she placed a palm against my cheek. "How did you come to find me here?" I asked her.

"I did what you asked me to do, Miss Emma. I kept an eye on Mr. Dobbs and his friend. When the friend went down Morton Hill, I went too."

"What about Mr. Dobbs? Did he leave the hill also?"

"No, miss, he stayed behind with the other dockworkers."

I looked up at Jesse. "All this time I'd been suspicious of Anthony Dobbs. I suppose I did him a disservice, didn't I?"

"Time will tell, Emma," he replied.

I turned back to Katie. "Thank you. You did well today."

"Oh, but if I'd only followed him more closely—oh, miss, I might have prevented him from hurting you. I didn't realize at first that you were here, too, and—"

"Nonsense, Katie. If you'd followed more closely, you would have been hurt, too. Thank you for doing exactly as you did."

A tide of crimson swept her face and tears sprang to her eyes. Jesse stood and helped her to her feet, then asked me, "Do you think you can stand? Or shall I send for an ambulance?"

I vehemently shook my head. "No ambulance." I reached out, and Derrick caught my arm. I leaned on him heavily as together we rose. I teetered a moment before my legs became able to support me, then widened my stance. "What about Mr. Ellsworth? Is he all right from his fall?"

"A few bruised ribs, but otherwise he'll be fine," Jesse replied. "He asked to be taken home. Dr. Kennison accompanied him, but I'll send for the doctor soon. I want him to take a look at you."

"I don't need a doctor," I insisted, resulting in some eye rolling from both gentlemen presently scrutinizing me as though I might shatter at any moment. "I'll be fine, I promise you. But Jesse, how is it you're here? I understand the policemen." I gestured to the two men conveying Mr. Hartwell away on the makeshift stretcher they'd fashioned from the blanket. There was always a policeman or two present at events of this size. "But you? Was I unconscious so long you had time to come all the way from town?"

"Indeed not, Emma." He removed his derby and swept the hair back off his brow. "I was already on my way here. We've been doing some checking. The onset of the burglaries happens to coincide with arrivals of both the Hartwells and this Jonas character. Jonas Boyd is his full name. I came to warn you both." He nodded at Derrick. "Considering all the other connections between Lilah, the Hartwells, the wharf, and the fact that this Jonas Boyd works at the wharf, I thought until we find out more there is no trusting any of them. It would seem I was right." A fond look softened his expression. "I'm only glad nothing worse happened to you."

Derrick took my hand and set it in the crook of his arm in a proprietary way. Jesse's mouth tightened, and an awkward silence fell. I cleared my throat. "Has anyone told the Hartwells what happened? They've lost a family member. They have to be told."

Derrick and Jesse both shook their heads. Derrick said, "We'd only discovered you minutes before we awakened you."

"I'll send a pair of officers to speak with them." Jesse's

manner changed, became brisk and businesslike. "Now that I know you're all right, Emma, I'm going after Jonas."

Derrick's jaw beaded. "I'll bring Emma home and then I'm coming with you."

"That'll take too much time," Jesse said with a shake of his head. "I'm heading back to town now. I want to check his boardinghouse. Logic says he'll be clearing out and trying to leave the island as soon as possible."

Katie stepped timidly forward. "I'll take Miss Emma home."

"I have a better idea." My comment led to groans from both Derrick and Jesse.

Derrick said, "Please, Emma. You've had enough excitement for one day." Jesse nodded his agreement.

"Take me to Chateau sur Mer. It's close and I'll be safe there. Someone needs to warn the Wetmores about Jonas and discover once and for all what the link is between them and Lilah. I don't think Mr. or Mrs. Wetmore has been intentionally holding back. Rather, I believe the link may be many years old, and I also believe I've pieced together enough of the story that with any luck, I might prompt a memory."

The men didn't like it; they wanted me home. But in the end, I had my way.

Chapter 16

Jesse and Derrick lingered at Chateau sur Mer long enough for Jesse to order the butler to admit Katie and me. Otherwise, Mr. Callajheue might have shut the door in our faces. I can't say I would have blamed him. A good butler is the first line of defense in his master's household, and I had no doubt my name had been linked to trouble and upset among many in that household.

Miss Maude and Miss Edith seemed even less inclined than their butler to show me much courtesy. The sisters met Katie and me in the Stair Hall—or headed us off, I might say.

"Miss Cross," the elder sister, Edith, demanded with arms crossed and face stony, "why have you returned? My sister and I would prefer you conduct all future communications, should such communications be necessary, by written correspondence. Things are bad enough without your stirring them up."

Again, I understood they were attempting to protect their parents, especially their mother, whom Maude perceived to have been agitated by my last visit. I wished to explain, but first I needed to sit down and have a few sips of tea. I longed for a cup of Nanny's strong Irish brew, and suddenly wished I'd allowed Katie to bring me all the way home. But no, while Jesse and Derrick brought Jonas Boyd to heel, it was important I discover why he included the Wetmores in his schemes.

I leaned against Katie's side while she supported me with an arm around my waist. From the corner of my eye I saw her color rise at Miss Wetmore's chastisement. Yet when I thought she'd cower and duck her head, she instead stood straighter and lifted her chin. "If you'll excuse me, Miss Wetmore, Miss Cross has been hurt. Attacked at the polo grounds by a beast of a fellow. He's run away and the police are after him, but it was in your mother's service that Miss Cross risked her life. She needs to sit down and rest, if you please."

Both Misses Wetmore looked alarmed by this news, and not a little chagrined. Miss Edith stuttered something unintelligible. Miss Maude took matters in hand.

"Edith, send for tea. Come this way, Miss Cross." She led us up the stairs. Katie and I followed slowly, each step renewing the ache in my head. If the throbbing didn't subside by morning I would indeed seek Dr. Kennison's expertise.

Miss Maude brought us to Mrs. Wetmore's upstairs sitting room. "Wait here. I'll tell my mother you're here."

"Thank you," I said rather weakly. Katie walked me to the settee and held my arm to steady me as I sank onto it. She did not sit, but stood vigilantly beside me until the door opened upon Mrs. Wetmore. Maude had not returned with her, and I briefly wondered whose idea it had been for her to remain behind.

"Miss Cross." Mrs. Wetmore swept across the room, and as she did so Katie moved away and took up position by the window overlooking the front lawn. Mrs. Wetmore sat beside me and took my hands. "Tell me what happened. Did that man really attack you? Why? Who is he? What has he to do with us? Oh, you poor dear, to suffer so on our account."

Her outpouring jumbled in my head so that I didn't know which question to answer first. I slipped a hand from hers and held it up. "Mrs. Wetmore, please let me explain in my own way. The man who attacked me was the brother, I believe, of the woman found dead at the bottom of your staircase. His name is Jonas Boyd. Does that mean anything to you?"

"Not a thing. Should it? I don't understand, Miss Cross."

"Then let me tell you what I've pieced together." I described Lilah's photograph album, the parents, Lilah, and her younger brother, and how some of the photographs appeared to be missing. "I think those missing pictures might have been of a third sibling, a younger one, who was adopted. Lilah might have removed the pictures to safeguard her sibling's new identity." I drew a breath. "I believe I know the whereabouts of that sibling. Does the name Hartwell sound familiar?"

"Hartwell . . ." A look of fierce concentration distorted Mrs. Wetmore's features. My pulse began to race at the thought that we were about to make a breakthrough. But the woman glanced up, shaking her head. "No, I can think of no significance to the name Hartwell as it pertains to me, my husband, or my family."

A breath of disappointment escaped me, but Mrs. Wetmore hadn't finished speaking. "However," she said, "as you know, Miss Cross, the fate of Rhode Island's orphans concerns me greatly, and the cause of finding suitable homes for such children has always been a vital one for me. Could the child in the missing pictures have been an infant? And perhaps a girl?"

My pulse sped up again. Was Mrs. Wetmore's work with orphans the link I'd been looking for? I moved to the edge of the settee and eagerly turned to face her. "I believe the answer to both questions is yes."

"One of the associations in which I became involved, years ago, focused on placing baby girls with wealthy families, often older couples with either no children of their own, or who had only sons and longed to raise a daughter. Boys are always far easier to place, you see, for everyone wishes for a son, and my colleagues and I saw too many little girls left behind. If a girl was too old, however, she would also be hard to place."

"Which might have been the case with Lilah," I supplied. My pain and fatigue forgotten, I all but bounced on the cushions in my excitement. "And her brother as well, no?"

"It's quite possible, yes. Unfortunately, most adopting couples desire infants or very young children. That was one circumstance we were never able to change."

"If we are correct, then Lilah's sister could very well be a young lady named Nanette Hartwell, who happens to be in Newport with her family. According to one witness, Lilah had been going to the Casino for no other reason than to watch the family. She never approached them. That to me signifies a singular interest in these people. Somehow, she must have discovered her sister's whereabouts, or perhaps found a way to keep track of her through the years."

Mrs. Wetmore frowned as she considered. "It may be that Lilah brought her sister into the room where the adoptive parents took possession of her. That was allowed, sometimes, to help with the transition, so that the older siblings could see that the adoption, while separating the youngsters, was in the best interests of the younger child."

I gasped as the many tenuous connections and theories I'd formed in the past days suddenly coalesced into a viable scenario. Both Jonas and Lilah had been left behind at the orphanage. But while Lilah felt gratitude toward Mrs. Wetmore on behalf of her sister, Jonas had perhaps grown bitter at being forgotten. I knew from my own observations at St. Nicholas Orphanage in Providence, where I often sent what monies I could spare, that the experience of growing up in such a place could be vastly different for boys than for girls. The girls typically looked out for one another, especially the older girls when it came to the younger ones. Boys, by contrast, sometimes formed bands and picked on those smaller and weaker. Had such been the case with Jonas?

His arrival in Newport at the same time as Nanette would have raised Lilah's concerns and her guard. She might have learned of her brother's plans and confronted him, ending in her death. And then he used his sister's body to gain revenge on Mrs. Wetmore by nearly destroying her life. To whom had Jonas been speaking the night Lilah overheard him plotting against the Wetmores? His friend and workmate Anthony Dobbs? Did Mr. Dobbs assist in Lilah's murder and in placing her inside Chateau sur Mer?

"Miss Cross, please tell me what you are thinking. What has all this got to do with my husband? And why would the brother have attacked you?"

It was my turn to take Mrs. Wetmore's hand as I delivered this next blow. "I believe it was the brother, Jonas Boyd, who murdered Lilah and left her here that night. And that it wasn't so much your husband he sought to discredit, but you, ma'am."

Mrs. Wetmore paled and whisked her hand from beneath mine. She set it, trembling, at her throat. "Good heavens, this isn't a man we're speaking of, but a devil." Her voice rose in pitch on that last word, just as a knock came at the door and it opened.

"Tea, ma'am." A footman bearing a tray shouldered his way into the room. Behind him came Miss Maude.

"Mother, you look distraught." Her steely gaze darted to me. "Miss Cross, were you even attacked as you claimed, or was that a ploy to gain entry into this house for the purpose of upsetting my mother again? I've a mind to telephone the police."

Before either Mrs. Wetmore or I could get in a word, Maude pivoted and strode back into the hallway. "Father! Father, come here, quickly."

Mrs. Wetmore gestured to the befuddled footman. "Set the tray down. I'll pour. You may go, thank you."

He seemed all too happy to retreat from the room. Before Mrs. Wetmore could man the teapot, however, Katie hurried over. Mrs. Wetmore signaled her to hand me the first cup. "Drink, Miss Cross. You look as though you could use it, and no wonder after your ordeal." She paused as she accepted her own cup from Katie. "Dear me, as can I."

Heavy footsteps resounded from the gallery, and a moment later George Wetmore appeared in the doorway. Though his house arrest had not yet been lifted, he wore a suit of dark clothes as if planning to go out. The thought of him intending to disobey the police took me aback until I realized the senator was simply not a man to lounge about the house in a smoking jacket, as my brother, Brady, might have done. He had probably holed up in his office all morning, attending to official responsibilities.

"Edith, what on earth is going on?" He recognized me and scowled. "Miss Cross, are you disturbing my wife?"

"She is doing no such thing, George." Mrs. Wetmore waved her husband into the room, prompting Katie to duck and scamper back to her place by the window. "Come in and shut the door. Maude, you'll excuse us, please," she added in a tone that allowed for no argument. With a harsh look, Miss Maude patted her father's arm and walked away.

George Wetmore lowered himself into an armchair that faced the settee. The change in his physical bearing these past days shocked me. The robust man who had presided over the first match between the Westchester and Meadowview polo teams looked almost shrunken in stature, no longer the influential senator but a man entering the first throes of old age, perhaps even infirmity. I thought of my uncle Cornelius, and how distressing matters had led to his physical collapse. I prayed that would not be so for Senator Wetmore, that once the strain of uncertainty about his and his family's fate lifted from his shoulders, he would regain his vitality and his zeal for shaping the politics of the country.

"Then what is this all about?" he asked wearily. He scrubbed a hand across his eyes as if to relieve them of their bleariness. "Why is Miss Cross here?"

His wife drew a breath and let it out slowly. "George, I hired Miss Cross to investigate that woman's death."

Florid color rose in Mr. Wetmore's ample cheeks. "Why on earth? Edith, what were you thinking, involving yourself in such sordid matters? Matters best left to the police, I might add."

Mrs. Wetmore was shaking her head. "No, George. The police were going to drop the entire episode, call it an accident and leave it at that."

"And what would have been the harm?" Mr. Wetmore clutched the arms of his chair and pushed to his feet. He took on a horrified expression. "Edith, do you not trust me? Do you believe I had something to do with that poor girl's death?"

"Certainly not, George. Please, do sit down and listen." He stood another several seconds, his complexion feverishly bright, before complying with his wife's request. "Now then," she continued, "I knew that without a thorough investigation, there would always be questions to haunt you and our entire family. Think about the children, George. Would you want the taint of murder hanging over their heads the rest of their lives?"

"No," he replied with a defeated air. "No, indeed." He half shrugged. "And as it happened, the coroner proved Miss Buford's death could not have been an accident. Thus I am under house arrest, suspected of murder. But why *her*, Edith?" He pointed none too politely at me. "She's a child."

I bristled slightly. Mrs. Wetmore came to my defense. "She may be young, George, but Miss Cross possesses skills of deduction that rival any police detective's." She leaned slightly forward and murmured, "I know. I have heard. I do have sources, George."

At Mrs. Wetmore's prompting, I once again explained my theories concerning the link between Jonas, Lilah, and the Hartwell girl. Now I had one more piece of the puzzle—the link between them and Mrs. Wetmore.

"Well, I'll be . . ." Mr. Wetmore sat ruminating over everything I'd revealed. "And you say Detective Whyte has gone after this swine, this Boyd person?"

Even as I nodded, the notion left me shaky and unsettled. If anything were to happen to Jesse and Derrick . . . I needed the fortification of another swallow of tea, and reached for the cup and saucer I'd placed on the table before me. A wave of dizziness swept over me and I knocked the nearly empty cup over. That brought Katie to my side. "Miss Cross needs to rest now," she said more forcefully than I would have given her credit for.

I awakened with a start to find myself in a room lit only by a thin strip of moonlight slipping through a gap in the curtains. Once my eyes fully opened, I recognized the velvet canopy above my head, while light snores from across the room told me Katie was with me, asleep on the brocade sofa.

How many hours had I slept? I knew only that the room had been bathed in late afternoon sunlight when I entered it. Which meant that Jesse and Derrick must still be out there, somewhere on Aquidneck Island, unless their chase led them onto the mainland. The uncertainty precluded the possibility of my going back to sleep. Gingerly I sat up, waiting for the throbbing in my head to renew itself. When it didn't, I rose from the bed. I was still fully dressed, my clothes rumpled and my corset stays poking my ribs where the garment had slipped a fraction to one side. Quickly I set myself to rights, but I didn't bother putting on my boots. Stockinged feet would better serve my purpose, for I had no desire to disturb the household. Then I took a folded coverlet off the foot of the bed and gently draped it over Katie, careful not to wake her.

The Wetmores surely had a telephone. I resolved to find it and contact the police station to see what, if anything, I could learn. The rumble of masculine snoring traveled the gallery, emanating from a bedroom door that had been left slightly ajar. I tiptoed past and down the main staircase, once again avoiding the side where Lilah had been found. The butler's pantry would in all likelihood be equipped with the telephone I sought, and I headed in that direction.

Yet as I entered the Tapestry Hall, I became aware of weeping coming from the library. Mrs. Wetmore? Had I distressed her to a greater degree than she had admitted? Guilt prodded, while the image of an avenging Maude Wetmore rose up in my mind.

I stopped to listen, debating whether I should go in or allow her her privacy. The latter notion won out, but before I moved on through the hall, a male voice stopped me cold.

"Stop your sniveling, Mrs. Wetmore. You'll wake your family, and then I'll have no choice but to kill all of you."

Jonas. My blood ran cold even as a cool breeze swept my ankles. Somewhere, a door to the outside had been left open. A door from the ballroom to the veranda, perhaps, where Jonas had entered once before?

An agony of indecision nearly immobilized me. I couldn't very well go charging into the library and demand Jonas give himself up. I gazed about the darkness for something to use as a weapon. But even armed, could I move quickly enough to prevent Jonas from harming Mrs. Wetmore? I could wake a footman or two, but that would mean retracing my steps, this time all the way up to the third or perhaps even the fourth floor. In so doing, I would be leaving Mrs. Wetmore very much alone, and there was no telling what could happen in the interim.

Jonas was speaking again, making quietly forceful demands. "I want five thousand dollars, Mrs. Wetmore. Now."

"W-what? We haven't that much cash in the house."

"Liar. You rich people always have plenty on hand. Where is your husband's safe? Or should I go ask him myself?"

"No! Don't do that, please. I'm telling you the truth. We never keep that much in the house." She yelped as if Jonas had struck her, and I lurched, nearly vaulting into the room. Mrs. Wetmore spoke again. "I can give you silver . . . and jewelry. As much as you want, worth much more than what you're asking."

"You think I'm going to risk pawning your things and getting caught? Stupid woman. It's cash I want. You owe me. You left me in that awful place to be beaten and spit on and laughed at every day until I was old enough to get out of there. The older boys, they stole my food, ripped the shirts off my back. But *you*—you didn't care about that, did you?"

"I . . . didn't know. I'm sorry, I . . ."

Summoning help from the police, and then perhaps taking the back stairs up to the third floor, seemed my best option as long as Jonas didn't hear my voice. Holding my skirts clear of the floor, I tiptoed to the dining room, intending to enter the service corridor where the butler's pantry was located. A footstep—not my own—sent my heart pounding into my throat and fear exploding inside me. Arms wrapped around me from behind, the muscles biting into my flesh. One large hand slipped over my mouth and pressed until my teeth bit into my lips. Sweat and coal dust invaded my nose. Had Jonas somehow headed me off? How? I struggled and tried to break free.

"Stop it," a whisper in my ear commanded. "Don't move. Don't make a sound." Despite the demand I tugged again, resulting in those arms tightening like a vise and a threat penetrating the roaring of blood in my ears. "Don't make me hurt you."

I went still. Yet it was sudden recognition of that voice, rather than fear for my life, that stole the fight from my limbs.

It was Anthony Dobbs.

Chapter 17

"All right?" he whispered, his hold on me loosening a fraction.

I nodded.

His hand remained on my mouth. "So help me, if you call out I'll strangle you and enjoy doing it."

I managed a shaky nod. Slowly, his hands receded. One settled on my shoulder and turned me about to face him. Like a beacon of danger, Anthony Dobbs's bulldog features gleamed with sweat in the darkness. His nostrils flared, and I braced for . . . what, I didn't know. Surely if he wished to harm me, he would have done so already. Wouldn't he?

"Stay put," he ordered, and slipped away into the Tapestry Hall.

I watched him, straining to see in the scant light. He paused by the fireplace and, with a stealth I would not have believed that large man capable of, slid the fireplace poker clear of its stand. Not the slightest trace of metal scraped against the bracket. But when I expected him to proceed into the library, he instead exited into the Stair Hall.

My initial fear surged. Armed as he was, he could only intend sneaking upstairs to the bedrooms. Mr. Wetmore and his two daughters would never see the poker raised above their heads, would never know what caused the sudden agony that obliterated their lives. Evil, evil man.

But not if I could do something to stop him. I followed as far as the Tapestry Hall, when Mr. Dobbs suddenly called out from the bottom of the staircase. "Edith? Are you down here?"

He had deepened his voice, lending it the roughness of recent sleep. With a gasp I realized he was pretending to be Mr. Wetmore, looking for his wife.

"George, run!" Mrs. Wetmore cried out. "Go back upstairs. Save the girls!"

Footsteps from the library sent me scurrying into the far corner of the Tapestry Hall. Jonas bolted out of the library and into the Stair Hall. A glint of light bounced along a knife with a curved blade some eight inches long. He held it out in front of him, ready to strike. Scuffling, grunts, and cries of pain echoed in the stairwell. Something heavy hit the floor with a crash, something else thudded, then screeched like chalk on slate, and another cry of pain followed. Shadows thrown by moonlight through the stained glass windows at the half landing formed grotesque shapes on the floor of the Tapestry Hall. I fled past those twisting shadows into the library, while the sounds of the skirmish went on.

Mrs. Wetmore, in her dressing gown and slippers, stood pressed into a corner of the bookshelves. She watched me with large eyes as I ran to the French doors. I tugged, but they remained steadfastly closed. I rushed to Mrs. Wetmore and grasped her hand. Like the doors, she, too, refused to budge.

"We've got to get out of this room," I whispered urgently. "Out of the house."

"George . . . the girls."

"We can do nothing for them from here." I yanked for all I was worth, dislodging her from her stronghold against the books. She stumbled once or twice before matching my pace. We ran back into the Tapestry Hall, and from there through the tiled hallway. The old front entrance lay at one end, but this, too, stood locked tight. I gazed wildly about the hall. It was Mrs. Wetmore who chose a direction and tugged to get me moving. We entered the Green Salon, but I didn't bother trying any of the doors here, for I remembered the cool breeze that had swept my ankles earlier.

"The ballroom," I said, and without bothering to explain, led the way into the cavernous room. To my relief, I hadn't been wrong. One of the doors rocked gently back and forth on its hinges as the breezes blew and subsided. I pulled it wider and Mrs. Wetmore and I escaped into the blackness of the damp lawn. At first we ran toward the south perimeter wall, but I remembered it had been at the Moongate that Jonas had first entered the property, carrying an already deceased Lilah.

"This way," I hissed, and changed our course to the front of the house. Before we'd taken many steps, an explosive burst shook the house and reverberated through the open windows. The shock of it thrust Mrs. Wetmore and myself to our knees.

All went silent for several resounding heartbeats. Then lights sprang to life in the upstairs windows, and Edith's and Maude's voices rang out.

"Mother, Father? What happened? Where are you?"

Mrs. Wetmore pressed to her feet and tensed to run back to the house. I grabbed her wrist none too gently and pulled her back to the ground. She struggled against me, and with little choice I rolled with her, propelling her to the ground on her back, with me looming over her and my hands pinning her shoulders.

"I have to go. Let me go," she pleaded. "George, the girls. They need me."

"No, Mrs. Wetmore. You can't go back in yet. I won't let you."

She attempted to push up from the ground. I heaved my weight more firmly over her until she lay limp against the grass. "We'll go back when we know it's safe," I told her in no uncertain terms. I'm sure she had never been spoken to that way before, at least not since she was a child.

It worked, for she nodded, even as I had when Anthony Dobbs bade me be silent. I eased off her, ready to spring on her again if need be. She sat up and raised both hands to the sides of her head. "George and that man, fighting. Oh, which was shot? Miss Cross, I shall go mad if I don't learn what happened soon. And if it was George who . . ."

In this, at least, I could ease her mind. "Jonas wasn't fighting with Mr. Wetmore. There was another man in the house. Anthony Dobbs, who used to work for the police."

"Another man? A policeman?" She looked at me in amazement, mirroring my own sentiments. I didn't bother to explain about Mr. Dobbs. If she wished to believe for now that a policeman had taken up the fight with Jonas Boyd, then let her.

"And listen. It's silent in the house." I tried to sound calm, reassuring. "The fighting has stopped." But I wondered if it truly had.

She clutched her hands together. "We don't know who has prevailed." Her voice threatened to splinter.

Moments later, lantern light swept the driveway as two vehicles turned in from Bellevue Avenue. Relief made me giddy as I recognized the carriage in the lead and the wagon that followed. Jesse and his men had arrived. "We'll know soon enough, Mrs. Wetmore."

"What is that?" She swept locks that had fallen from her braid back from her face as she peered at the approaching vehicles. Her eyes once more grew large with alarm. "Miss Cross?"

"It's the police. It's over." I let out a long breath as the last of my energy drained away. I tried to wave to the vehicles, tried to stand and call out, but I couldn't summon the strength. I wanted only to lie back against the damp grass and close my eyes. When Mrs. Wetmore scrambled to her feet and urged me to hasten across the lawn to meet these latest arrivals, I gestured for her to go on without me.

How long did I sit there, breathing heavily, my thoughts wandering unfocused, while the night dampness sent a chill through my skirts? I couldn't have said. Little by little the downstairs windows began to glow with lights from inside. Voices drifted to me as if from far away, from another world. I heard the Wetmores calling one another's names, the police shouting orders, my own name being called. The shadows closed around me, sealing me in a cocoon from which I couldn't seem to stir. Then, abruptly, doors opened onto the veranda and two figures came at me through the darkness.

"Emma, where are you?"

It was Derrick who called, but I knew even before I could make out their features that they were both there: Derrick and Jesse. They reached me and fell to their knees on either side of me. I felt arms around me and hands seeking my own. Questions concerning my welfare barraged my still-dazed mind. Terms of affection grazed my ears.

I forced myself to shake away my lethargy. "Yes, yes, I'm all right. I wasn't hurt. But Mr. Wetmore, the girls, are they . . . ?"

Jesse, holding my hand, rocked back on his heels to better meet my gaze. "They're all fine, Emma."

"I heard a gunshot."

"That was Mr. Wetmore's revolver." Derrick, too, sat back a bit. The two men regarded each other, each having claimed one of my hands. Derrick coughed; Jesse cleared his throat and glanced away. They both released their holds on me, yet neither backed away. "He heard Boyd and Dobbs downstairs, realized his wife wasn't in the bedroom with him, and grabbed his gun."

"Was anyone hit?"

Jesse shook his head. "The shot startled them enough to stop their fighting, and the senator threatened to shoot them both if either moved a muscle. Not that either man escaped unscathed, mind you."

"They're both bleeding." Derrick reached again for my hand. "Can you stand?"

I nodded. "I think so."

I found both my hands once more engulfed in theirs. They helped steady me as I rose, and at my silent look they released me. "Dobbs—I don't understand. Why was he here?"

"I'd like the answer to that myself." Jesse gestured to the house. "Let's go inside."

The ambulance wagon waited while Jesse stopped the orderlies from loading the stretcher bearing Jonas into the back. An officer and my old friend Scotty Binsford would be accompanying Jonas to the hospital, and then to the jailhouse once the doctors released him.

Jesse scowled down at the prone man. Jonas bled from multiple cuts on his face, hands, and groaned with each breath, indicating broken ribs. "Jonas Boyd, you are under arrest for the murders of Lilah Buford and Donald Hartwell, multiple burglaries, arson resulting in the death of Ellsworth

Cigars manager Bertrand Styles, and illegally detaining and attempting to blackmail Mrs. Wetmore." Jesse smiled grimly. "In short, you'll never have the chance to bother anyone again."

However much Jonas Boyd deserved his punishment, I couldn't help a shudder as I pictured the hangman's noose. Derrick stood beside me, a little behind Jesse. "And while you might not be able to prove it, he'd also been blackmailing Donald Hartwell since the Hartwells first arrived in Newport."

Jesse went on to explain that when the police officers went to break the dismal news to the Hartwells about their patriarch, they had learned of Jonas's blackmail from young Gerald, with whom I had danced at the Casino assembly ball. I'd had a sensation then that Gerald took pains to hide something. It wasn't guilt, but the knowledge that Jonas had been threatening to reveal Nanette's origins to all of society, thus destroying her chances of making a good match. To protect his granddaughter, Donald Hartwell had been paying Jonas large sums of money, meeting him at different locations in town for each payment. One of those payments had occurred on Carrington's Wharf, and there Lilah had heard Jonas telling Mr. Hartwell of his bitterness toward Mrs. Wetmore, and his desire to hurt her and her family. The two men had obviously planned to meet for another payment behind the grandstand at the polo grounds, where I had stumbled upon Mr. Hartwell.

As Jesse concluded his story, another shiver traveled my length, and not because of the night air. If I hadn't interrupted their rendezvous, would Mr. Hartwell still be alive now? That was something I didn't dare dwell on. At least, as Jesse said, Jonas Boyd would never have a chance to harm anyone again.

"Don't forget his assault on Madam Heidi," I said, "for I'm certain now it was Jonas who beat her. She must have seen or heard something and confronted him. Perhaps she even suspected that Jonas murdered Lilah. His own sister— his flesh and blood." I scoffed at the man to whom I had once believed I owed a debt of gratitude. It might have been beneath me, but I couldn't help a parting taunt. "I hope you'll find it was all worth it."

He glanced up at me through the swollen slits of his eyes. "I should have killed you at the polo grounds."

I nodded. "Perhaps you should have."

"And I should have strangled Mrs. Wetmore while I had the chance."

I smiled at him as Jesse had—coldly and without pity. "Your greed got the better of you, didn't it?"

"Take him." With a jerk of his chin, Jesse set the orderlies in motion. "Get him out of my sight."

Inside, the Wetmores gathered around their dining room table. Upon reuniting, there had been tears, embraces, and praises sent heavenward by parents and daughters. Even Miss Maude, typically so imperious and stoic, had broken down in her parents' arms.

They had since calmed and requested food be brought up to the dining room. Jesse, Derrick, and I joined them now. As I took my seat, I could hear the last creak of the ambulance wagon as it turned from the driveway onto Bellevue Avenue. The family occupied one end of the long table. Anthony Dobbs sat a few seats away, sipping coffee and munching on a sandwich. Though sporting multiple bruises, a black eye, and a split lower lip, he appeared to have fared better than Jonas. He looked up as we took our seats. The glower he sent in my direction puzzled me, but no longer had the power to intimidate me.

I merely raised my eyebrows at him and reached for the coffeepot.

A policeman had followed us into the room. He sat at the

head of the table, opened a writing tablet, and held a pencil over the blank page. Jesse consumed a sandwich in about three bites and swallowed several gulps of steaming coffee. "All right, Tony. Give me your account."

Mr. Dobbs sent a gaze around the table. "Here? In front of everyone?"

"The Wetmores have a right to hear what brought both you and Jonas Boyd to their home tonight." Jesse sat back in his chair and folded his arms across his chest.

"Indeed, out with it, sir." George Wetmore held his coffee cup in one hand and his wife's hand in the other. He frowned. "Perhaps Edith and Maude should return to their rooms."

This raised an immediate protest. "No, indeed, Father."

"Really, Father, don't treat us like children. We won't be shooed away."

Mrs. Wetmore settled the matter. More calmly than I would have expected, she said, "Let them stay, George. Their lives were as much at risk tonight as yours or mine. They deserve to know why." She turned her attention to Mr. Dobbs. "Please enlighten us."

He took his time, finishing his cup of coffee and pouring another. He plucked another sandwich off the platter near him, then held it up and stared at it a moment before setting it, untasted, on his plate. He heaved a sigh and then, without glancing up, spoke to those two thick slices of bread and the deviled ham between them.

"I began to suspect Boyd after the first few robberies. He'd be nowhere to be found, then suddenly show up at the Blue Moon or the boardinghouse where we both had rooms. Then the night of the fire, he pushed Miss Cross—"

"You saw him push me?" My mouth dropped open on a burst of indignation. "And you said nothing?"

He avoided my angry gaze. "I saw him push past you, and

you fell into the street. I couldn't prove anything—it just seemed suspicious. And he'd been gone again—another one of his disappearances." He shrugged. "Without proof, what was I supposed to say? Besides, there's a dockworkers' code of honor."

"A dockworkers' *what?*" The notion galled me. "I could have been struck by falling, burning roof timbers, and you were concerned with—"

Jesse held out a hand, signaling for me to be silent. I closed my mouth and gritted my teeth. "Then what?" Jesse prompted.

"It was Miss Cross accusing me of hitting Madam Heidi that really got me thinking. I knew I hadn't done it, but I also knew there wasn't a thing that happened on that wharf or the immediate vicinity that she didn't know about. And I began to think, if Jonas was up to something, she'd know, just as sure as she knew her own face in the mirror. She must have said something to him, maybe about Lilah. Maybe about the fire. And he beat her to shut her up."

He had just confirmed my own theory about Jonas and Madam Heidi. As he spoke, he'd taken on the mean, bullying look I knew so well, but this time with a difference. For once it wasn't aimed at Brady or me, but at the idea of Jonas using physical violence to frighten and intimidate a . . . a what? What exactly did Mr. Dobbs consider Madam Heidi? A neighbor? A businesswoman? A fellow Newporter? A hapless victim? All of those things? Suddenly, I saw an entirely different side to this man—a man willing to risk his life for a wealthy family he didn't much know, and for a woman— me—for whom he had no regard. It was confusing, disconcerting, and not a little astounding.

"I'm sorry I accused you," I mumbled.

He again shrugged one of his hulking shoulders, made even bigger by the manual labor he'd been engaged in since leaving the police force. "Don't think this changes anything.

I don't like your family, Miss Cross. Not your good-for-nothing brother, and not you with your meddling and bossy ways."

"Bossy? That's the pot calling the kettle black, wouldn't you say, Mr. Dobbs?"

"That's enough." Jesse glanced at the policeman taking notes. Derrick caught my eye and winked. "Tony, how did you happen to know what Jonas intended tonight?"

Was there the faintest note of accusation in Jesse's question?

"When he left Morton Hill today, I decided to follow him. I saw him knock out Miss Cross behind the grandstand."

I tossed up my hands in frustration—and anger. "Again, you watched him assault me and did nothing?"

"Your little maid was already on hand," he said defensively. "Isn't it better I followed Jonas to see what he planned next?"

"You could have alerted the police." Derrick's hands balled into fists against the tabletop as he spoke. "We could have avoided the entire scene here tonight."

"Good heavens, man!" George Wetmore shoved back his chair and came to his feet. "You endangered my wife and daughters so you could play the hero?"

Mr. Dobbs's shrug was becoming intolerable. "The police department and I are not on the best of terms. For all I knew, they wouldn't have believed me. And our Miss Cross here believed it was me that killed Lilah. Didn't you, Miss Cross?" I admit I squirmed a bit as his scrutiny shifted to me. "Besides, alerting anyone would have meant letting Jonas's trail go cold. I stayed right behind him all the way to town and back, and he never knew it. I didn't spend ten years as a police detective for nothing."

There wasn't much more to say, and Anthony Dobbs was allowed to return to town. He left with heavier pockets than he had arrived with, for Mr. Wetmore insisted on showing his appreciation in the form of a generous monetary reward. To his credit, Mr. Dobbs hesitated before taking it, looking very much as though he were about to turn it down. Sensing his disinclination, Mr. Wetmore pressed the stack of bills into Mr. Dobbs's hand. Mrs. Wetmore expressed her desire to pay me as well for the services for which she had hired me, but I assured her there was no hurry for that, that I knew her payment would arrive in good time.

Jesse took statements from each of the Wetmores and from me. Then he offered to drive me home, but I instead accepted the Wetmores' offer to have their chauffeur bring me. I had seen the look of displeasure on Derrick's face when Jesse made his offer, and I was simply too exhausted to cope with the ongoing rivalry between the two men. I found Nanny awake when I arrived at Gull Manor. As I creaked my way up the stairs, her bedroom door opened. Never have I been so happy to walk into her welcoming, and slightly admonishing, embrace.

"Will you stop your snooping *now*, Emma?" she demanded after I'd told her everything that happened. I merely smiled, kissed her cheek, and took myself off to bed.

And yet I slept little. Instead, I lay awake, not reliving the fear of the past day, but wondering about tomorrow, and all the days to follow. I needed employment, and quickly, for though my great aunt Sadie's annuity allowed for the general upkeep of Gull Manor, there was still food and fuel and clothing to buy. How could I continue taking in women in need, or helping the children of St. Nicholas Orphanage in Providence, without an income?

The question of what I would do plagued me until sunrise.

Chapter 18

❦

"Miss Cross, I do hope we aren't being too forward in coming to see you. Nanette insisted and, well, we owe you so very much."

Mrs. Hartwell's statement left me momentarily dumbstruck. The entire family—those who remained—had telephoned first, and then driven out to Gull Manor shortly after breakfast. They were leaving Newport on the first available steamer, but wished to have a word with me first. I hadn't known what to expect. I certainly didn't expect the Hartwells to feel in any way indebted to me.

I gestured at the shabby furniture that inhabited my parlor. "Please, do come in and sit down. May I offer you tea and refreshment?"

The family did as I bade, but as to my question, Mrs. Hartwell pressed her hands together. "No, we wouldn't hear of putting you out in the slightest. Besides, our boat leaves within the hour. No, Miss Cross, we merely wished to express our gratitude. And our regret, for your having been caught up in our family's difficulty."

Young Nanette was nodding vigorously. Mr. Hartwell also nodded, but solemnly, meeting my eye only briefly. But then, it was his father who had died at Jonas Boyd's hands. Gerald merely stared across the sofa table at me, his eyes lit with an admiration I didn't feel I deserved.

"Mrs. Hartwell," I began, then addressed them all by encompassing them in my gaze. "I only wish I had been more alert to the danger Mr. Hartwell Senior faced. Perhaps I might have done things differently, and avoided—"

"Oh no, Miss Cross," Nanette said, her golden hair piled beneath a simple straw hat trimmed in pink satin. Once they arrived home, they would order appropriate mourning attire and begin the funeral arrangements. "You mustn't blame yourself. It was my brother." I flinched at this, and again the girl nodded. "My parents have confessed all to me. I admit it's all quite shocking and difficult to accept. I imagine it will sink in at some later date and I shall cry buckets over it. But I know now that I'm adopted, and I know the truth of why my grandfather died."

I stared at my hands. "He died to protect you, Miss Hartwell."

"Please, call me Nanette. Yes, he died to protect me—he'd have done anything for me."

"As would the rest of us," her father put in quietly, a rumble from deep in his chest.

A blush suffused Nanette's cheeks, and her eyes shone with unshed tears. "I know, Papa. And I do understand why you never told me the truth about where I came from, or that I had a brother and sister somewhere in the world." She turned to me again. "What can you tell me about my sister, Miss Cross?"

"She was . . ." I hesitated, wondering how much, if anything, Nanette knew about Lilah and the Blue Moon. I decided it wasn't my place to enlighten her on those details.

That would be up to her parents. "She was well-liked. And respected. And very brave, as it turns out. Somehow, she followed your progress through life, and took particular interest in you when you came to Newport. How your brother came to be here is not completely clear to me, but once Lilah realized the danger he posed, she resolved to intervene."

"But you say she took particular interest in Nanette," her mother said. "Why did she not simply come to us and tell us of Jonas's plans?"

I had wondered about that myself. Why had Lilah been so intent on warning Mrs. Wetmore and not the Hartwells? "She must have known Jonas was blackmailing your grandfather and perhaps decided to leave it between them. How else to shield Nanette from the truth of her origins?"

"I didn't need shielding." The girl's chin came up, hinting at the spirit beneath her refined exterior.

"Perhaps not," I conceded, "but your sister must have believed it was up to your parents to decide. She wished only to prevent an incident due to the good turn Mrs. Wetmore, and others like her, did you when you were a baby. Jonas was very bitter about being left behind at the orphanage. Perhaps with good reason, but Lilah was also left behind, yet seemed to bear no ill will toward anyone because of it."

"She was a good person." Nanette's expression brightened as she spoke.

"I'd say she was." I came to my feet. "Wait here, I have something for you."

Their curious stares followed me from the room. When I returned, I placed Lilah's photograph album in Nanette's hands.

"What's this?"

"It is about where you came from." I experienced a sudden doubt and darted a glance at her mother. Mrs. Hartwell nodded, closing her eyes for an instant. When she opened them, they held tears. "There are no pictures of you, I'm afraid. Either Lilah couldn't bear to gaze upon them for missing you too terribly, or she sought to erase your past once the Hartwells adopted you."

"We have pictures of Nanette as a baby." Her mother smiled shakily. "We'll add some of them to the album."

Gerald had stood and walked behind his sister's seat on the sofa. Peering over her shoulder as she slowly turned the pages, he scowled. "You might wish to remove the photographs of *him*." He pointed to a young Jonas.

Nanette shook her head. "No, I should like to think he wasn't always evil. Once perhaps, he was a fun-loving boy who cared about his family. Who cared about me, perhaps very much." She raised her chin to look up at her brother. "Even as you do, Gerald."

They left soon after. I lingered in the parlor, thinking about the future, although not my own—not just then. I resolved to speak with Flossie at the first opportunity and offer her an alternative to life at the Blue Moon. She was still young. Perhaps she could be spared the tragedy that all too often befell women in her position. Thus determined, I rose, but on my way to join Nanny and Katie in the kitchen, a knock came at the front door. It was Derrick, and judging by the looks of him, he was here about an urgent matter.

"I've got a solution to both our dilemmas," he said in lieu of a greeting. He dragged his hat off his head as he stepped into the front hall. "It's perfect, Emma, and I'm hoping you'll give it serious consideration."

With a laugh I led him into the parlor. "Give what serious consideration?"

"The Newport *Messenger* is for sale, and I'm considering buying it. What do you say?"

He stood practically toe-to-toe with me, rather crowding me, if the truth be told. High color suffused his cheekbones, and his smile was infectious, or would have been, if I had better understood his intentions. As it was, I gave a small shrug. "It sounds like a wonderful opportunity for anyone wishing to break into small-town newspapers, but are you serious about this?"

"Of course. Why wouldn't I be?"

"Derrick, the *Messenger* is little more than a news sheet with a very small subscription list."

"I'll build it up."

"But are you certain you want to remain in Newport?"

"Why not?"

He seemed determined to answer most of my questions with other questions. "For one thing, your father is very likely to relent about his decision to disinherit you. He's angry about Judith—hurt, really, to discover his daughter stepped beyond the bounds of propriety. Any father would be. He's lashing out at you because, frankly, with Judith so far away, he can't lash out at her."

"Father can keep the Providence *Sun*. I no longer care. I want to begin anew with my own paper. Buying the *Messenger* is the perfect way to do that. The offices and the presses are already there. I'll rehire the existing employees, and . . ." He lowered both his voice and his chin, speaking to me on an even level. "And I want you to be part of it, Emma."

A knot began to form in my stomach. "Derrick, I'm not sure that's a good idea just now."

His eyebrows converged. "Whyever not?"

"Well," I began warily, "just exactly what do you have in mind concerning my participation?"

"Full partner."

"I haven't the funds to invest in a newspaper, no matter how tiny it is."

"That doesn't matter—"

"Derrick, do you not know me at all? Do you not understand that it matters to me, very much?" His exuberance melted away like snow in a January thaw. I was not only disappointing him, I was hurting him as well. But I couldn't help it. I knew any other woman in my shoes would have snatched at this opportunity; would have considered me mad for pushing it away. But accepting such terms—in essence, allowing him to pave my way through life—would obligate me to him in a way I could not countenance. Not until I had reached some decision concerning my future. Were I his wife, we could have been partners and I would have gloried in our joint business venture. But I was not his wife, nor were we merely friends either. Too much history existed between us, along with too many future possibilities, and decisions I was not yet ready to make.

No, those decisions must be made first, and only when they became perfectly clear, both to myself and to Derrick, could he and I speak of a business partnership, or any kind of partnership. Until then, accepting his offer would have been wrong, and might have been misconstrued by him.

The telephone rang, and it was with some relief that I went to answer the call.

"Miss Cross, I'm glad to find you in."

"Mr. Bennett?"

"Indeed. Miss Cross, I've thought long and hard and I've made a decision."

There was that word again: *decision.* I couldn't pretend I didn't know what he meant. That knot in my stomach pulled tighter, not from apprehension this time, but from sheer excitement. Mr. Bennett was about to solve my dilemma, both concerning my need for employment and Derrick's untimely offer. I could barely contain my eagerness. "Yes, Mr. Bennett?"

"The *Herald* could use a reporter like you, Miss Cross."

"Really, Mr. Bennett! This is wonderful news."

"How soon can you relocate to New York?"

"I . . ." The receiver came away from my ear and I stared into it. Surely I had heard wrong.

"Miss Cross? Are you there?"

I raised the ear trumpet back into place. "I'm here, Mr. Bennett. It's just that, well, I'd hoped to work from Newport. To report on this town and the outlying area, and wire my stories—"

"No, no, that won't do. I need you in New York. What do you say, Miss Cross? This is quite an opportunity I'm handing you, and I'll need an answer soon. Quite soon."

"Yes, Mr. Bennett, I'll give you my answer . . . soon."

"Good. I'll wait to hear from you."

The line went dead, but for several moments I remained staring at the call box, holding the ear trumpet. Leave Newport? Even now, the sounds of pots clunking, water running, and Nanny's and Katie's voices traveled down the hallway from the kitchen. Leave them? Leave this house where Great-Aunt Sadie taught me to rely on my wits and skills, to be independent, to answer to no one but myself? Granted, I would not be utterly alone in New York, for my Vanderbilt relatives lived there for much of the year. But I wouldn't be here, in this city, on this island I loved so much. Could I leave this place that was so much a part of me, that had shaped the person I was, that seemed, sometimes, the very source of my strength?

Was employment—even the dream of achieving the status of a hard news reporter—worth all that?

"Emma, is something wrong?" Derrick stood in the parlor doorway.

"I don't know," I mumbled, and gently set the ear trumpet on its cradle.

"What?" He frowned in concern and crossed to me. When he reached me he took my hands and held them against his chest. "Who was that? What has happened?"

"It was . . ." I swallowed the bitter taste of indecision, of wondering what it was I truly wanted in life. Of wishing the answers would fall into my arms. "It was nothing pressing. Never mind. Come, let's see what Nanny is preparing for lunch later. And then, why don't we take a walk along the water's edge? I haven't done that in rather a long while."

He smiled. "I'd like that. And about the *Messenger*. I realize I came rushing in here all half-cocked. It's merely an option. Perhaps we can discuss it further."

"Yes, we'll talk about it," I said, and together we made our way to the kitchen at the back of the house.

Author's Note

Chateau sur Mer and the Wetmore family might not be quite as well-known outside of Rhode Island as The Breakers and the Vanderbilts, but both the house and the family were no less significant in leaving their mark on Newport's history. George Peabody Wetmore, son of China trade merchant William Wetmore, served as a governor of Rhode Island, and a U.S. senator. Though born during a family trip to England, George Wetmore was raised in Newport, and is buried in Newport's Island Cemetery. Upon his father's death, he inherited Chateau sur Mer, an Italianate villa completed in 1852 and remodeled in the Second Empire French style in the 1870s. He continued to live there when his duties didn't take him to Washington, D.C.

What set the Wetmores apart from most other Gilded Age families was a quiet dignity that was never sacrificed for the sake of ostentation. Rather like the Astors, they were secure in their place in society and had little to prove; they were neither publicity seekers nor scandal courters. While society matrons went to great lengths to marry off their daughters to titled Europeans, the Wetmore daughters, Edith and Maude, remained single during their entire lives. The sisters would marry for love, or not at all. Their younger brothers having passed away at early ages, Edith and Maude inherited their father's vast wealth along with his properties. They split their time between Chateau sur Mer and an apartment in New York City, but it was Edith who truly continued to call Chateau sur Mer home until her death in 1951. Both sisters were active politically—both Republicans, like their father—with Maude holding office in the National Civic Federation, the American Women's Association, and the Women's National Republican Club.*

Chateau sur Mer was the grandest house in Newport until the Vanderbilts began building their palazzos in the 1890s. It's now considered one of the smaller "cottages" in Newport. But don't be fooled into thinking the visitor will come away disappointed, or that the stoic Wetmores were frugal in the design of their home or the comforts they enjoyed. On the contrary, the house is a treasure trove of architectural delights and ingenious innovations that made life for the Wetmores luxurious. For anyone visiting Newport, I highly recommend taking the house tour, which is much more intimate in nature than the tours of the larger houses. The enthusiasm and knowledge of the tour guides present a very personal view into the history of the house and the Wetmore family.

I decided to use a fictional name for the wharf where the "Blue Moon Tavern" is located. The wharves present at the time of the story still exist today, but what was once (even in my own memory) a somewhat rough and rundown part of town is now prime real estate filled with condos overlooking

---

* Kathleen Kennedy Wood, *Chateau sur Mer: A Child's View of Life at the Famous Newport Mansion*, Morgan Hill, CA: Bookstrand Publishing, 2015.

Narragansett Bay; I thought it better not to imply that one of them once housed a brothel. However, Blue Moon Gardens was a "restaurant" in Newport for several decades during the twentieth century. There are numerous articles about the establishment in the Newport newspapers, none of them flattering. Located on Thames Street and popular with sailors and lobstermen, the place was often cited for serving liquor after hours and to minors, frequent fights, and the antics of intoxicated patrons. For instance, in 1951 a drunken sailor attempted to steal a wallet and a "spangled brassiere" from a dancer after following her into her dressing room. On another occasion, one of those dancers was arrested for intoxication and "indecent dancing." The place certainly had a reputation, as any longtime Newporter can tell you.

James Gordon Bennett's Casino is now the Tennis Hall of Fame. The story of why he established the Newport Casino was taken from history, but exactly where truth leaves off and legend begins, no one is quite sure. While wagering probably did take place there among male patrons, this was never a gambling establishment. *Casino* is an Italian word for "small house" or "small villa." Bennett's residence across the street, Stone Villa, was demolished in 1957 to make way for the Bellevue Shopping Center. It's one of many casualties of post–Gilded Age Newport.

The Stanford Whittaker character in the story is based on Stanford White of the architectural firm of McKim, Meade, & White. White was well-known for his innovative and exciting designs in commercial, civic, and residential architecture, including the Newport Casino, but also for his scandalous lifestyle. The fictionalizing of his name is more for the purpose of not confusing the reader with the character of Jesse Whyte, as similar names are something authors try to avoid.

The Westchester Polo Club Grounds are now located in Portsmouth, at the north end of Aquidneck Island; the grounds described in the story arew now a residential area just west of Morton Park. The Westchester Polo Club was America's first polo club. The Meadowview Club mentioned in this book, however, is fictional.